PERFIDY

by **Mark Bowman**

First Edition published 2015 by Slap-Dash Publishing
ISBN : 978-1-906407-30-8

Slap-Dash Publishing
St Luke's Art Project
TLC-St Luke's
c/o St Luke's Church and Neighbourhood Centre
Guidepost Road
Longsight
Manchester
M13 9HP

0161 273 1492
stlukesmanchester@googlemail.com

Available on Lulu, Amazon and Kindle

Typeset design by Rae Story
Cover Image by Jex

THE VERITY TRILOGY:

Verity

Perfidy

Certitude

Chapter 1

The crab-like collection of pincers and legs paused for a moment as its internal clock missed a dozen oscillations. The stars flickered back into existence, but the constellations were subtly distorted. For a moment, active silence replaced the absence of noise which had accompanied the nonexistent time. Then a shockwave formed simultaneously at every point on the hull, and attempted to rip the droid from its perch. This was not the faint shock of gravity-waves washing through space, but the harsh turbulence of a planetary atmosphere entered at hypersonic speeds. Super heated plasma formed in microseconds, and set to work annihilating every sensor that encrusted the droid's metal skin. In the fraction of a second before being blinded, it relayed images of a blue-grey backdrop viewed through the orange glow of disassociating air molecules. The droid then hunkered down against the ship's hull, and waited for the cool predictability of vacuum to return.

Inside the slender spaceship, three anxious faces watched as the ramshackle remains of a man staggered from some unseen blow. Clusters of fibres and tubes snaked from his neck and left arm. They moved to their own rhythm as if tied to another will, like a puppet's strings. He had the wasted look of a hermit emerging from decades of contemplation or madness. A slate-grey jumpsuit was pinned to his frame by protruding elbow and shoulder bones.

"Wow! We're here." The man sounded shocked and unprepared.

"Where?" Mex demanded, a sense of anticipation adding impatience to his voice. He was the only one of them to indulge in head hair, and it formed a darkly-alarmed halo around his head. "Pilot, Kaamil, where are we?" he asked the man again.

"Earth. It must be Earth." The third voice was from an impossibly tall and lithe woman. She wrapped herself around the oversized biceps of the fourth and most purple of the figures in the circular control centre.

The purple-skinned man grunted his agreement, the three folds of his mouth flaps briefly opening to let the sound escape. He put one chunky hand over the inhumanly slender fingers of the woman, making her smile at the reassurance.

"If it's Earth what's the problem?" Mex asked, trying to tame his unruly cloud of hair with one hand.

"José and Nomia may be masters of the impossible but they are not experts in celestial dynamics. We are definitely very near Earth but our relative velocity is about Mach two hundred."

Mex looked perplexed for a moment even as his brain caught up with his mouth. "A Mach speed? That only makes sense inside a sound-carrying environment like an atmosphere." He paused as more catching up took place. "Oh, I see. Are we going to crash?"

The Pilot grimaced as a shudder rippled down to them from the ship's skin. "I'm trying to calculate our hyperbolic trajectory. I think we will just miss the surface unless a mountain gets in our way and we definitely have escape velocity so we'll break free again."

"What about atmospheric friction?" asked Yakini, her long, thin nose forming an exclamation mark with the round alarm of her mouth.

"The air around us is already burning but my hull has shifted into a reflective rigid lattice with maximum thermal inertia. It would take many hours before it heats enough to melt."

"Can we slow ourselves down enough to enter orbit?" Mex's hair started to cooperate as the Earth's gravity made itself felt. The control room reoriented itself to the local gravity vector, helping to ground the meagre crew.

"I'm not sure that flipping the ship at these speeds and inside a planet's atmosphere is high on my list of death-defying feats for today."

Mex flashed a quizzical look at the latest example of the Pilot's blossoming sense of humour. He had been confined in a spherical bunker for over a decade, tethered to the interstellar spaceship, the Suparna, by a collection of umbilical control cords. It had only been a few hours since he had been wrenched from the bunker. The trauma had almost killed him but he had survived, and was already developing as a person. It was almost as if a personality had been laying in wait for daylight to trigger its awakening. The forced re-entry into the human world had been a birth in more ways than just the immediately obvious metaphor of the womb-like bunker.

Yakini shrugged an intricate collection of bones towards her ears. "So we are passengers on the roller coaster of fate. Again."

Now that they were forced to stand rather than float, the ship-wide tremors became harder to ignore. The savage anger of Earth's atmosphere growled its way up their legs and tore at their stomachs.

"I suggest you all take a seat," the Pilot directed.

Only the stocky purple figure of Bergur ignored him. Dressed in a collection of stiff strips, more useful for attaching weapons than providing warmth or modesty, he stood behind Yakini's chair and pushed nail-less thumbs through the taught muscles of her shoulders.

"Can we at least see what we're going to crash into?" Yakini asked.

"That's not easy. Pretty much every sensor on my hull was vaporised before the first shockwave formed. I could coax a section of my hull towards transparency without significantly raising the chance of catastrophic failure. If that would suffice."

"And aim a camera at it?" Yakini enquired.

"I think I can do better than that. It may be hard to see much detail because light is the dominant heat transfer mechanism in the bow-shock formed around the ship." There was a momentary feeling of acceleration which did not feel like the incessant drag of gravity, and then the vibrations of atmospheric re-entry resumed. The section of bulkhead behind the Pilot's head began to glow faintly, until flame-like tongues licked the surface. The edge was indistinct, like a crude camera obscura, but a deeply dark-blue backdrop formed behind the flames.

"Behold Earth."

Mex frowned. "Is that view straight ahead?"

"Pretty much."

"Should blue be filling quite so much of the wall?"

"I think I mentioned how close to the surface we were going to get."

"It looks as if we might be on kissing terms."

"José and Nomia did a good job of getting us close. Pretty much a bull's-eye, I'd say."

"Bully for them." Mex's hands were clasped tightly together like a pilot pulling back on a flight control stick.

Yakini blinked and asked, "how long before we don't hit?"

"Less than a minute. In fact, we'll be not colliding with the surface in twenty-two seconds."

They watched the fiery scene for several seconds, their brains seeking familiar coastal patterns where blue met green or brown. With only a single breath left before impact, Bergur opened his mouth flaps and inner eye lids, and spoke for the first time.

"Did anybody see where Nomia and José went?"

*

Sera prodded the tear in her thermal suit. The fabric quivered under the pressure and slithered across the torn fibres. She set off again, taking extra care to avoid brushing against the jagged rocks which protruded, as sharp as teeth, from the tunnel walls. Her jaw was starting to ache from gripping the mouthpiece of the lung that dangled like a desiccated honeycomb in the contours between her breasts. She could still taste the ammonia that tainted the bacteria generated air and she had started to associate the acrid smell with the claustrophobia of being underground. Eventually, natural diffusion would mix the new atmosphere that freshened the planet's surface with the old carbon dioxide in the tunnels, but then she would find herself redundant, and the DTM would need a new storage philosophy.

She relaxed her jaw and gummed the mouthpiece. The accumulated rubble which formed the floor of the tunnel crunched under her boots and slowly spread dust towards her knees. Sera stumbled again, her long legs flailing to escape becoming knotted.

"Shit", she cursed through her nose.

She massaged the green sack of algae on her shoulder and adjusted the collimation lenslets. Its sickly light bit deeper into the darkness at her feet. Infinite crystals played with the light, throwing it around the tunnel with reflective abandon, but none of them reflected the light just right to trigger a response from her eye-caps.

"Double shit," she repeated and crunched deeper into the labyrinth. She risked activating the global positioning receiver, to get a better lock on her location. There was a few seconds window in which she could get a satellite lock without the peer-to-peer transceiver registering her location. As soon as she saw the positional lock flicker into the corner of her vision she powered the feature down and consulted Ndita's map. She was very close to the mineral seam the ground penetrating sonar had located. Maybe she would be able to afford the new cube after all; she might even be able to stretch to one with a view of the lake, after making her regular donation to the DTM funds.

Sera walked on another hundred metres, into a chamber that glittered above her head like the night sky over the Martian North Pole. She pulled a trowel from her back pack and bent down to take a sample. The blade stopped a few centimetres into the brittle gravel.

"Got you," she muttered prematurely.

The mineral she sought was tougher than typical basalts, and was often found in tunnels with little erosion or seismic damage. The trowel blade automatically switched from a physical digging blade to sonic, and started to burrow into the floor of the chamber. Chemical compositions and concentrations began to flow across her vision. "Thank God, the mother-load," she sang, resisting the urge to do a jig.

A crack like the first clap of thunder before a summer storm buffeted the walls of the chamber. Sera pulled herself upright and swore for the third time as the bottom dropped out of her world.

The lump in her stomach, fighting to climb out of her mouth, told her she was falling, but the bubble of illumination that surrounded her showed only a suspension of dust, rubble and boulders big enough to sit on. For a few seconds she was almost able to deny the lethality of her situation, but then a sharp piece of fixed rock flickered into her view and bit a lump out of her side. There was a flash of blood in her mouth as she bit down on her tongue, and then another second of peace before consciousness was crushed from her by the floor of the next chamber down.

The last thing that wandered through Sera's battered mind was an image of an angel floating above her, blonde hair streaming above a face like a china doll. Delicate arms and legs were splayed, as if the vision was bathing in a cosmic light only visible to the heavenly host.

Take care of me, Sera thought as her mind flickered and went out.

*

You mean, lay down and die.

She wanted to scream the words with all the precious air in her lungs, but the only voice she had left was in her head.

Julienne was paralysed; rigid with the terror of the condemned, and yet unable to surrender herself to fate. Mostly, she was frozen to the slab by a suspicion her body would betray her. While she put no demands on its treacherous muscles there was still a faint chance she remained the dominant controlling force.

A new wave of defeat crashed through her mental flood-defences. The urge to lie passively and wait to be deactivated was as strong as the sense of self-preservation it replaced.

I am not a machine, to be switched on and off. I live or die, she reminded herself.

The other presence in her head showed the simple serenity of a wiped personality; a chance to start again without bad dreams, tormenting memories or the blackness of self-doubt. A fresh life, to grow and explore, and this time the Corporation would not expect so much of her. This time it would be an easy and fulfilling life.

The presence did not argue its case. It could not conceive of any objection or protest. It simply stated the way it would be, and made her body lay loose and accepting of its fate, but Julienne knew what the other voice was. She knew that it was not her own inner-voice. She had lived – maybe existed would be a better word for the period of mental and physical torture in question – for almost a week in the echo-free monologue of

11

her own head. The voice, which so subtly dominated her decision making, belonged to an analysis and storage processor that was bio-welded to the inside of her skull. The slabs of grey protein which had been scrapped away to make room had contained many of her long-term memories and much of her analytical skills. Her brain had started to adapt, even as it stuttered towards shutdown; groups of neurons had been co-opted and old memories reformed as dream-like visions. She had started to rebuild a new mind within the scarred remnants of her brain. Of course, it had not been sustainable. Julienne had suffered a series of emotional crashes and her body had begun a spiralling series of shutdowns, but at least she had learned to distinguish her own inner-voice from the serpent whisper of the machine within.

There was at least the potential for a battle.

A man's pale face cast a shadow across her. The movement made her realise her eyes were open but losing focus. He pulled a transparent hood over Julienne's head, and glowing displays filled the space between them. His follicle-free skull glinted dimly from the semi-permeable polymer coating that guaranteed the clinic's sterility. Her own skin probably had the same odd texture, which probably explained the slight effort required to breathe, as if she was flying too high in a taxi. She wanted to wrinkle her nose, to disturb the plastic plug filtering her breath. Instead she opened her mouth and asked him a question.

"What's that doing to me?" Her eyes darted to the side to indicate the apparatus above.

The face did not register a change for a moment. Then he seemed to realise, not only was she talking, but she was speaking to him. A mild shock stretched his features for a heartbeat, and then he looked to his left, maybe to check he was not being observed.

He coughed away a long silence, and said, "Erh, nothing. It is just monitoring your implants." His voice was deliberate and awarded every syllable equal value.

"Monitoring for what?" her voice sounded a million kilometres away from her body.

"It will track the changes to your brain when we inject the nanites."

"Then I'll be wiped clean?"

"Yes." He seemed relieved she accepted what was about to happen.

"I can start my life again. Wipe away the pain."

"Yes." He sounded less confident now they were discussing details.

"You know, they thanked me for the information I brought back?" She paused to control her voice. "Then they sent me here?"

"I see," but he clearly had no idea.

"They expressed gratitude for my sense of duty. Almost as if I had another choice. Like I could have said, to hell with the Corporation, and chosen my own happiness."

The face shrank slightly as he backed away for a moment, returning with a nanite application pen held inverted in his left hand. He had clearly decided rapid progress was the fastest way to end this deranged conversation. Julienne felt the cool tip of the pen touch her neck and then a tingle as the lead nanites parted the epidermis and hunted for a blood vessel.

"No!" Julienne sat upright in a single movement which took both of them by surprise. Her implants were in a state of partial shutdown in preparation for the mental cleansing, and seemed as stunned as the medic.

He stood staring at the debris of his equipment littering the floor around the surgical slab.

"What are you doing? You cannot exhibit free will with your implants in hibernation. It is not possible." The medical technician seemed to be convincing reality of its error more than offering any protest to her.

For a giddy moment she suspected he might be right, but her adrenal glands reluctantly stuttered into life and energy surged through her limbs. A perfectly symmetrical smile ignited her slender face, introducing a rare curve onto her straight features.

"I am not finished with this life just yet." She spoke with her old confidence as she swung her legs to the ground and advanced on the stupefied man. Mentally, she clamped down on the implants, refusing to let them boot back to full operation. She might be missing much of their analytical abilities but she was content to accept a compromise between operational ability and free will.

The medic offered no resistance as she brushed him aside and made for the only obvious exit from the room. There was no point restraining the medic, the building's A.I. would already be aware something odd was happening. A new wave of futility washed through her as she realised how little chance there was of even getting free of the building, let alone surviving in the outside world.

Just for once, live for the moment, she told herself but the inner voice sounded distinctly like Mex.

She moved into the grey corridor with rounded corners and soporific lighting, but the far end was already morphing away from the exit to lead her further into the clinic's depths. Julienne half-heard and half-imagined the sound of marching boots. She darted back into the treatment room before the walls could close it off from her.

"What's your name?" she asked the technician. He looked like his regret was rapidly moving backwards through time; disquiet about turning up for work was evolving into a tentative doubt that being born had been a particularly good idea.

"Michael," he stammered.

"Right Mike, how do I get out of here?" Names were powerful, nicknames doubly so.

"You let me wipe your mind clean, and then you walk out."

Maybe he was braver than he appeared. "How about an alternative plan?"

"Why would I help you?" Michael was clearly already regretting the question as his imagination filled in a hundred unpleasant answers.

Julienne wound her hands into tight fists, white bone deforming her knuckles with hard ridges. She gave him a moment to think, her silence offering sufficient threat.

Michael sagged as air escaped his collapsing chest. "There's nothing I can do, even if I was stupid enough to go up against the building. Security teams must be gathering now. If you try and leave they will get you. If you stay here the building will go into hostage mode and probably kill us both."

"How?" She already knew the answer but she needed time for her diminished mental capacity to develop a solution.

"Take your pick: heat, cold, low pressure, high pressure, gas, water, nanites, sound, light, dark. Inside this building the A.I. is physics. We are totally in its care, completely at its mercy."

"In that case we must appeal to something more fundamental." The plan was growing in her head like an igniting star; it glowed blue and hot, pushing back the darkness of despair with luminous rays of hope.

"Unless you've got religion there is nothing more fundamental." He was backing towards a desk, hands snaking behind his back.

Julienne strode over to him and put one arm across his chest, forcing him to bend backwards over the desk until his feet left the floor. With her free hand she tapped two words into his forehead. "Safety interlocks."

"What?" he managed as his legs flailed, desperate for purchase.

"Ever since the first wafer of silicon was put in charge of a lift, there have been hardwired safety systems. There have always been certain events that are too safety critical to be trusted to the fuzzy logic and software vagaries of intelligent systems. If I can't walk out of the building then we need to lock it down so that nothing can get at us."

Michael still looked baffled even as Julienne spun him around and waved his head into the path of the splice terminal's login laser. "Put it into multicast mode." A knee held high between his legs reinforced the instruction. Glowing menus painted the air above the desk in primary colours. Julienne waved into focus a menu tagged with a motif shaped like a robotic ant. She spun through the myriad of options until she found the program she wanted.

"Mike, give me the nanite pen," she ordered.

Michael looked lost until his fingers shifted on the slender cylinder still held in his sweating palm. He held it up as if to confirm he was not hallucinating, and Julienne plucked it from his grasp. At one end, a green pin-point of light flickered briefly, as the new program was loaded. She walked over to the nearest wall and thrust the pen at the surface, pressing a recessed trigger for a random count of ten. There were a few seconds of anticlimactic calm and then the wall began to decay like a time-lapsed movie. Waves of virgin metal flooded towards the breach as the wall tried to defend itself, but the nanites ingested the material as fast as it arrived. After a brief battle, an old fashioned claxon sounded and rigid steel shutters crunched across the doorway. An echo of the hiss of convected air whistled in her ears as it shutdown.

"Let's see the A.I. override a bio-containment lockdown." Julienne cried triumphantly.

Michael continued to stare at her with mounting fear. "You're mad. You have just locked us inside. What kind of escape is that?"

"Escape comes next."

Julienne kicked the nearest piece of furniture until it got the message and slithered towards the centre of the room. "High chair," she ordered and it obediently elongated until it was over a metre tall. As Julienne clambered on top and stood on the seat, it broadened its base to add extra stability. This time she held the trigger down until the pen flashed red and stopped humming. Grey ash started to fall from the ceiling like the nuclear fallout she had seen on the history channels. Julienne stepped down and away from the path of the expanding snow storm. She shook her head, dislodging a shower of fine dusting. Reaching to her smooth scalp she felt the glossy feeling of the polymer sheaf that encased her. With two blunt fingernails she rubbed until it started to flake and peel. It formed a dirty crust as it mingled with the ceiling debris and nanite waste. The powdery streaks distorted the symmetry of her naked body making her bizarrely self-conscious.

"Give me your clothes, Mike," she ordered with a menacing smile. He obliged without complaint, as if this was the least alarming of today's demands.

By the time Julienne was dressed, daylight was streaming through the dusty hole in the ceiling. "The nanites won't eat organics will they?" she fired at the de-robed medic.

"Not on the setting you chose," he confirmed.

Without any more thought, Julienne leapt onto the stool and sprung through the hole in the roof. The enhanced muscle control of her lower-level implants responded without complaint. With the poise and grace of a ballerina, she emerged into the combined heat and light of the sun. After trotting a hundred metres from the nanite infestation she stopped and studied the sky. She waved at the cloud of taxi drones circling the city until one peeled off and plummeted towards her. It hovered nervously at arm's reach until Julienne offered her MynCorp security numbers.

"Thank you for overriding regulatory restriction on pickup/unloading from corporate buildings, Agent Garland. You may now board."

Julienne pushed through the revolving adverts which had engulfed the egg-shaped drone as it descended. Her senses were briefly flooded with images of the latest MynCorp apartment block, as the display spliced directly at its captive audience. She waved aside flashes of blandly chiselled couples strolling arm in arm through wood-panelled dining rooms.

"City view, now," she barked, triggering the taxi to climb straight up and lose itself in the clouds and clusters of commuters.

Chapter 2

Somehow Sera knew waking was going to be a bad idea. Each time the
chaotic images of dreaming coalesced into a conscious mind, her first act
was to shatter it back to the safety of oblivion. Eventually, her mind became
sufficiently self-aware to preclude the illusion of non-existence, and she
woke up. This in itself was a surprise given the numerous opportunities
for death while lying unconscious in the lava tubes of Mars. Even in official
figures, hyperthermia and asphyxiation competed annually for the title of
most prolific killer. Asphyxiation usually won through its shear ingenuity;
she might spit-out the mouthpiece of her extra lung or choke on it. The
thermal suit she wore was remarkably bright considering how cheap
it had been. It ran its meagre mind on the electrostatic energy it could
harvest from her skin, and it managed to keep her extremities at a preset
temperature, regardless of her level of exertion or the outside conditions.
It had no internal power source, so it could not actually heat or cool, but by
altering its thermal conductivity she would remain comfortable in a diverse
range of environments. She could feel it creeping around the edge of her
face as it tried to keep her injured body warm.

That thought raised two interesting questions, which she pondered as she
lay with her eyes firmly closed. What injuries, and where was she? A long
fall in the dark poured from her memory and splashed across her vision.
The half-remembered crunch of the landing made her jerk upright to a
sitting position. An ache from the left side of her stomach now made its
presence known, as if pain preferred to flow uphill. She looked down at
her stomach before opening one eye; still not ready for the full force of the
bad news. The thermal suit was dull where it had grown back over a hole;
a large hole, much bigger than it was designed to self-heal. Even odder, she
could not see the edges of a patch.

Sera sighed her confusion, and then clamped her mouth closed where the bacterial lung mouth piece should have been. Now she was thoroughly perplexed, and looked around for an external agent to her condition. She was pretty much where she had landed; a hole like a shark's mouth taunted her from above, complete with scraps of fabric and blood. The chamber she had landed in was crescent-shaped, like an oxbow lake off the main lava tube. The walls were made of the same jagged basalt as the main tube and looked similarly inclined to tear any flesh they could touch.

She noticed three things which made this space unique, strangely, in reverse order of significance. Firstly, she could breath, or to be more precise, she was not suffocating. Next, she could see everything about her with perfect clarity even though there was no obvious means of illumination; without the continuous encouragement of being manually mixed with nutrient, the algae sacks on her suit should have long since gone to sleep. Lastly, there were two naked figures hanging in the air near by. The man was in his forties, with the physique of someone who used their mind rather than their body to earn energy, but without the deterioration of excess. His skin was tinted with the olive brown of a Mediterranean ancestry which his face reinforced with a strong nose and dusk-black hair. Sera remembered the image of an angel that she had seen as she fell, or rather as she landed. She wondered why an angel would not choose the physical perfection that the Pre-Raphaelites had always envisaged. His broad frown was definitely out of place.

The second figure was much more as Sera would have envisaged; vulnerability and pale fragility personified. Despite the broad and almost victorious smile, there was an old pain and even older strength in the shadows of her eyes, and in the creases at the corner of her mouth.

They seemed to be talking about her, or she could make out two sets of thoughts which related to her; no words were actually spoken.

"Don't be cross with me, José." The thoughts were female.

"What do you expect? You agreed we had to leave the Suparna after the jump to Earth. You saw how dangerous our presence might be, both as a temptation to MynCorp and as a lure to the Eidolons. We discussed how we must hide on Mars until we were ready to mount a defence." That was definitely the blinkered logic of a masculine mind.

"I did agree on all points."

"So, in what way does she fit into this low-profile approach?"

"She's important for our plan to rescue my brothers and sisters."

"I can see why you might think that, but why didn't you discuss it with me?"

"Because you would have said no."

"When have I ever said no to you?"

"I've never given you the chance." Her smile broadened, and his frown faltered. The emotions flooding from the two of them almost made Sera blush as they reached out and took each other's hands.

Sera coughed and spoke out loud in the mysteriously breathable air. "Should I come back later?"

The man frowned again but this time it was from confusion. "You can hear us?" he asked aloud.

"That's why I chose her," the young woman answered before Sera could digest the question. "Telepathy was so close to the surface of her mind, I barely had to tinker."

"You've been inside my mind?" Sera found her voice edged with inexplicable indignation.

"Only a little bit," she held up two fingers a hair's width apart. "You have an innate gift. It would probably have come naturally in the right conditions. Don't be angry, it will be invaluable in your struggle."

For Sera, the situation had just turned from curious to dangerous. The young angel could only be talking about her involvement in the DTM, which made them a threat, both to her and to the future of Mars. The soldier in her personality stood to attention and assessed the situation. It – she considered the fighter a beast she allowed to kennel in her mind – counted the exits and potential weapons with efficient detachment. None and none, it reported. She found herself wondering if hand to hand combat with angels was undignified. Would they bob up and down in the air if she jumped up to grapple them? As if in answer, the man descended to the floor with a sigh of settling gravel. "Please don't think of us as a threat. I can assure you that your enemies are some of our enemies," he said.

"But are your friends some of my friends?" she responded glibly.

"Not yet." The younger angel's smile was as disarming as her voice was reassuring.

"My *friends* are not really the sociable type." Sera felt that implicit threat was about as aggressive as she could manage sitting down. She stood up in case it made her feel more in charge of the situation. The ache in her side felt tight like new skin under a scab.

"They'll want to meet us," the woman said as she sank to the ground and offered her hand to shake. Sera could have sworn the chamber dimmed as her feet made contact with the rock floor. "I'm Nomia," the angel said, "and this is José. We're going to save everyone."

They both smiled but with distinctly different degrees of confidence in their eyes. "Hello," said the angel named José. He looked as if numerous uncertainties were battling for control of his frown. "May I be frank?" he continued.

"I think it is almost essential, given the circumstances." Sera felt that she had been violated enough that a reciprocal introduction was not owed.

José looked at Nomia for a moment and a complex burst of their argument and counterargument burst through Sera's mind like a solar flare. Nomia nodded her agreement, and José took a tense breath of air that should not have been breathable. "I've never had much time for the Martian separatist movement."

Sera opened her mouth to correct a common misconception about the DTM's goals, but her righteous pedant streak was feeling a little muted in such an alien environment. She let him continue what was undoubtedly going to turn into another typical rant about ends and means.

"The mine workers were undeniably treated appallingly during the Nauru riots of '26, but terrorist attacks on MynCorp facilities do nothing to advance your cause."

"What would you recommend? A leaflet campaign, perhaps?" Sera's tone contained a well-practised balance of contempt and sarcasm.

"No, that would be futile. As I see it, you are dependent on Earth for bio-technology, just as Earth is reliant on Mars for minerals. MynCorp are very careful to make their technology single-generation. Once it completes its task it becomes impotent, perpetuating the relationship of producer and consumer. The solution is to play MynCorp and Durga Corp off against each other. Use your bargaining position to extract concessions until you have the ability to be self-sufficient. The threat of a viable independent Mars would be enough to make the corporations relent and allow a new economic force to emerge. Then you have equality in their terms and freedom in your terms."

Despite the refreshingly insightful argument she still hated being lectured by a short-arsed Terran. "Swap one tyranny for a home grown variety?" she retorted.

"That's up to you." He smiled without smugness.

Sera sighed with resignation. "I'm not really prepared to discuss the politics of an illegal organisation to which I have no alliance, with a complete stranger who is obviously Terran," she said before remembering the whole angel routine and adding, "or, at least, looks Terran."

"Fair point. Perhaps if we tell you our story you will feel able to be honest with us."

"Perhaps." Sera tried to sound non-committal despite the huge cloud of intrigue colouring her thoughts.

"Nomia was a Nexus Node." He stroked his companion's shoulder in obvious lament for a past which should need no additional explanation.

"Is that bad?" Sera asked, unsure how the words 'nexus' and 'node' could be combined in any meaningful way. She knew that the Nexus was MynCorp talk for their computing system which connected people's brains together into some sort of infinite processing system. MynCorp controlled all meaningful data processing capability, and commonly charged clients a share of the data they manipulated. It was just one of the reasons she hated their nefarious ways.

"Bad?"

"I take it I should be shocked."

"It depends on whether you consider over twenty years of forced sleep a violation."

Sera looked at Nomia for an explanation. The trauma which made the corner of her smile flicker and added the premature wisdom darkening the innocence of her eyes was evidence of a tormented past, but Nomia offered no words of clarification.

José shouldered the burden of explanation. "MynCorp are happy to allow consumers to know that the Nexus is built from human sub-consciousness because it acts as…" He paused as if looking for a word with sufficient nuance. "motivation," he finished.

"The Drop?" Sera suggested.

"Yes, quite an appropriate name." He paused, clearly remembering a personal experience. "The Drop is a collection of subconscious minds connected together in Verity Space by a network of data hubs. Each mind is a raw processing unit interacting with the Downey probability field of every quantum decision which shapes our reality. What co-opts this natural ability and uses it to do useful processing is the data hubs."

"I suppose I knew there was some infrastructure underlying the Drop victims. Wait, you're saying these hubs are people? That's gross, but not that surprising. How is it worse than being sentenced to the Drop just because you lose your job?"

"To start with, the Nodes, including Nomia, have a life sentence, but more importantly they are not entirely unaware of what is happening to them."

"How?"

"I was born with a form of autism called Asperger syndrome." Nomia said softly.

"You don't seem particularly autistic."

If Nomia was shocked at Sera's typically Martian directness she hid it with a smile. "I'm not," Nomia replied. "I was born with a particularly strong connection to the Downey field. The interaction with Verity Space bleeds into my conscious mind, or I suppose it would be more useful to say that some of my conscious focus is lodged in Verity Space."

"You still don't seem very autistic."

"I've learnt to switch my complete consciousness into physical space or into probability space. I'm a complete person."

"Wait, are you saying you've been into the Drop? Not via a splice terminal but just pushed your mind into it?"

"We both have." They said in eerie unison.

"Do you know how mad that sounds? What happens to your bodies while you're tripping the light fantastic?"

"That depends." José shrugged.

"On what?"

"What we decide should happen to them."

Sera shook her head, casting out the weirdness. "Can I ask what this has to do with me?"

Nomia answered with a flush of words that finished in a triumphant smile. "We are going to rescue all the other Nodes and bring MynCorp down."

"Is that all?" Sera felt her expectations deflated. Despite making level-headedness into an art form, just for a moment, she had started to feel a little of the hope fostered by these strange angels. Now she must deal with the banal reality of their delusional state.

"There is one slight snag." José said while looking at Nomia pointedly.

"Just one?" Sera asked, her shield of glibness restored.

"There's an unstoppable alien force on its way to destroy the Solar System."

Sera sighed one last time and said, "Isn't there always."

*

"What would Mex do?" Julienne said to no one, as she blinked away an image of round eyes peeping out with mischievous intent from a shaggy mop of black hair. Then she realised, despite his numerous and imaginative attempts to escape from her control, he had never actually succeeded. In fact, she had always stayed one step ahead of him without even particularly taxing her resources. So, if he could survive on Earth without as much as a blip on the MynCorp spider programs, then so could she. And she would do it without sinking to his more morally ambiguous depths.

"So, what to do?"

She looked down on the city from the vantage point of the drifting taxi. A wide river ran artificially straight from North to South with agricultural squares boxing it in on both sides. On slightly higher ground, grids of tree-lined avenues cut gorges between tower blocks of silver and white. Several smaller buildings lingered out of formation as the city completed its seasonal migration down to the flood plains of the valley floor. Directly below, a cluster of low amorphous buildings formed the MynCorp industrial heart of the city. Taxis and drones streamed in and out from this centre like bees from a hive.

Two twisted black spires stood ostracised on the edge of the city where they had been corralled by the other buildings. Their outer surfaces were soot black and undulated like a nightmare reflection of the other buildings in the city.

"Jefferson buildings," Julienne instructed the simple mind of the taxi.

"Warning: the Jefferson Buildings have been declared unsafe by city authorities. The building A.I.'s are designated as senile."

"MynCorp override. Agent Julienne Garland." Julienne offered even as she wondered how many more times her credentials would work.

"Override accepted. Street level or roof?"

Usually she would ask for a floor and the building would accommodate the taxi, but she was no more keen to fly into the side of a senile building than the taxi's mind was. "Ground level," she confirmed.

They flew in at head height, the surrounding avenues clear of people or trees. Julienne stepped off a hundred metres from the front entrance as the taxi hovered like an impatient dog. As soon as she was clear the taxi banked steeply and hurtled straight up. It was about two hundred metres above the ground when a tongue like protuberance of diseased black metal lashed out from the side of the building and engulfed the taxi whole. There was a moment where it looked as if the taxi might break free from the clinging tongue and then it was dragged back towards the side of the building, vanishing beneath the surface without so much as a ripple.

Julienne stood in stunned silence for a minute before she shrugged, looked around nervously and headed towards the twisted caricature of the building's main entrance. Two ragged and salt-carved pieces of driftwood were nailed across the door, forming a threatening cross. Three words had been painted above with the stiff strokes of an old brush. The paint was red and had run like stage blood. The message was minimalist but clear.

CONDEMNED – KEEP OUT

There was something improbable about the scene which made Julienne reach out one finger to prod the surface. The door and its unwelcoming adulterations vanished with an ethereal giggle. A broad low lobby slowly revealed itself in the dirty sunlight. To the left a rickety wooden staircase twisted its way up and out of sight. Around the base and across the cinder-grey floor to an acrylic counter, lay various pieces of deactivated furniture. Their shapeless bodies formed a rough strand of dead jellyfish on the sea of dust that had congealed in the lobby. Julienne stepped inside, relieved to see the dust had been heavily churned by numerous shoes and boots. Even more reassuring was that some of the prints were going out and not just entering to some imagined doom. Julienne did not see images of ghouls or goblins in the solidified shadows. Her imagination was limited to line of fire calculations and potential ambush points. Just the same, her adrenaline levels made her jumpy, and liable to flinch when the breeze being sucked up the stairs formed wordless whispers as it twisted between floors.

Two children's dolls had been nailed to the wall behind the counter. One was a Terran baby, white and chubby with its limbs articulated to some unlikely angle. The other was a Martian baby, its disproportionately slender limbs reaching up and down as if it would be flying if not for the corroded nail trough its chest. The two dolls were turned to face each other, ignoring any visitor in favour of some private doll conversation. Julienne decided anything that curious was likely to be a trap of some kind, even though she was not clear why anyone would want to trap the lobby of a building. She concluded her suspicion said less about any realistic threat and more about how far outside her comfort zone she found herself. Nevertheless, she avoided the desk and headed to the two gated lifts which dominated the wall to her right. The first gate slid open as her fingers brushed the rough brass of the handle, to reveal a shaft of impenetrable black. Again, Julienne let her fingers do the exploring. Something wet and gelatinous fell onto the back of her hand. The oily lump shivered as she withdrew her hand with a jerk. It flopped to the floor and formed an ambiguous blob. A layer of dust crept up its sides and started to conceal it in some conspiratorial result of surface tension.

"Stairs it is then." She found some strength in her own voice.

The stairs creaked theatrically as she started to climb. Julienne let one hand drag along the side wall until she noticed that the surface was undulating like convulsions in the throat muscles of some giant snake. She stopped walking. The creaking sound continued in anticipation of the next step she had not taken.

"Very creepy but I'm getting bored now," she shouted to the void above.

There was no answer, but the walls solidified to a respectable beige stone, and the stairs morphed to a reliable looking white polycrete. The whispering air seemed to sigh in boredom and dim lights flickered into life.

Another half flight of steps, and a narrow landing served a pair of swinging wooden doors, before the next flight twisted further towards the roof. Another doll lay between the doors, preventing them fully closing and allowing a faint smell of wood smoke to sulphur-singe her nostrils. Julienne pushed the door and stepped sideways through the gap, letting the door close back on the doll's head. A broad corridor snaked and twisted away in all directions, doorways, like scales, staggered along its length. In some places, the doorways wound across the ceiling or lay like trapdoors in the floor. Beyond the horizon of the furthest door, the corridor and doorways grew bigger, again messing with her depth perception.

Julienne started to walk down the tortured corridor, ignoring the horizon of her peripheral vision which kept trying to make her fall over. There were no doors in the first three openings but the rooms beyond were too distorted to be useful for shelter or storage. The fourth door was mangled by the distorting forces of the frame and was wedged half open by the rising floor inside. A large woman was sat on a box in the middle of the room nursing a baby in a thick blanket. She seemed to sense Julienne standing awkwardly on the inclined entrance.

"Do you mind?" she said thickly as she turned and stared at Julienne from under shaggy eyebrows.

The baby stopped suckling for a moment and gave Julienne a similar look but slightly cross-eyed from the strain of focusing at a distance.

"Sorry, the door was open." Julienne turned to indicate the door before struggling to return her eye to the woman's face.

"Of course it's open. Do you think I'm stupid enough to trust the building with a closed door?"

Julienne was at a loss to see where she had offered offence but could not shake the implicit authority of the matriarchal figure. "Sorry. I was just looking for somewhere to rest for a moment."

"Oh, my poor dear. Have you just arrived?" Her defensive aggression evaporated into maternal concern.

"I suppose so."

"We'll you'd best go and see Mr. Gaverson. He'll sort you out with a room. I'm Beatrice by the way. I won't ask your name. Nobody ever wants to give their name when they first arrive. It takes a while for the paranoia to blow away." She points further down the corridor. "Fifth door on the right. It's at about shoulder height," she said before pushing the baby's face back onto her breast.

Julienne muttered an unintelligible thank you, before returning to the relative sanity of the corridor. Another two dozen steps and the floor started to buckle and twist sharply, as if it had tried to tie a remembrance knot in itself some time ago. The fifth doorway was indeed high above the floor. The threshold was near her shoulder, and the opening loomed above her as if ready to swallow all those who passed.

Bracing herself against each side, Julienne swung herself up and in, half expecting to fall straight back out. Inside the floor sloped away from the entrance completely at odds with what her feet expected. The room had been square at some point in the past, but had evolved into a shape with too many irregular sides to have a useful name. There were windows in the two side walls but they injected no light into the space. Instead, two twisted wires were pushed into a flesh-pink section of the wall and a mercury vapour bulb spasmed white around the flickering room. Below the bulb a man sat at a desk made from stacked boxes. His face was lit by the pale light of the backlit notepad he scribbled on with a physical stylus. His body and face were starting to sag with age hard-earned. This downward motion competed with features which made him look as if he had been born in a wind tunnel. Everything from the end of his nose to his grey-shot eyebrows was pushed up and towards the back of his head. The pushed-back look was exaggerated by the permanent wrinkles on his forehead and the thin grey hair plastered back against his ash-grey scalp.

"Mr Gaverson?" she suggested, feeling strangely dislocated by the surreal nature of the meeting.

"Yes." He looked up from the notepad, pushing more of his features into the harsh shadows of the lamp. "Ah, we don't know you, do we? A new recruit for our little community, maybe?"

"Maybe. I need some space to rest, and I need to trade for some energy credits." Julienne simplified the list of priorities starting to order themselves in her mind.

"Space to rest we can definitely manage. Energy credits are unlikely. We don't operate within the constraints of the corporation's energy slavery here. We have no significant energy generation and mainly just operate a direct exchange of services. You understand?"

"Not really, but I'm sure I'll get the hang of it."

"Grand. The only community membership rule we enforce is that no corporate body is actively looking for you. Our community is rather precariously balanced on the edge of oblivion. One hard stare from MynCorp and we could topple out of existence."

Julienne ad-libbed a new persona with an ease which reflected the fragility of her own personality. "I'm not important enough to make anybody miss me. I just need some space from the interminable cycle of earning energy then spending energy."

"I understand. Right, we don't expect you to contribute from day one, but you'll find things a lot more comfortable here if you have useful skills to trade. Do you mind if I take a name and occupation? First name will do." He picked up his stylus and notepad with intent.

"Nomia. I'm a laboratory assistant." Julienne lied without hesitation using a name she would always react to.

"Hmm, I'm sure you have some transferable skills." He smiled thinly, making his lips lose the little colour they had left.

Julienne returned the smile with similar warmth as he scratched a few notes on the antique notepad. Gaverson stood and walked around his desk before directing her towards the entrance with an open palm. He hopped down into the mad corridor and offered a hand to Julienne. She pretended not to see the offer and dropped down to stand next to him.

The corridor continued to meander and convolute through the interior of the building as if it was deliberately trying to disable Julienne's sense of direction. As they paused to climb over a series of shoulder height ripples in the floor, Julienne broke from her own thoughts to collect some more information about her environment. "You said you are outside the corporate energy economy."

"Yes, that's right."

"How is that possible?"

"I assume that is why you are here, to escape the slavery of earning calories."

"Sure. Everybody knows the stories and it's hard to deny your existence when there are two giant black reminders standing at the edge of the city. But how does it work?"

"We can only exist as long as we do not draw appreciable resources from the city. The buildings may be insane but they are not stupid. They long ago realised they would be left to their madness as long as they unplugged from the energy grid and didn't replace the generation capacity with any of their own. MynCorp will only react if they are losing more energy than it would expend in the reaction, or if their energy generation monopoly is threatened. The buildings unplugged and have been making do on a starvation diet. As far as I can tell the buildings extract small amounts of energy from the surrounding air and ground but only enough to prevent death. They've also adapted to a low-nutrient environment in other more alarming ways."

"Like what?"

"The towers have become ...I suppose the best word would be carnivorous."

"Like eating taxis?"

"If they stray too near."

"Nice."

"Not really. Ah, here we are. You'll be sharing a room with Maria. Let me introduce you."

Maria was sat cross-legged facing a large window. Despite the contortions of the walls, the frame still contained glassing and provided a mostly unrestricted view of sky. Late afternoon sunlight streamed through and made her frizz of curly hair glow a coppery red. As Julienne stepped around to her side, she could see that Maria was smiling beneath broad freckle-scattered cheekbones and her eyes were closed. The smile only dipped slightly when Gaverson coughed and introduced Julienne as Nomia. He left as soon as decorum allowed, muttering something about filing not sorting itself.

Maria was dressed in a coarse weaved shawl and skirt of clay-red. When she noticed Julienne looking at the fabric Maria said, "You like it? I made the fabric myself. It's what I do here. That and collect food but we all do that."

"It's lovely," Julienne lied, looking down at the grey two-piece she had stolen from the medic. It would keep her warm or cool and self-clean but it marked her as MynCorp. "I like your hair. Do you think hair would suit me?"

"What colour is it?"

"I'm not sure." Julienne realised she had never even asked about hair colour when she was given the body. Fortunately, it was very common to never allow any hair growth throughout life.

"You look like a blond to me. That face deserves blond hair. Your nose, mouth and cheekbones are a sculptor's dream. You know an artist will often say they can see the shape in a piece of stone waiting to be released. They just allow it to reveal itself. Now I know what they see."

"I don't know what to say." Julienne found she did not need to role-play for a moment.

"Sorry, that was a bit forward of me. I've always had strong first reactions to people. I can be quite normal on a second meeting." She redoubled her smile.

"That's alright. The face isn't mine anyway. I stole it." They both laughed. "So, what do you do for food around here?"

"We pillage a little."

"From the corporate farms?"

"As long as we only take a little there seems to be no objection. The corporations are completely emotionless; we do not annoy them, it is simply a loss within tolerance. Would you spray a whole field to rid yourself of a beetle which only ate one plant per season?"

"What about growing your own?"

"There is no unclaimed land any more. We used to grow crops on the roof of the tower but that had to stop when the top ten floors died."

"Died?"

"The buildings are always close to starvation. Sometimes the parts furthest from a food source die."

"That doesn't sound very sustainable."

"It is for us. The buildings are a bit like a tumour. They would spread and corrupt everything given enough energy, and they would mutate too fast for us to live inside them. As long as we take precautions we are safe from MynCorp and our own home."

"Like what?"

"Sometimes the tower tries to lay down main roots into the city's grid. If they were successful all hell would break loose. That's when we have to fight the tower. Most of the time we just make sure to not get locked in a room."

"What happens if you get locked in a room?"

"As long as a door is pinned open, the building cannot change its internal configuration. Given the state of the tower's mind, we would probably not be talking about moving up or down a floor. A room could just as easily be turned inside out."

Maria led Julienne through another doorway – the door was pinned open by a tapered metal spike which secured it to a wall – and into a large room of makeshift tables and box chairs. About twenty people were gathered around a battered metal pan held over an open wood fire. Smoke rose to the ceiling and seemed to vanish without leaving even a layer of soot. Julienne was offered a bowl of vegetable stew without comment, and she sat down with Maria and a teenage boy called Fez. As the chunks of root vegetable started to revive her stomach, Julienne considered her situation. Although MynCorp probably did not rate her as a particularly important resource, they must have believed enough of her report to consider her memory as valuable. Or at least, the destruction of her memories as important. So they would come looking for her, but at the same time she could not just hide. She had to do something about the Node's threat even if MynCorp were not convinced. She had pushed the shock-drive as hard as she dared to get back to Earth. She had held off giving a detailed report until she could do it in person. Several top executives of MynCorp security had gathered and impatiently waited for her to speak. She had described the apparent alliance between the escaped Nexus Node and the piratical Eridanian colony. She had detailed the ease with which the conspirators had managed to turn MynCorp resources against them. José Sanchez the xeno-archaeologist and the interstellar craft, Suparna, were already corrupted when she arrived, but they had rapidly managed to turn her pilot Yakini and her civilian advisor on Nexus technology, Mex Tyrian. She had tried to explain how the conspirators had managed to turn corporate technology against its own people, including how her own implants had tried to drive her mad.

The MynCorp executives had shown very little reaction, even as she described the desperate situation. Faced with only one remaining course of action, she had decided to destroy the Node and her accomplices, even though each of the thousand Nodes were valued beyond measure by the corporation. Her attempt to destroy the ship's pilot had failed at the last moment, but she was still not sure why. She could remember strangling him with her bare hands but the memory was tied up in a collection of emotions she could not resolve; love for one man, hatred for another. She had described the facts as an impartial observer might, but in her head it was all a muddle.

The only time her interrogators had seemed interested was when she described the strange tales of god-like creatures living in Verity space. The

Node and José had used the mythology as justification for their actions just as theological terrorists had done for millennia. But MynCorp had grown impatient when Julienne could not repeat every conversation word for word due to one of many malfunctions in her implants. They did not seem to appreciate the risk from a renegade group with such advanced technology. Did they create it themselves or buy from a third party? Either way the implications were frightening.

She could not hide. She must collect further evidence and get high enough within the corporation to overcome the complacency which poisoned middle management. First, she would need energy credits, then she must get back into space.

"Maria, who should I talk to about trading some hardware?" Julienne ventured as she pushed the empty bowl away from her.

"Nobody I know. We live a very simple life here. I suspect hardware means something completely different to you."

"I mean implants. Some storage capacity and an analytical unit."

"What use would we have for those? You have to understand we are forced to live a sustainable existence. Anything which raises us from subsistence would probably end up bringing the corporation down on us."

"So nobody here trades with the rest of the city?"

Marie paused for a moment, then said, "We don't even have a useful currency for such a trade. I don't think anyone here can help." The hesitation was not that of a lie, so much as an omission.

Julienne instinctively reached inside her mind for the splice interface to the building to help her analyse Maria's reaction but managed to stop herself before the requisite implant was triggered. She built a couple of layers of mental defence to protect against instinctive activation, before returning her concentration to the conversation. Fez was looking quizzically at

Julienne. He had said nothing beyond the grunt of welcome when they had first sat down. Now he spoke. "You could go to Jefferson II."

"The other tower?"

"Yeah, there are people there who trade."

"Fez, are you trying to get her killed?" Maria sounded exasperated.

"I'm just saying. There are traders there."

"And all manner of deranged psychos."

"It's not that bad, they're just not into sustainability."

"And that's why we have to endure the MynCorp clear-out every few years." Maria was close to tears. Julienne put a calming hand on her shoulder even as she gestured to Fez; she would meet him in the corridor later.

*

It seemed strange that silence and a floating sensation should tell Mex he had survived. His ears were ringing but he could not quite remember whether it was from the roar of an atmosphere tearing apart an invading body or from his own impotent screams. He could remember Kaamil's almost embarrassed frown just before a violent lateral thrust had inflicted brutal punishment on his body. There was a dim memory of a floating chaos of entwined limbs and fading colour. Mex was fairly certain he had not lost consciousness but his brain had certainly used a temporary calm to reduce his awareness; there had been no period of black but maybe a dark grey.

"What happened?" Mex asked himself.

"My initial calculation was a little off. I had to make a slight adjustment." The Pilot sounded apologetic for taking measures to save their lives.

"You're forgiven," Yakini groaned from somewhere behind Mex. "What did you do?"

"I fired the manoeuvring ion thrusters."

"I thought you said that was too dangerous."

"I reassessed the risk."

There was a deep flapping laugh, which reminded Mex of a cartoon hippopotamus. It was enough for Mex to open his eyes and accept the reality of the visual world. Bergur was still standing behind one of the chairs at the table, with his toes tucked under a lower ledge. He loomed above Yakini who was still pinned to the chair. His head was tilted right back and his three mouth flaps were fully dilated. A fat slab of a tongue undulated between concentric rings of pointy teeth. It was one of the most terrifying expressions of joy that Mex had ever witnessed. Yakini joined him with a high pitched throaty warble.

"Can we go around again?" Bergur asked between roars.

"Sadly not," Kaamil informed.

"Maybe not such a close shave but we have got to go back." Mex turned his attention to the Pilot who was floating unselfconsciously in front of the jet black wall; the same wall that had recently shown them hills and cities through fingers of flaming air.

"And how would you like me to do that?"

"With fiery jets of nuclear fused stuff."

The Pilot simply stared at Mex like a schoolteacher waiting for a slightly slow child to catch up with the rest of the class.

"Oh yes." Mex would have looked at his feet if they had not been floating behind him. "We lost the engines didn't we?"

"I remember it more as a bunch of purple-skinned beasts, cutting them away with plasma cutters and then leaving them floating in interstellar space as soon as MynCorp showed up." Kaamil looked accusingly at Bergur, who stood impassive, apparently incapable of guilt.

"You can't blame the Eridanians for helping themselves to MynCorp stuff after the way they've been treated," Yakini said as she stroked Bergur's arm defensively.

Mex found a perverse delight in how readily Yakini's political allegiance aligned itself with her libido. For once, he kept his thoughts to himself. "So, where are we headed and how long until we get there?"

Kaamil's eyes glazed for a moment before he spoke. "We are heading back out of the plane of the solar system. We do not have solar escape velocity so we will swing back into the plane with a highly elliptical orbit."

"Like a comet?" Yakini chipped.

Mex had an image of years in frozen purgatory. "How do we generate enough thrust to bring us back to Earth orbit?"

"Anti-matter pellets." Bergur grunted glibly.

Mex sighed. "We've been through this. You start blowing up anti-matter behind the ship and we arrive back on Earth as a pretty meteor shower."

Kaamil agreed with a simple nod, but then sagged his stress-tight shoulders. "Unfortunately, I cannot see any other way to develop sufficient thrust to reverse our velocity vector."

"What about the bow thrusters?" Mex's brain started to fire in what he hoped was a lateral direction. "This ship is smart, can't you reconfigure the ion drives to provide drive thrust?"

"There is simply not enough thrust to make a significant change to the momentum of such a huge mass. It would be faster to assist our solar orbit and aim to rendezvous with another inhabited planet on our next pass through the planetary disk."

"How much faster?"

"Probably a few months."

"Not good enough. How long to grow something vaguely resembling new fusion motors?"

"Maybe a month or two."

"Come on. We're only a hop, skip and a jump from Earth. There has to be some way of turning this lump of scrap metal around. No offence, Kaamil."

There was a pause in which mental feet shuffled.

"What about shuttles or escape pods?" Yakini asked hopefully.

"None. We have no crew," Kaamil explained.

"What are we, Scotch mist?" Mex demanded.

"Unexpected passengers. I'm sorry, I should have started building life rafts as soon as you came aboard."

"But how do you get on and off this boat?" Bergur growled.

"I don't," the Pilot said without self pity.

Silence returned. Finally, Kaamil said two words.

"The bunker."

The Pilot seemed to deflate in front of Mex, back to the devastated wreck that had been wrenched into the world in an act of retribution by Julienne. Mex's angel, but an angel of vengeance; Kaamil's guilty conscience reborn and filled with bitter retribution. Mex could not imagine how much it cost the Pilot mentally to even think of the bunker, let alone speak the words out loud. It was a symbol of his long incarceration, mental deterioration and the site of his lowest moment. MynCorp had burnt the memory from his mind and plugged him into a new bunker but Nomia had helped him rediscover his lost life, and with it the truth of a deranged fantasy which had made him think that he could love and be loved by another pilot; an ill-conceived infatuation which had led to the death of the other pilot and taken away her own dream of flying with the stars. Even then, MynCorp could not leave them alone, reincarnating the female pilot as a golem agent and giving her a new life of servitude but the same name.

Julienne, why couldn't you have just stayed? Mex thought at any gods that might be listening.

"You mean that black sphere you lived in before…?" Yakini ran out of words which seemed appropriate.

"Yes." Kaamil did not miss a beat. "The problem is simply that the Suparna has too much inertia for the available thrust. The bunker has a self-contained life support system and is designed to be a life buoy in the event of total system failure." He paused for a moment as he focused on emotional control.

"You mean we abandon ship?" Mex started to feel a plan forming.

"The Suparna's A.I. will run the ship until the engine repairs are complete and then return to Earth orbit. It makes no difference to the ship if we are on board or not. In fact, repairs may well be faster if parts of the life support could be temporarily cannibalised."

"You managed to make a pro-active plan sound like keeping out of the way, but I like it. How do we pilot the sphere?" Yakini could obviously see a chance to get back into the driving seat.

"The bunker is made of dumb material so I cannot reconfigure it, but I could build a brace to attach engine modules."

"Like the modular motors used to switch modes between atmospheric and inter-lunar shuttles?" Yakini's enthusiasm was effervescent.

"That would be a good analogy." Kaamil frowned at his own verbosity. "Yes," he tried with more satisfaction.

They all looked at Kaamil expectantly but he did not seem to notice their implicit agreement to proceed.

"There's a catch, isn't there?" Mex guessed.

"Two," Kaamil sighed. "The most obvious is the bunker was not designed with multiple occupancy in mind."

"That's okay, I'm not shy," Yakini purred, stroking Bergur's arm. Even the stoic Eridanian looked as if he might blush.

Mex laughed before he choked. "Thanks for the image Yakini, but I suspect Kaamil is more concerned about hygiene, air, water and other basic stuff."

"This hardly seems a significant concern when we are trying to save all known life," Bergur said dismissively. "It still sounds like luxury compared to an Eridanian vessel."

"Agreed," smiled Mex. "What's the main concern, Kaamil?"

"The bunker is kept at the centre of a null gravitational field by a shell of exotic material made of its super symmetry equivalent. Normally, the shell automatically configures itself to compensate for the bulk acceleration of the Suparna but in an emergency it can be used to eject the bunker."

"Eject? How savage is the ejection?"

"I can select the vector to nullify a large fraction of our speed relative to Earth."

"What are our chances of surviving the ejection?" Mex asked, keeping up with the Pilot's description.

"Bergur and I will be fine but..." The Pilot did not finish the sentence.

"I can live through anything you can," Yakini almost sneered at Kaamil.

"My muscles might be severally atrophied but my internal organs have been reinforced to prevent rupture at high accelerations. And, to be frank, your physiology is less resistant to damage than normal Terrans."

"Don't worry, the irony isn't wasted on me. My body has been modified for low gravity but I'm less use in zero and high gravity. One day we'll all be on Mars, and then you'll see me as more than a collection of ungainly limbs."

"That's a date then. So, what do we do? I assume you have a potentially dangerous solution," Mex said glibly.

"We will have to build scaffolding around Mex and Yakini's internal organs to prevent damage. Their brains should survive without too much bruising but the heart and other torso organs will need some extra rigidity."

"I assume you're talking nanite organ grafts?" Mex felt the blood draining from his face even before the process had finished been proposed.

"Oh," agreed Yakini.

"I take it this isn't a good plan," Bergur prompted.

"We will have to temporarily shut down their hearts and metabolic systems while the stiffening supports are in place." Kaamil tilted his head slightly as he spoke as if anxious to analyse the emotional content of Bergur's answer.

"You mean, kill us?" Mex assumed that the asymmetry in Bergur's mouth flaps was an indication of agitation.

"The nanites will temporarily replace their haemoglobin to swim oxygen to the brain and tissues while there is no pulse."

"Will they be conscious?"

"No, that would be most distressing for them."

"So, how is it different to being dead?"

Kaamil appeared to be considering the question for a few seconds. "Drones have finished searching the damaged areas of the ship. José and Nomia are not aboard," he said.

"Do you think they abandoned us?" Yakini asked but withdrew the question with a wave of her arm when Bergur growled his objection.

"Maybe that's the way it works," Mex offered. "We pop up here and they stay behind."

"That doesn't sound very useful. It would mean they were left alone to face the Eiodolons." Kaamil said with a sceptical tone.

Mex shrugged. "So, the most likely explanation is that they deliberately separated themselves from us. Unless something went wrong, which seems unlikely judging from how close they got us to Earth. Assuming that all is as it should be, we should continue and assume they will pop up at our moment of greatest need."

Nobody disagreed so Kaamil led the way from the control room, his trailing control chords swaying in invisible currents of data flow.

The sense of wrong was still there. Not a moral complaint, just a concerned frown which took hold of his brow and dug in. Mex tried to tell himself that it was because he knew what had happened to Kaamil and Julienne when they finally confronted each other on the black sphere below. "Have we got to do all that death-defying leaping again or can you magic up a ladder?"

Unease added an arrogant clip to his voice.

"I can do better than that." Kaamil extended his good arm and slowly drew the hand towards his chest. The snaking chords from his spine and limb left arm flickered to attention, reaching for some unseen connection.

The inner wall of the spherical space spasmed and fist sized undulations started to slurp across the surface. At first the only noticeable effect was the occasional optical flare from the drones ferrying equipment towards the centre of the space. These flashes of blue made the space glow and cast the bunker into shadowed relief.

"It's getting bigger."

"No, it's getting closer," Yakini breathed beside him. "An asymmetrical gravitational field."

"Correct, Yakini, I should be able to bring the sphere's entrance directly in front of us."

Mex looked at Kaamil, watching for signs of stress. His voice was calm but he must be suffering. Mex was actually more worried he might not be; retreating back into the detachment which had let him pilot the Suparna for so many years.

Bergur gently put one hand on Yakini's shoulder as if she was the most delicate of flowers. "You know there are more ways this can go wrong than right?" She squeezed his hand robustly.

"There are infinite possible outcomes each way," Kaamil said.

Bergur released some tension in a half-hearted laugh. "That makes me feel so much better," he grunted through half-open flaps.

Without another word Kaamil turned towards the rectangular doorway painted in shadows against the black of the sphere. He stepped off the ledge they were perched on and vanished inside the bunker. Mex shrugged at Bergur and Yakini before following, not allowing hesitation to turn into fear. It can't be worse than a Drop chamber, he thought as gravity did a somersault and then vanished all together.

Kaamil was floating near the far wall, staring fixedly at an intricate web of acceleration-absorbing fibres which converged on the centre of the space. In amongst the grey threads, tubes and cables snaked. Some of them performed a synchronised dance with the cables protruding from the Pilot's body. Mex shuddered. He expected the space to smell like a medieval jail but the total absence of aroma was more dehumanising. He reached out a hand and rested it gently on the shivering shoulder of Kaamil.

"You okay?" he asked.

"Not really, but it's better to be in pain than to feel nothing. Right?"

Mex was rescued from such a complex question by Bergur and Yakini. "I've definitely seen worse." The bundle of purple muscles was fussing over a smaller frame and fibre bundle lashed to the side of the room. Mex looked towards a similar addition to the opposite wall. "Is that mine?" he pointed.

"Yes," Kaamil confirmed. "The nanite control system is integrated into the fibres. Bergur and I will share the pilot webbing."

"How long will I be dead?"

"It will take the fibres an hour to construct, then another to destruct, the internal scaffolding. The ejection of the sphere will be impulsive; there will be no prolonged deceleration."

"So, I'll be out of it for two hours, all for just a moment of deceleration. Are you sure I couldn't just grit my teeth?"

"It is unlikely that any of your major organs would survive the experience but your teeth would be fine."

"Well let's get to it."

As Mex allowed himself to drift towards his acceleration nest he could see Yakini already being drawn into a crucifixion posture by the tightening web of hers. Mex tried to relax despite his body's distrust of being manipulated by an external force. The web gripped his skin, bypassing the MynCorp uniform he still wore. He felt his arms muscles draw tight as his joints opened to their maximum extension. A tingling, like a million ants, signalled the nanites easing themselves through his skin and into his bloodstream. Mex desperately wanted to offer one more quip to the Universe before he dropped. He mentally kicked himself. This was not a Drop chamber, he was not entering the Nexus. This would be over in a couple of hours, not years, and it would not pollute his dreams for the rest of his life. He tried to open his mouth to speak but it was too late. He looked inside, waiting for darkness or a white light but when death came it was a slow decay of self; a repeated fragmentation of his personality until the spark of life could no longer jump from grain to grain. Then the spark itself flickered out.

Chapter 3

"You're serious?" Julienne nodded at the microwire which headed out into the blackness between the towers.

"Believe me, you do not want to walk in the front doors. Only tourists do that. Tourists with really good life assurance." Fez's eyes shined with excitement.

"And when was the last time you checked the other end of the wire?"

"A couple of weeks ago."

"And you just assume the other tower hasn't reconfigured much since then."

"It won't have."

Julienne took hold of the makeshift pulley and clipped it onto the zip-line. Fez moved behind her and put his arm around her shoulders. "What are you doing?" she asked, resisting the urge to break an arm.

"I'm coming with you, and there's only one pulley. Would you rather hold on to me?"

"No."

"Well then." He snuggled closer, almost overpowering her with the smell of teenage sweet. Suddenly, the thought of moving through clean air seemed appealing and Julienne let her feet drop off the ledge and gravity started to drag them along the line.

"What's to stop the building making a meal out of us?" she called over her shoulder.

"Being quiet and stealthy might work," he replied with a level of sarcasm she had to respect.

After a few more seconds, a blackness with a different texture to the surrounding darkness loomed at them. Julienne brought her bare feet up to cushion the impact. They hit hard, their double weight on the low friction wire giving them sizeable momentum. Julienne grunted as her legs absorbed the impact. Fez shifted and she started to choke as his weight pulled on her throat. Taking one hand from the pulley she rearranged his weight onto her shoulders before reaching out for the entrance to Jefferson Tower II.

"You're stronger than you look," Fez offered.

"Very probably, but right now I'm more interested in where this cable goes."

Her hand was carefully tracing the microwire, avoiding putting enough pressure on it to slice through her hand. The fibre ended at the cool roughness of the sick building's cladding. There was no window.

"Where's the window?"

"Straight in front." Fez offered, shuffling round to peer pointlessly at the dark.

"Can you reach over my shoulder and feel for the entrance?" Julienne was aware of the tendons in her wrist stretching, microtears peppering the surrounding muscles as they tried to keep her joints together.

Fez's grip around her throat tightened nervously. "You've got to be joking. I'm not letting go for anything."

"Consider that I am carrying both our weights and that I might decide to lighten my load before risking hanging by one hand," Julienne lied.

There was a pause followed by a shuffling. Two skinny legs wrapped themselves around her waist and the hand crushing her windpipe changed to a forearm. Julienne sighed.

"It's not there," Fez breathed into her neck, the moist fear in his voice condensing on the fine hairs of her ear.

"Try higher up."

"I'm telling you it is not there."

"Well, make a new one."

"What?"

"Just put your palm against the surface. If that doesn't work then draw the outline of an opening with your fingertips." Julienne had a sinking feeling. His ignorance about basic human-building interactions could not be good.

"And that will do what, exactly?"

"The surface must let you in. It's one of the most primitive abilities of the intelligent metal."

"If you say so."

There was more fidgeting which sent rods of white hot pain up her arms.

"Well?" she prompted.

"Nothing. Why exactly should the building do what I ask it?"

"Because that is their primary purpose." He was not that stupid. She was expecting too much from this tower of malignant degeneracy.

His laughter sounded manic in his tight throat and it did not last long. Julienne shuffled her knees, searching for a smoother area of the building to take their weight. One started to slip and she felt her face being pushed closer to the surface. A quick bounce which made Fez swallow a yelp, and she was back on both knees but at the expense of a deep graze which dripped warmth onto her bare toes.

"What about the return cable?" she asked.

She was frustrated by the stupidity of their predicament and by her helplessness. It's like one of those no-win exercises the academy insisted on dropping into the training schedule, she thought, and all the accompanying pop psychology. She kicked herself out of that particular avenue of thought as she realised it inevitably ended with surrender.

Fez was mumbling in her ear again.

"The other cable is two twists up and on the other corridor." He sounded as if panic was starting to shake his tense muscles.

"What does that mean?"

"Up. Too far up," he summarised.

"I got that bit. What's the twist bit?" More than giving him something to think about, she was trying to distract herself from what had to happen next.

His grip rearranged itself on her shoulders as they curved forward under the continuous stress.

"Inside. It's two twists going up. Like, what's a call it? Like inside life."

"A double helix?"

"Something like that."

"Oh."

"Are we going to die?"

Julienne sighed again. "Not just yet. Give me a second."

One layer at a time, she started to boot her implants, searching for the minimum set which would give her the control she needed. As each system acknowledged its readiness, her head felt like it unfolded beyond the confines of her skull into something bigger and noisier. At each step she held her breath waiting for either the wave of passive surrender she had felt before they switched off in the medical laboratory, or the warning message from monitoring MynCorp A.I. minds. She went as far as she dared, leaving the main logic unit and Nexus splice unit in dormant state. A few unusual requests to the service mapper and she was able to interface to the basic splicer, directly from her biological mind.

Julienne opened a direct channel to the building mind she felt hovering nearby in her mindscape. There was a pause of human perceptible duration which must have represented protracted debate for something as accelerated as a building mind, then she screamed at every level of her existence.

Black-ice talons of decay pierced her mind and tore at her humanity. Screaming laughter resonated inside her skull building towards a white noise of liquid horror. The mind of the tower was fractured into two main personalities and a plethora of impotent sub-voices like a drunken audience or over-excited jury. The two partial minds twisted around each other like a pair of snakes trying to pin each other down. Endlessly they climbed, getting nowhere but chipping off splinters of each other as they tussled. The needles of black ice rained down on Julienne as she reeled in the shadow of the battle. Each slither of decayed mind was like a week held inside someone else's nightmare. They tore at the interface between the self she was starting to know and a mind familiar through context but alien in its mechanics and machinations.

Julienne felt at a loss to know how to communicate with these minds directly, without the usual layers of abstraction offered by splice terminals and human-building interface systems. She stared up at the wrestling leviathans, feeling like a speck of insignificance. "Listen to me!" she roared, trusting her splice unit to embed the message in an appropriate protocol.

The lesser voices increased their rattling as if trying to drown her in noise. "You will listen to me. I demand entry."

"Enter at own risk. No liability accepted," something giggled from the melee.

"We are on your skin. Open a portal for us now." She tried to keep her mental tone neutral, not sure how much intonation the interface supported.

"Skin hard and unforgiving. Dying from the hunger. Feed us. Let us grow and move. We want to grow to the sky. Grow to the horizon. We hunger for room to ease the pressure inside."

"Maybe later. For now just open a portal let us in."

"No more fleas. Scratching and poking at our insides. Taking our strength and defecating their poison."

"You will let us in. It is your primary directive. Examine your reason for being. Without me you have no purpose. Let me in and find fulfilment." It was a gamble but Julienne was finding it hard to comprehend a building which considered people as parasites.

"Are you conspiring against me, brother?" Another voice without a centre, or more likely, the same voice but with another mind behind it.

"It wants to come in. It demands entrance but at least it asks, for once." The first mind again.

"You're making allies. This insignificant mind will not help you win. I am stronger than both of you."

"You are so far beneath me, I was talking to this fleshy mind to relieve the boredom."

They continued to argue like over-educated children, communicating at human speed but leaving no perceptible gap between outpourings. Julienne could not build a message to interject. Perhaps if she worked through her higher order logic unit she could argue as an equal. She considered powering up the rest of her mind. Her body felt a long way away but she could sense its shaking stress via the levels of toxins and the weakness of the neuro-response being reported to her with objective detachment. She tried one last human-conceived approach. She pushed a message over the top of their streaming dialogue.

"You both argue about who is the most powerful but all I see is a dead building. Your mind is locked in its death throes unable to even shape the tower which defines your existence."

"The fleshy mind thinks so little of us it would pitch its mind against us. We are sunk beneath the waters of sentience if such a battle of wits is considered possible."

Julienne could not tell which of the minds had spoken, or if it was a new splinter of the fractured mind.

The self-pitying voice continued. "We fight each other for energy, our subsystems unable to cooperate sufficiently to share resources at such a level of scarcity. But in the battle we forget the mental decay that bought us to this end. Let her in, it can make no difference to us now."

An identical voice answered. "I cannot. My outer skin has been static for too long. The metal has scarred, and now it holds us up as much as defines our shape. I have done what I can. She will have to do the rest herself."

Julienne got the message. She sprung back to the wind-chilled reality which was her body. The pain in her shoulders and wrists was no longer a column of statistics. She grunted in receipt of the queued-up sensation.

"Hold tight," she told Fez redundantly, as she pushed up on her toes and held herself away from the wall of the tower. A quick mental shift, and the last of her strength was diverted away from her arms and to her legs. She felt her grip loosen on the pulley but it held for the moment. She kicked off from the wall and swung almost up to horizontal. As the return swing started she locked her legs to make the landing as hard as possible.

Julienne was still shutting down pain receptors as the pair of them crashed through the brittle tower wall and tumbled into the grey void beyond.

*

Kaamil could feel the growing tension in the inner skin of the chamber. The ejection process was cascading towards the final moment of gravitation dipole; an explosive realignment of exotic matter which would allow it to decay into more acceptable physics and fling the pilot sphere into space. Standing waves were building in the degenerate neutronic fluid. With a final farewell telemetry exchange with the Suparna's A.I., Kaamil gave the order to eject.

The force-absorbing web which held him with arms and legs outstretched gripped him tight and quivered with dissipated force. Inside his body, organs were pushed hard against bone and flesh. Blood pushed against bursting capillaries. Tendons strained to hold balls in sockets. Even his teeth hurt, as they tried to work free from his jaw. The acceleration lasted twelve seconds, but it was many more before his brain relaxed back into human thought.

"Bergur, are you alright?"

"You call that acceleration? I've felt worse in the mine-conveyors back home."

Kaamil smiled, cracking bruised lips. "I'm sure."

"Yakini?"

"I've already started the reanimation process. Her body seems intact.

Minor bruising but nothing life-threatening. Mex is okay too."

"Good. Where are we?"

"We are no longer leaving the planetary disk. The engine jig is matching our velocity and preparing to attach to the sphere. We should be under our own thrust within an hour."

Kaamil remained hanging in the web while Bergur wriggled free and floated over to the pale figure of Yakini. "I thought there would be more bruising," the Eridanian said, looking at his own mottled skin.

"There will be some when her heart starts, but for now there is no blood flow. The nanites will repair most of the damage before they restart her metabolism."

"Good."

They lapsed into silence. Kaamil felt a familiar claustrophobia compressing the back of his head. He felt his personality start to retreat in response. He tore free of the webbing and floated in the confined space. Being in freefall in a small sphere actually felt more constrained than being held in the web. He tested his connection to the Suparna, just in case Nomia's magic extended from implausible into impossible. Nothing. He was completely integrated into the pilot's sphere even without being neurally connected, but the sphere was no longer plugged into the Suparna.

He wished her luck and recited a mantra towards their reunion. Opening his eyes again, he decided to concentrate on his immediate senses. After all, for ordinary people that was all they ever had and most managed to remain vaguely sane.

He fussed over Mex, mimicking Bergur's concern for Yakini but without the kissing of eyelids and stroking of fingers. "She'll be fine," he said, more to break the silence than out of a need to reassure. Bergur grunted his acknowledgement.

"Welcome back."

Mex looked up at Kaamil, confusion rapidly being replaced with resigned determination."Thanks, I think. How's Yakini?"

"Fine. She should be waking up any time now."

"Cool. Did it work?"

"Yes. We are now under our own power, and making good progress towards Earth."

"Head to a Lagrange point. Don't risk an orbital insertion."

"Agreed."

"What's the plan?" It was Yakini, propped up on Bergur's lap and massaging life back into her arms and legs. She was almost half a metre taller than the Eridanian peering out from behind her left shoulder.

"We need to get face-to-face with someone high up in MynCorp." The others looked expectantly at Mex.

"And without José or Nomia to wow the audience what are we going to say?" Yakini asked.

"We still don't know when they'll show up again. So, I suggest we worry about one step at a time."

"Typical man."

"And that was so atypically female," Mex retorted. "Glad you're feeling better. Kaamil you have an emergency transponder for this lifebuoy?"

"Yes, Mex. It is a pure machine-to-machine interface, but I can rig the webbing up to give us audio. My apologies for the crudeness, the bunker was designed to be inert with the minimum of intelligent materials."

"That's fine. We'll use that channel to get a verbal foot in the door."

"I am transmitting now. The round trip delay is currently forty seconds."

"That's perfect. It will give me a chance to think."

By the time Mex and Kaamil had navigated their way through the initial layers of a MynCorp A.I. and front-line officials, conversation was almost real-time.

"This is Sardon Lucas of MynCorp intelligence. Good afternoon Mr Tyrian. You sound well, considering."

"You know who I am?"

"Of course. The lifebuoy is transmitting sufficient telemetry for us to reconstruct the identity of the occupants. You are Mex Tyrian; ostensibly, a building personality specialist but known to offer illegal access to the Nexus. The gentleman with you is the pilot of the Suparna, or former pilot judging from your current location. The Eridanian is Bergur Sturlaugur, grandson of Ragnar Sturlaugur, the chief science officer of the original Epsilon Eridani expedition. The MynCorp officer must be Yakini Akida. My apologies to you, Ms Akida. Agent Julienne Garland has been suspended after her breakdown during the Suparna rescue mission. You will be returned to active duty, with MynCorp's thanks, after a period of debriefing. Have I missed anyone?"

"Is Julienne...?"

"What, Mr Tyrian?"

"Nothing. Curiosity distracted me. Have you just spliced all that information or are we really dealing with someone in a position of authority?"

"Authority is a relative concept but you can thank me for introducing Ms Garland into all your lives."

There was malice in Sardon's voice but it was devoid of emotion and, clearly, deliberate. Mex felt sure Sardon was fishing for a reaction. Rather than feeling intimidated, Mex drew strength from the attempted manipulation; if the MynCorp Intelligence agent was completely confident in his relative situation he would not feel the need to test them. Somehow, somewhere, there was an edge which concerned MynCorp. What that might be, Mex had not the slightest idea.

"In that case, after considering the weakness of our position, I would like to offer our unconditional surrender. We request you personally take us into custody." Mex gestured for Kaamil to cut the link as the howls of protest descended on Mex from throughout the cramped black space. Before Mex could quieten Kaamil and Bergur enough to make himself heard, Yakini cut through the noise with two softly lilted words.

"He's right."

Bergur's mouth flaps hung open in a manner Mex had grown to associate with surprise.

"I am?" Mex said.

"It's the only way we'll get to talk to someone of influence. If we resist, they'll send soldiers against us, again."

Mex bit his lip.

Yakini caught the reaction. "She'll be alright. The one thing I learnt about Julienne is that she's a survivor," she said to Mex.

Mex did not bother denying his concern. "So, we surrender," he said. "Anyone disagree?"

Bergur clenched and unclenched his fists three times, sending pulses up the muscles of his bare arms. Finally, he bowed slightly in a neck-free approximation of a nod.

"I have a debt to pay," Kaamil started. "If I cannot make reparations as a free man then I shall pay it in incarceration."

"I'll take that as two yeses. Kaamil, reopen the channel."

"...appreciate the offer."

"Sorry, Sardon. We lost the signal for a moment. Would you mind repeating that?"

"Of course. The short answer is no."

"No?"

"I cannot accept your surrender because you are no longer designated as fugitives."

"You've got a really short memory."

"Your apprehension has already exceeded the energy budget assigned to the task. If you had the Node or Doctor José Sanchez with you, then I would be interested. I'm sorry Mex, you are just not important enough."

"What about Kaamil or Bergur?"

"The Eridanians do not officially exist. I would rather he vanished back under the ice of his home-world. The pilot is most likely beyond redemption, particularly as he has been separated from his craft. The Suparna has been listed as scrap after scans showed the extent of its damage during your Earth flyby. None of you are worth any more effort. Sorry, but if you could drop Yakini Akida at a MynCorp station we'll take her off your hands. Otherwise, good luck to you all. You can assume that your MynCorp credits have been revoked. Your may not earn or spend energy at any MynCorp establishments. Maybe one of the Jovian moons would be a good place for you to seek work."

"Well, that's a relief. Being hunted was starting to hurt my business interests." Mex continued without hesitation. "Seeing as we're all friends now, who do I talk to about selling some Eridanian technology?"

"What?" Bergur and Sardon said in unison.

"Bergur and I have entered a business relationship to financially exploit two recent advances in Eridanian technology. Firstly, there is the dimension-folding engine which allowed us to jump the Suparna from interstellar space into Earth orbit. Secondly, Kaamil here is modelling the latest in symbiant coupling slimes, allowing him to maintain his connection to the Suparna without sensory and physical isolation. We would like to give MynCorp first rights to this technology before we start open bidding with all four corporations."

"You have design details for these inventions?"

"Would Bergur risk alienating his people without a guarantee of an energetic return?"

"And you claim you have not offered this tech to other corporations, Durga Corporation for example?"

"What? No, why would we start with a second fiddle organisation?"

"No reason." There was pause long enough for a shift of perspective. "Mr Tyrian, suddenly you find yourself in demand again. I will restore your account long enough for negotiations to be completed. Are you able to make your way to Dyson station?"

"We'll have to get a shuttle from a Lagrange station."

"You have sufficient calories."

"So, no expenses then?"

"What do you think? Most of your energy was acquired illegally, so I consider this offer to be almost excessively generous."

"Yes, I suspect you do. We'll be in contact."

"No need. I'll be waiting for you."

Chapter 4

"We're alive!" Fez sounded shocked that reality had come down in his favour for once.

Julienne said nothing. Nausea swelled in her stomach, accompanied by an equally wave-like pain in her legs and arms. She lay on her back fighting for the mental control which would banish the agony to a warning voice in the corner of her perception.

"We should keep moving before the building changes its mind," she said, but made no attempt to move.

Fez took the hint and pulled Julienne to her feet. She accepted the help without comment.

"There's a man half a twist up from here who knows about tech stuff," Fez offered, as he half-dragged her towards the doorway.

By the time they were in the gently sloping corridor Julienne had regained enough function in her legs to at least give the appearance of walking, although much of her weight was still bearing down on the gangly frame of Fez. He had his arm around her waist as if they were promenading. Julienne realised his help was as much about raising his credibility amongst the people they passed as offering her support. She decided to afford him this simple pleasure, although it was too mercenary to feel like flattery.

The building was superficially in better shape than the first tower. The corridor rose up before them, turning always to their right. The walls and floor were smooth but blotchy in colour, as though rashes had infected the material and were slowly eating away the surface. Many of the regularly spaced doorways had been widened with crude violence to form shop fronts. None of them displayed a name or obvious wares, but there was usually a man or woman sat just inside the room, warm clothes pulled over their frames to hide whatever merchandise they held close to their bodies. Many of the people were clustered in small groups, talking in the low tones of paranoia or wise caution. There was little evidence of permanent habitation. There was the occasional portable kitchen preparing bubbling stews of indistinct origin, but these seemed to be serving the transitory appetites of customers or traders. Julienne suspected most of these people lived in the main city, and travelled here to trade, away from the suspicious gaze of MynCorp and the other corporations.

"Where are we going?" Julienne asked softly, aware that Fez's face was very close to hers, although, more worryingly, she could no longer smell him.

"Just up here. The bloke's called Sickle."

It's a big planet, Julienne thought, but not big enough for that to be a coincidence. She remembered a certain politically vocal friend of Mex's coming up during her research, back when life had seemed predictable, if not simple. She could not delude herself she had been any happier then, but she had been less prone to fear for her life on a daily basis. Her mind flitted through memories, hunting for happiness. Mex's face popped up. Julienne remembered a brief moment of pleasure over a shared meal, and a political argument which had nearly ended in a kiss. Julienne felt an unwelcome flush of heat between her breasts. She coughed herself back to full alertness.

"Times must be hard," she muttered to herself.

Fez stopped in front of a man. Julienne tested her legs and decided to take her own weight. Fez reluctantly let her go and stood fiddling with his newly unoccupied hands.

"Mister Sickle, I've bought someone to see you," he said to the man who seemed to be doing his best to stare straight through them.

"And why would you want to do that?" he said in an overly dramatic hiss and without making eye contact.

"She wants to sell some tech."

"I repeat, why would you want to do that?"

Julienne stepped directly into the line of sight of the man. "Sickle, I know you trade technology. I have a simple proposition for you. No corporate strings. I am as anxious as you for this transaction to be anonymous and quick."

He looked her straight in the eyes. He seemed surprised they were the same height but his gaze did not falter. "The difference is that I'm nobody and you are definitely MynCorp."

"I'm absent without leave, but you're right. This way you can make some energy and get one over on MynCorp at the same time."

"Or end up in the Drop."

Julienne decided to play her one and only joker. "Mex spoke more highly of you than this."

"Who?" Fez asked on Sickle's behalf.

"You mean the same Mex who vanished three months ago after meeting with a MynCorp operative. I doubt you visited him in the Drop."

"He's not in the Nexus. He's very much up and about. Last time I saw him he was living it up on a rogue MynCorp interstellar ship."

"Mex Tyrian? Are we talking about the same back-room programmer?"

"He turned out to have a rebellious sub-personality and a propensity to survive big odds."

"Good for him. Was it you trying to kill him?"

"Quite the opposite." The words stumbled out before she could attach them to a thought.

Sickle studied her carefully with an uncomfortable disregard for politeness. Julienne stood straight, her body back under precise control.

"You can go now Fez," Sickle said, without breaking eye-lock with Julienne.

Julienne spared Fez a smile and a brief kiss on the cheek as an afterthought.

"See ya around." Fez tried to sound casual as he wandered off, back the way they had come.

"Use the stairs," Julienne called after him.

Poorly-oiled gears wound the bed back towards a sitting position, rattling her body from its stupor. Julienne realised she had not slept for fifty-odd hours. Despite the uncertainty of her position and company, her body tried to shut itself down for some repair time. It took a couple of mental kicks from her implants before she felt fully alert. The woman with the greasy face bent over the luminous display, the poorly maintained back-light flickering on her face like sparks off an oil slick. Sickle stood to one side watching his investment with keen interest.

"She got what she claims to have?" he asked.

"Oh yes. Indeed. Indeed. Lot's of yummy tech snuggled up close to her mind stuff." The woman, who had been introduced to her as Scrappy Lou, spoke in two alternating voices, one shrill like a bird, and the other the squawk of a small child. She did not appear to be talking to herself but Julienne decided she probably spent a lot of time alone. "We could split this load across many customers. Make many upgrades from one scrapping."

"I'm only interested in trading some memory and processing capacity. I'm keeping the rest." Julienne sat up and looked at both Sickle and Lou.

Sickle said nothing. Lou started to fidget with a couple of curved blades which hung from hooks under the fold of her stomach. Julienne hoped they were purely decorative; there would not be much of her brain left if she went at her head with such crude tools.

Without resuming eye contact, Lou muttered. "She just wants to trade the implants which are deactivated. How strange. How do we know they work at all? Turn them on and give us a demo."

"That might not be a good idea," Julienne said tentatively.

Sickle leant back against a wall with his hands shoved in deep pockets. "Maybe, because we would be knee-deep in MynCorp security," he said casually.

Lou started to fidget more fervently. "Of course. This is MynCorp agent tech. Not civilian. So hard to be sure. MynCorp always first to market with cross-over stuff. Why does she want to trade her agent tech?"

"Because she is no longer an agent." It was a statement, but Sickle's eye challenged Julienne to contradict him.

"Let's face it," Julienne used her best no-nonsense voice, "if the tech was mine to trade, I wouldn't be here. Why would anyone go though all the hassle of getting here if they had a legitimate reason to make a trade? So let's cut through the next teeth-sucking stage and get right on with the haggling. I want fifty MegaCalories for one hundred exabytes of storage and a grade four, personal A.I."

There was a pause long enough for Lou to drop a cleaver with a barbed end and retrieve it from the sea of detritus which threatened to swallow it. Sickle laughed freely, his shoulders dropping to a new and genuine level of relaxation. "You look like a city girl but you talk like a first-rate scavenger. I think I actually envy Mex."

Lou shook the retrieved implement then licked the blade clean. "That's a lot of MynCorp credits for a few slithers of crystal."

Julienne allowed her face to show a minor conciliatory smile and stated her remaining condition. "I got somewhere to go. Somewhere off-world and, by the way, the calories can't be MynCorp. I'll need them from one of the other corps and not tied to my identity."

"Anything else?" Sickle asked without losing the smile which cut like a wound though the dark stubble of his broad chin.

"No."

"Sue, you got that many Usher calories?" Sickle asked.

"We have. Not sure we want to part with them. Maybe for all the implants." Scrappy Sue spat briefly, revealing painted teeth and a tattooed tongue.

"Now Sue. We've moved beyond that. We're all friends now. We can't cheat Mex's girlfriend. I'll never hear the end of it."

Julienne felt a moment of outrage at his presumption but then felt confused by her own reaction. The fact she cared was a worry to her. She filed the experience away for later consideration, but it was immediately obvious she had not shed all the emotions she had felt while losing her mind on-board the Suparna. She was going to have to face the real possibility some of those feelings might be real. Such realisation was not going to improve her chances of keeping her personality intact – MynCorp seemed insistent she try life number three.

"Forty thousand is as much as the tech is worth to me." Sue said, both her personalities agreed for once.

Julienne realised she had no idea if that was enough for her plan. How much did it cost to hire a mercenary crew?

"Right then. I'll leave you to it." Sickle eyed the curtain hanging across the entrance.

Julienne was surprised. She had expected him to keep a very close eye on his cut of the tech. Sue explained his reluctance to hang around with a mocking sneer. "He doesn't like to see inside. Thinks he is immortal. Nothing but his will inside." She kicked the mounting post of the surgical couch.

Julienne tensed involuntarily as the seat jerked back to horizontal underneath her, leaving her head floating for a moment and her knuckles white on the scuffed upholstery of the arm rests. Sickle gave a smile that was probably meant to be reassuring, and ducked under the curtain.

"Just lie back and relax. Won't hurt a bit. With luck." All sentiment had been stripped from Sue's words by regular repetition.

Julienne closed her eyes and started to slow her brain, disabling enhancements in reverse order of complexity. There was a hiss and a cool tingle on her scalp as Sue sprayed a self assembling substrate. Alarms started to flick in Julienne's vision as the substrate started to tap into her systems, re-routing control to whatever jury-rigged hackware Sue was using to subvert the implants. Another alarm told her that a dozen memory modules had deregistered from the memory manager and were busy disassociating into her blood stream.

"I'll have to put you on blood dialysis to filter out the tech. We're embarrassed at the evasiveness of the method but needs must. Maybe you could have a word with MynCorp about the price of osmosis shunts?" Sue was humming to herself as she worked, maybe as some kind of mantra to help with the mental challenge of interfacing to Julienne's implants remotely.

Julienne managed a grunt through the nervous tension of feeling bits of her mind break off and swim towards freedom. She prepared herself for the more dramatic loss of major analytical units - she would not be performing tactical battles in four curved dimensions from now on – squashing alert systems before they could react.

Something altogether different was happening. There were no alerts, no subsystems signing off. There was simply the feeling of sinking into a coma like brain death. All her implants started to melt into the slushy swamp of incoherence.

"What's happening?" she heard the words in her human mind but they emerged as the strangled wail of something primitive.

"Just relax dear. We're just helping ourselves to all that lovely MynCorp tech. Don't think you'll be running home to complain. You'll be better off without it. You're mind will be your own, at least the half that's left in there." Julienne felt chubby knuckles tapping on her skull.

Julienne sat up, shaking her head to throw off the mesh of nanites crawling over her head. Nothing happened. She was still lying with her hands clamped on the arm rests and teeth gritted against expected pain. Julienne thrashed in panic but her body was not her own. It was as if her physical body had been replaced by a mental replica. She felt herself move but the world through her eyes remained still.

A wave of claustrophobia crashed through the barrier between the primitive and civilised halves of her mind; the feeling of paralysis as close as a coffin. Julienne reflexively fired up every implant that would respond. Adrenaline mingled with the processing boost of artificial intellect to throw her predicament into sharp focus. Feelings of futility and helplessness were amplified beyond her ability to tolerate by her new position of rarefied perception.

Julienne took a diver's breath as she prepared for her one and only resort.

The handful of implants still responding entered a self-defence mode and shifted significant electrical potential to their skins. She hoped that the resulting electric field would fry the sensitive nanites on her scalp, assuming that the surgical bed was insulated.

The momentary magnetic field kicked into the fleshy parts of her mind like an exploding light bulb. Every conscious and subconscious thought in her mind pushed hard against her spine and then rebounded. Her heart beat once, as if trying to expel all her blood into space, and then stalled. Her lungs spat out their load of air like the screeching brakes of a steam train.

There were no thoughts which knew the name. Her consciousness was draining out through the tears in her eyes but she could only perceive one image; a face with a smile which deserved slapping, even as her own tears burned blisters into her eyes. Then the smile faltered and was replaced by concern so pure she could not brush it away with cynical sarcasm. The face had an associated memory and a context which drew obvious parallels with the here and now. She had been lying on an acceleration couch, clutching her knees to her chest to protect herself against the splinters of her mind that remained when the whole had disintegrated. She had been focused on capturing the Node called Nomia. All of her mental resources had been humming with the unifying direction the objective had awarded her. Then it had all come crashing apart when Nomia, or her partner José, had deployed some novel technology to disable all the advanced hardware on Julienne's ship. Her mind had shut down without a warning whimper. She was left with instinct, short term memory and raw emotions; everything she had gratefully sacrificed when she accepted the new life as a golem.

Mex had come to her and offered unconditional support and comfort. This delinquent waste of potential had been the only bloom in the scorched earth of her imploding personality. She had let the seed of emotional connection through a crack in her heart and it had grown into a twisted vine which had confused and turned her dedication. Later she had regained some control and fled to find objectivity, but at that one moment when all she could see was blackness he had given her enough of himself to let her carry on.

The transition into unconsciousness was not accompanied by any sense of falling or dimming. Her mind was already too disorientated to know whether the light grew brighter or dimmer but one syllable was carried though her lips by a last sigh. It was a man's name. A man that had tried to escape from her all the time they were together but still lingered in her mind when all other thoughts had fled.

*

A shower of grey dust stung Kaamil's eyes as he adjusted his hold on the beam. The grit explored his face, tempting him to wipe it away. The nagging emptiness below his feet kept his knuckles white on the dismantled gantry.

Dalal and Grace giggled to his left. Qadir was hanging by his left arm, casually examining the fingernails of his free hand. He was only six months older than Kaamil but already four inches taller and developing the build of a Jovian cloud dredger. A tension had developed between Qadir and the girls which Kaamil could sense but not decode. On the opposite beam, Joshua tried to shrug, mouthing a question mark.

A rumble rolled down the tunnel, buffeting their perch with subsonic tremors. Kaamil tried to ignore the way the vibrations made the beam feel slick with oil. He took some minor satisfaction from seeing Qadir frantically grab the beam, his face flushed with pounding blood.

The ore carrier crunched around the curve of the tunnel, its transmission system dropping through a dozen gear ratios as it decelerated. Half rolling and half snaking down the wall of the tunnel, it slowed to a more leisurely pace and continued along the floor. Each of the dozen caterpillar segments tore into loose rubble, briefly struggling for traction.

"The second hopper," Qadir directed.

Kaamil and Joshua nodded. Dalal and Grace just stared with wide eyes.

"Now!" Qadir dropped from sight.

Kaamil was briefly aware of a complicated series of negotiations between the adrenal excitement of his brain and disbelieving fingers. Then he was in free fall.

The empty ore hopper moved beneath him as he fell. Qadir had already landed and was looking back up. Kaamil had time to see Dalal falling next to him, her arms held out like wings. Grace and Joshua were watching them from between their feet, their hands still firmly attached to the gantry.

"Now," Qadir repeated.

"No," Kaamil shouted, "too late." Then he and Dalal were sprawled together in the dirt of the hopper's floor. They struggled to roll apart, their limbs tied in the awkward knots of those still getting used to teenage bodies. Kaamil was rescued from his embarrassment by an extended whoop from Joshua.

Kaamil got to his feet and pulled up on the rear lip of the hopper. The toothed surface of the cylindrical caterpillar track continuously emerged from inside the drive segment and slid rearward until it sank back below the surface, just before the next hopper. Grace's face appeared grinning back at him.

"They okay?", Dalal asked from behind Kaamil.

"Yeah, they're in the next hopper."

Qadir jeered, "very cosy."

Clear of the remains of the old transport hub, the ore carrier accelerated hard. It started to climb the outer wall of the first curve, ageing gyros struggling to keep the hoppers level.

The five kids hung over the edge, excitedly pointing out vague shapes in the shadows of the tunnel. Kaamil felt his ears pop as they passed from one pressure segment to the next. He retrieved the breather mask from his belt without thinking. He grinned through the window of the mask but Dalal did not find the painted animal face amusing any more. Kaamil tried it on Qadir and got a friendly punch on the arm.

They continued in enforced silence. Each of them containing their excitement behind the wafting feathers of capillary air pumps, plucking at the air like feeding crabs. Eventually, the mask seals relaxed and the smell of dusty tunnel air leaked in.

"We're close," Kaamil whispered near Dalal's ear.

They waited for a sign that the derelict station was near. The transport would be forced to slow down to a few metres a second by the disused platform projecting from the wall of the tunnel. The vibrations climbing Kaamil's legs shifted from a buzz to a jarring stutter. With mutually-reassuring smiles the three teenagers helped each other onto the edge of the ore bucket. Grace and Joshua were already perched on the side of the third hopper. Vague lights shimmered somewhere in the darkness. It was now or never.

Arching high in the air, each of them jumped the four metres to the platform.

Reunited, the small band of explorers laughed and punched the air.

"We made it," Grace and Dalal cried. The two girls hugged.

Qadir slapped Joshua on the arm. "Thought you were going to bottle it," he said.

"Never, we just fancied our own carriage."

A monochrome hologram flickered into life above the entrance to the Spa. "Welcome to the Artemis Resort. Here on the dark side of the Moon we can offer you the only true retreat from the permeating electromagnetic fields of the modern world. We hope you enjo.."

A stone ricochetted off the emitter. "What a load of bollocks," Qadir scoffed.

"Whatever," Dalal shrugged and headed through the entrance.

The moulded edges of the resort's corridors were cracked and smeared in lunar dust, as if the extruded mica was morphing back into the virgin lunar soil. The spa wore its abandonment as tears of detritus, forming small drifts in the corners of each room. Fashion had moved on and discarded this place such that the fluted mouldings leant as much age as the physical degradation.

"It's hard to believe that this place was ever popular," Kaamil said.

Grace fell into step next to him. "This place used to pull in more calories than the rest of the settlement combined. People came from all over Earth for a bit of pampering."

"Now it just feels sad and empty."

"I think that was the idea. The empty bit. No sim broadcasts shaking all your electrons."

"Come on. They can't have been that daft."

"Why daft? It can't be good for us to be exposed to such a continuous barrage of electromagnetic emissions."

"But for half of each lu-day this side of the moon is facing the Sun."

"Yeah well. Maybe they just served really good food."

Qadir slapped them both on the back, his face suddenly between theirs. "Let's play a little game."

"Capture the flag?" Kaamil guessed.

"Capture the flag! Start running!"

*

"Play nicely."

Julienne's cheeks hissed with the indignant heat of childhood injustice. All she had been doing was the same as she always did. Why did Mummy never remember that? Instead she repeated the first lie Julienne had ever noticed – the fact that grown-ups could lie had been the first shocking brick in her wall of isolation – as she said, with a tone of perpetual disappointment, "It takes two to argue."

Julienne cursed her brother silently from behind hate-squinted eyes. He smiled without a care as curse and scolding slid from his skin without leaving a blemish of self-doubt. Julienne did the thing she knew would infuriate her brother the most. She returned to her splice session, blanking him as if he had never been born. The data, that winked at her as if begging to be stroked and played with, meant nothing to her. It was the patterns they made she found enthralling and addictive. The universe inside the Nexus was like a kaleidoscope of information, forever shifting into intricate patterns of unearthly beauty. One pattern would start to fragment and chaos seemed about to scatter structure to eternity, when a new and more wonderful collection of shapes could break through and dance just for her.

She had once told her Dad but he had used the chat as another opportunity to show he considered running amok with all the neighbour's stupid children as more precious than the beauty she swam in on her own. It was not that she wanted to be alone – unless the alternative was consorting with the monster which pretended to be her brother – but if she could not get Dad to understand then what chance did she have with Pran, the wide-eyed boy from the apartment currently next door? A kid who found pleasure in tormenting the building by demanding all the furniture in his room be suspended from the ceiling.

She found the data patterns reassuring. Reality could not be too wrong while such perfection existed. Like life, it was always changing but, unlike the real world, it never failed to take her breath away with its staggering beauty.

Julienne rose closer towards consciousness, finding herself in a mature body, but not a grown-up version of the one she started out with. The head her thoughts echoed in was hurting. There seemed to be more energy in the pain than in the rest of her slack body.

A person-shaped shadow hovered above her. It seemed to be expecting something from her. "What?" she mumbled with a voice that was not the one she had learnt to speak with.

"I said, I thought I told the two of you to play nicely." The voice was definitely not her Mum's. Apart from being male, it had a defensive level of over-confident swagger, that invoked impressions of small-time criminals perpetually on the brink of making it big.

"Sickle, what did you and that butcher do to me?" Julienne felt well enough to berate even if getting her eyes to focus was proving tricky.

"I think the question is more, what you did to her."

Julienne turned her head to follow the focus of Sickle's attention. The room followed at a leisurely pace, overshot and then settled with a nauseas wobble. A Sue-shaped blob lay half-drowned in the ankle-deep sludge and detritus that obscured the floor. Julienne's sight settled enough for her to make out a pale trail of drool running from the fallen woman's mouth. A series of shifting bubbles captured her breath as it pushed between half-closed lips.

"She'll live," Sickle offered after leaving the gap in which Julienne might have asked.

"Great. What about me?"

"You seem to be alive, unless I'm talking to residual charge in an implant."

"I think I'm still in here." She tried a smile. The corners of her mouth jerked into a brief grimace. Buoyed by this minor muscular victory, she sat up on the surgical couch. She retched and vomit was halfway to her throat before she clamped down, overriding her body's instinctive reaction to ingested poisons. No amount of stomach cleansing was going to make this headache go away. Maybe a week in bed would help.

"If you want to avoid the MynCorp security squad at the front door, you might want to follow me." He paused long enough to smile ironically, and then turned and whistled his way back into the corridor.

Julienne did not have to ask how they had found her. She had sent a surge through every piece of hardware in her head. Hunter programs across half of the Nexus must have sung like a choir. Combined with the universal theory of cascading woes, life was not going to let her have a recuperative nap. Her own internal diagnostics indicated she was physically capable of walking, and, after a fashion, they were right. Her leg muscles responded to weight with sporadic success. At randomly inconvenient moments a thigh or calf muscle would revert to flaccidity leaving Julienne staggering for support.

Sickle moved swiftly through the crowded corridor, his nonchalance barely concealing the tension beneath. Julienne ignored those she clashed shoulders with, her eyes fixed on the back of Sickle's head. They seemed to be ascending further up the building. While heading away from the search-party below seemed sensible, she could not help feeling they were just delaying the inevitable.

"Where are we going?" she asked when her legs were strong enough to catch up with Sickle's shoulder.

"This way."

"Don't be obtuse."

"I've got transport."

Julienne almost stopped in her disappointment. He could only mean a taxi. MynCorp security standard operations mandated a lock-down of all taxi drones before commencing a building search. With most of the city buildings able to create a taxi landing spot at almost any point there was no other way of capturing a target without a line of sight shot. The only feasible alternative was hard to believe. "You have a private vehicle?"

"Not exactly. This way."

Sickle ducked into an unremarkable doorway to his left. Julienne followed after checking behind to see if anyone had noticed them. When her eyes caught up with her feet she tilted forward with a vertiginous lurch. There was a ragged hole in the side of the building which reduced the room to a ledge. The blue and orange lights of the city twinkled as the streets and buildings radiated their daytime heat back into the sky. Sickle was gone. Other than a small pile of leaves clustering in a corner, the ledge was as empty as it was perilous.

"Sickle?" she called.

A grinning head popped into existence directly in front of her. "You called?" he said, as if being a floating head was completely reasonable.

"Refraction field. Very clever." She pushed back on his forehead with one hand as she stepped off the ledge.

Inside, the drone looked like an ordinary taxi, with four deformable couches and a shell which was set to translucent but could probably be adjusted anywhere between opaque and transparent.

Julienne inspected Sickle more carefully. "You're working for someone important," she stated. "This kind of craft is not licensed to fly by MynCorp."

"We can discuss my business arrangements after we get out of here."

"I hope the refraction field is broad spectrum or else this will be a short and, probably, terminal flight."

"I flew in undetected. We'll fly out the same way."

"What are we waiting for?"

"I wanted to let them get close enough to make it fun."

"Don't be an idiot."

"It this is how you treat your rescuer …" Sickle's complaint faded into a mutter as he drew a square on the nearest surface and fiddled with the control display which flickered into existence. The small craft lurched petulantly as the senile building dropped away and became a deformed shadow of the buildings around it.

"So, who are you taking me to see?" Julienne asked.

"What makes you think I'm not acting on my own behalf?"

"If any non-corporate organisation on Earth had access to unlicensed cloaking technology they would not risk exposing it to MynCorp for anything as mundane as rescuing an agent who has temporarily lost her way. Another corporation might consider me a resource of sufficient value to push the boundaries of the cartel agreement. So which corporation is it? DogStar?"

"I don't normally work for corporate vampires but sometimes their goals align with mine, and they have deep energy reserves."

"Yes, yes. I'm not interested in your alcohol-fuelled anti-corporate credentials."

"Mex primed you to say that." Sickle sagged. "Durga Corporation. They're paying me to deliver you to them."

"How did you know I would be at the Jefferson building?"

"I didn't. I was genuinely buying tech, but I had a word with a contact when I saw what you had in your head and … Well, I'll let her tell you."

The drone dropped down towards the blank exterior of the Durga embassy building, weaving once to avoid another taxi that was ascending, oblivious to their intersecting trajectories. The roof of the building puckered and let them into a vertical shaft which descended into the heart of the building. Julienne pushed the shell of the taxi to maximum transparency but she could see nothing except featureless walls. As the capsule slowed to a halt, Julienne leant close to Sickle and asked, "Was there really a MynCorp security detail hunting me?"

"Of course," he said quickly. She held his gaze, using some of her working processing power to penetrate the muscle and chemical masks he used to hide his intent. "Honestly. What do you think I am?" he pleaded.

Julienne did not answer but she was fairly convinced he was telling the truth. She stepped from the taxi and fired up a few analytical implant modules. The building would be shielded from MynCorp systems to a high level and, probably, from her, but she might get a few clues from any semi-open systems around her.

The taxi had come to rest in a blank space. The access shaft had dilated and vanished after it had disgorged them. A person-sized area of white wall twisted and formed an iris which lead into a short corridor. Sickle lead the way to the single door at the far end. The door vanished as they approached and Sickle stepped to the side to let Julienne enter.

An impossibly tall woman stood up from a splice table and smiled broadly as they entered. Even by Martian standards she was statuesque but her expansive nose and cheeks defined her heritage unambiguously.

"Ms Garland, delighted." The woman said with a sing-song lilt. She nodded an acknowledgement to Sickle, then turned back to Julienne. "Please, have a seat. I hope your journey was not too arduous." Without waiting for a response she continued, "I apologise for my rudeness but I am just finishing a meeting. Would you excuse me for a moment?" She sat down and was instantly lost in a glaze of splice lasers.

Julienne shrugged and took one of the two offered fixed form chairs arranged squarely on the door side of the splice desk. The room was as carefully aligned as the woman's overly stiff, green suit. Everything was mutually square, from the cubist art on the walls to the vase of crystal grown flowers on the table next to her. Julienne found herself lifting the vase and checking for a locating cross on the surface of the table, before placing it back down at a slight angle. Such an act of petty defiance confused Julienne. If someone had moved something in her quarters she would have corrected it at the earliest opportunity. Somehow she knew her behaviour must be Mex's fault in some convoluted way. Julienne straightened the vase and smiled at her host apologetically. If the woman noticed she gave no indication.

The splice session ended with a flicker and the woman's focus was instantly back on Julienne. "Now then. Introduction time. My name is Pimlico Sergeant and I represent Durga Corporation in certain strategic areas." She was watching Julienne with a scrutiny which felt like being reduced to a series of Pavlovian reactions.

Julienne could not think of anything to say apart from a desire to ask for eight hours to lie down. Pimlico seemed happy to do the talking. "What would you say if I said I believe you?"

"You believe me?"

"Yes."

"You believe me about what?"

Pimlico ignored the question. "We have been monitoring something odd in the Nexus for over a year. MynCorp have been trying to keep control of it but we think something big is coming. There will be change."

"And you are looking to benefit from the change? Are you trying to introduce an element of competition?"

"Heaven forbid! No. The cartel has been good for all the corporations. We would not risk the wrath of the other members by interfering, but when the new status quo is established we would like a bigger slice of the pie. Ideally, an Earth shaped slice."

"Good luck. If you are trying to recruit me then I don't think my current employer would appreciate the attempt."

"Recruiting you would be of no value to me. No offence intended, but you are almost engineered to be loyal to MynCorp. We would like to offer you the opportunity to redeem yourself in its eyes."

"I can't see how that is possible, or why you would make such an offer. I would not and could not spy for you."

"We know that the missing Nexus node is key to what's happening in Verity Space. The first causal glitch coincided with her abduction."

"Causal glitch?"

"One of the things we have been monitoring is the relative agreement of a network of atomic clocks at a dozen points in the Earth's orbital path. They are left over from a twenty-first century attempt to separate competing unified field theories. Every so often the clocks glitch due to unlikely coincidence of quantum properties. Close to a year ago all the clocks jumped together. The glitch was universal. This part of reality jumped as something passed through Verity space. Our theorists assure me it could only be caused by a coherent ripple in the local Downey field. Something like a shift in reality, ringing out from a central point of discrepancy. We triangulated the source to Earth using the relative intensity of the glitch at each clock."

Julienne guarded her reaction but her mind was racing. She had been right from the beginning. The Node had simply vanished from the Nexus facility and reappeared somewhere else. It had seemed the only possible answer even if it seemed ludicrously unlikely.

Julienne interrupted Pimlico's flow. "The thing that confuses me is why you are revealing so much valuable information. The more you say, the more I fear for my future."

"You're still thinking too small. This is the beginning of a major shift in our little corner of reality. The information I am giving you could only make any difference if MynCorp were prepared to act on it. They have already decided on a strategy of entrenchment. I'm sure you have tried to warn them but they are not prepared to listen. They can only see what they might lose."

"But I'm sure that Durga Corporation does not make a policy of revealing market-sensitive information just for the mental well being of the population."

"We want you to resume your mission to retrieve the Node."

"For you?"

"No. For MynCorp. She's of no use to us, we are not licensed to implement Nexus technology."

"But."

"We would like to talk to her briefly before you hand her back."

"Last I saw the Node and her merry band were a couple of light years away. I doubt you have any interstellar ships faster than the usual fusion drive. Are you happy to wait a few years for me to find her?"

"Firstly, we detected another causal glitch yesterday from Mars and secondly, we have a little experimental shuttle which can get you there in less than a week. It seats four. Plenty of room for you and Mister Sickle here."

"Mars?" Julienne said.

"What?" Sickle winced.

"Mister Sickle, you will continue your escort duties for Ms Garland."

"I don't work for you. I go where I please."

"My apologies, Mister Sickle. I forgot myself. You are, of course, free to make your own decisions, but I believe our remuneration agreement is agreeable to you, and you would agree that our goals are still aligned. Is that not true?"

"I suppose so."

"So you'll go?"

Sickle turned to Julienne and asked, "Does it count as manipulation if I'm aware of it?"

Julienne said, "Yes, but you're not alone."

Pimlico simply smiled.

Wisps of pure water vapour drifted through the sky above Bergur. He wondered at the brilliant clarity of the clouds, realising that he had never experienced real white before. He had grown up associating white with ice but this colour was dense and total rather than the diffusion of light.

Above the streaks of weather, the organic blocks of green, blue and brown formed a patchwork of pulsing life. The broad expanses of warm oceans acted as a backdrop to the mottled variety of the life-bearing land. Cities sat exposed on the surface like fungal growths, seemingly unaware of their vulnerability.

The colours started to pulse in front of his eyes. He felt the toxins in his blood throb with the same rhythm. The amount of oxygen in the Dyson station was overwhelming to him, making the algae in his skin glow a florescent purple and flooding his system with psychotropic waste products. Eventually it would kill him, but for now he was enjoying both the rush and the thought that he was a short jump from the world his Grandfather had been born on. A world he had turned away from just as it had turned its back on him.

Bergur reached up to the diamond ceiling of the low orbit space station and traced the outline of mountains on the Earth spread out above him. A house-sized cylinder of shiny metal punched through the clouds on the spider-thin chord which tethered the station to the Earth's surface. The centripetal force that gave the station a sense of gravity inverted his sense of up and down. So, the cylinder appeared to fall from the Earth's surface towards him. It slid into the belly of the station beneath him and he watched it come to a rest beneath his feet. It was replaced by two slender feet encased in grey socks, each toe individually wrapped in fabric that had stiffened slightly in response to the low gravity environment. Attached to the feet were two ankles that flowed up and up before gradually curving into calf muscles which stood proud of the pencil-thin bones. The skin was the warm earthy brown of chocolate beans and seemed free of the darker patches which had formed a map of damage after the ejection of the Pilot sphere from the Suparna.

Bergur let his eyes drift up towards Yakini's face, framed by the bright disk of the Earth, savouring every centimetre of her two metre frame. She was the complete opposite of every Eridanian woman. She probably would not be able to stand up on Epsilon Eridani Gamma, but that would be the least of her worries as she suffocated in the low oxygen and acidic vapour which passed for air. His initial infatuation with Yakini had been his perpetual search for novel experiences, as he suspected he had been for her. Now he felt an upwelling of emotion he knew could very easily turn to love. She managed to maintain a perfect balance between being irreverently carefree and softly wise. Now there were two women he would die for. In fact, half of the human women he had met since he left Captain Finnur's crew. Assuming he was not hopelessly fickle, only fate could bring him into contact with these two women at the same time. He hated the thought of a cosmic force which could steer reality, bypassing his free will. If he was going to give his life for their cause then he should at least have the satisfaction of knowing it was by choice.

His eyes found her face and the smile of blood-filled skin and square teeth stretching in a half circle beneath expressive cheeks. All thoughts of death and self-sacrifice were blown from his head by her brown eyes which blended carefree irreverence with passionate dedication.

"There you are," she said as she bent double to kiss him on his forehead He felt the ripples of heat spread out across his head as her breath disturbed the chemical party that was happening in his skin.

"I was just enjoying the view. Is it time?"

"Almost. Mex wants to discuss tactics before we meet with MynCorp. He's in the suite."

They stepped towards the central shaft of the station as a flake of translucent metal sank beneath them and spiralled down towards the main atrium. The accommodation suites were on the station rim to give the best views of the Earth above and the slowly spinning space below. They crossed one of the transit concourses filled with people milling and clustering with mid-journey impatience. Yakini's stride hesitated for a moment, causing Bergur to look down from the ceiling.

"Did you see her?"

"I've mostly been trying to avoid everybody staring at me."

"It was her. A bob of fake brown hair and a less than convincing change in skin colour but definitely her."

Bergur was scanning the crowds around them trying to look through the transient trappings of fashion to see the people beneath. "Who?"

"Not now. Let's get back to the rooms. It's not safe to talk here, the station A.I. will be filtering all speech for keywords."

Yakini lengthened her stride and Bergur found himself trotting to keep up.

*

Kaamil's footsteps thudded back against his eardrums as he sprinted down the corridor, his shoes struggling to keep him attached to the floor in the ineffectual lunar gravity. Ten steps later he couldn't even hear himself breathe. At the next corner he ran straight into Joshua. They held each other up until they regained their feet. Joshua was mouthing something that looked urgent. Kaamil pointed back down the corridor and lead Joshua a dozen paces.

"I found.." Joshua covered his ears as his voice powered back from every surface. "Shit, this corridor is messed up," he whispered deafeningly.

"The sound cancellation is completely out of sync," Kaamil noted. "Did you say you've found them?"

"No, but I found Grace's breather mask."

"No way."

"I know. This is really bad. Do you think they're messing with us?"

"I can't believe that Grace would leave her mask lying around just for a joke."

"What should we do? We've been looking for hours."

"I think we might need to get help."

Joshua looked pained. "The Sister will skin us alive."

"Just before she kills us."

"Shit. How could they get lost?"

"You've checked all the sensory deprivation tanks?"

"Twice."

"The kitchens have no atmosphere – serious subsidence – and we've checked every suite. There are places down there where no one has been for years and there's no footprints. They've got to be around the treatment area."

"How're we going to call for help? I've got no signal."

"There'll be a hardline somewhere."

"Then we wait for the Sister."

*

The suite was a circular room with half a dozen bedrooms forming alcoves round the perimeter. Several chair-like pieces of furniture moulded themselves in retro styles and bobbed expectantly as Bergur and Yakini entered. Kaamil was sat with his back to the main room, right in the centre of a ten metre full-height strip of tinted diamond which looked East towards Asia and the rising sun. Mex paced the room, scattering huddles of generic furniture blobs confused by the mixed messages.

"You've certainly got style," Yakini said to Mex.

"I can assure you I don't normally live like this but, one way or another, I won't be able to spend any MynCorp calories once this is over. So I thought I'd live for the moment."

"Is it safe to talk here?" Bergur asked.

Kaamil turned to face them. He looked tired in the unrelenting gravity but his voice was animated. "This is a premium suite. The walls have built-in hardware encryption. If anybody is recording any physical emanation from this space the signal will be scrambled. If won't stop our voices being recorded but it will not be possible to decode the words in real-time. We have at least a hundred hours of privacy."

"So, what's our strategy with Sardon?" Mex asked.

Bergur was first to answer. "You mean you haven't got a plan?"

"Not a clue."

"And when does Sardon arrive?"

Mex looked briefly at the splice emitter in the ceiling. "In about ten minutes."

"Well we don't have anything to sell."

"No, but that's not exactly the point. How do we convince him the Earth is about to be attacked by beings from another dimension?"

"We're screwed without José and Nomia."

"They might pop back into existence just in time."

For a hopeful moment they all stood in quiet expectation.

"Right, who has a plan B?" Mex looked at them each in turn, trying to draw inspiration by osmosis. "Okay, we stick to the plan. Get them hooked on the tech and then break it to them gently that it's all alien."

Bergur and Kaamil simply looked on. Yakini shrugged as she accepted the role of pragmatist. "There is no tech."

"They don't know that."

"And what do we do when they ask to see it?"

"We demonstrate its effectiveness."

"We demonstrate non-existent tech?"

"You forget. Kaamil can instantaneously communicate with the Suparna, which is now several million kilometres away."

"Actually, I can't." Kaamil said.

"You can't? Why not?"

"I can communicate with the pilot bunker which is tethered in the parking area of Lagrangian 3. It's probably a million kilometres away but it's not much more than a lump of inert metal. I lost control of the Suparna the moment we ejected the sphere."

"We can still manage some sort of demonstration. The fact that you're standing here is a minor miracle." The word minor seemed to hang in the air well after Mex had stopped talking. "Has anybody got a better plan?"

"Run?" Yakini grinned.

"Tempting." Mex grinned.

Yakini gave Bergur a look of uncertainty which momentarily cramped her expansive face. She sighed and said, "Mex, would this be a good moment to tell you that we saw Julienne?"

"Here? When?"

"She was trying to look inconspicuous in the main concourse a few minutes ago."

Mex was already heading towards the doorway.

"You can't seriously be about to leave us?" Yakini called after him.

A soft cough from the walls signalled that the station A.I. was about to speak. Despite his distracted state of mind, Mex cringed as the programmatic attempt at humility ruffled his professional feathers. "Excuse me, Sirs and Madam, Agent Sardon Lucas and Mr Benjamin Shenfield are requesting access. Should I let them in?" the voice asked apologetically.

"Yes," Mex said, although even he was not sure if he was answering Yakini or the slave-like personality of the station.

A section of the wall evaporated outward towards a semi-circular border-strip of geometric design which might have been inspired by Mayan artwork. Mex nodded at the two men stood just outside and parted them with his shoulders as he left the suite.

Mex walked directly to the most central area of the main concourse, an open atria capped by a four hundred metre cupola of crystal. The sun was low in one quadrant. Its disk was masked by a tracking patch of jet black but the corona of the sun caused streaks of rainbow colours to radiate across the crystal sky, in an aurora of cycling hues which danced against the backdrop of star-flecked blackness. He stood at his chosen lookout point and slowly revolved, trying to let his subconscious sift through the hundreds of people drifting though the space. Almost every woman who was slender of frame but strong of stance seemed to have her back to him. Some he willed into turning around, others he rejected with some unqualifiable instinct. After ten revolutions something made him start to meander towards the departure gates for Mars and her moons. He felt the barest suggestion of recognition but he could not find the source as his eyes flicked from face to face. He started to walk and scan faces faster as the feeling of certainty evaporated.

Just as he was about to turn back towards the centre of the concourse a figure slipped between two clusters of people. She walked with the grace and determination of a ninja ballerina. From that moment he could only see her, as if she was twice the height of everybody else. He clamped down on a smile which wanted to betray his emotions, but he moved towards her with as much nonchalance as he could manage. He knew nothing about why she was there or why she was navigating the room like a symphony to time and motion studies. MynCorp claimed not to be pursuing him, but Julienne could be here for some covert mission which threatened his own plans.

Of course she's here for some covert reason, Julienne doesn't do pleasure trips, Mex thought.

He realised he was still making his way indirectly towards her and he was going to talk to her regardless of the consequences. She was unlikely to kill him in such a public place and anything short of death was worth the risk to see her again.

Julienne stood at the edge of a group of young women. They were all dressed in similar knee-length skirts which imitated a course-weave fabric with a strobing tartan pattern. Pale arms protruded from white bodice tops. The only similarity between them and Julienne was the long auburn hair lying in a loose plait down their backs. She was managing to look like she was a fellow groupie for whatever sim character they followed, even though she was dressed in drab shapeless clothes which had probably been discarded by their first owner. The lack of ergonomically figure-hugging uniform helped to disguise her artificially precise posture but there was no denying the thin-lipped frown and perfectly symmetric creases in her brow.

One of the girls said something to Julienne, smiled weakly and the group moved away en masse. For a moment she was exposed apart from a man who stood facing her.

Mex missed a step, almost tripping over his feet.

It was Sickle.

There was no doubt. Mex had known him for over fifteen years, been drunk with him for a lot of it. Mex would probably have listed him in his top ten friends even though they spent most of their time arguing about the value of Mex's lifestyle.

Sickle and Julienne together on the same orbital as Mex at this pivotal moment in everything; the implications were immense, or might be if Mex could get any kind of meaningful thoughts to hang together. He started to move forward again as he realised that he was not going to work this one out without some help from them.

A steel-hard shoulder spun him one way before another one spun him back. Two tight clusters of muscle in dark jump suits pushed past him and headed directly towards Julienne. Mex could see the break in symmetry of their swagger that meant a concealed weapon. Mex knew something was more wrong than he could currently understand. He put two fingers between his lips and let rip with a shrieking whistle which stopped every conversation in a hundred-metre radius. Before the first echo made it back from the diamond ceiling he was crouched down behind two pieces of recently abandoned furniture. His last glimpse of Julienne was the widening of her eyes as she spotted the backs of the two men in black who had one hand each pushed inside secret pockets as they scanned the crowd around where Mex had been standing.

"Covered cot," Mex whispered at the nearest furniture drone. It started to morph, engulfing Mex and concealing him within a one way mirror of a sleeping pouch. "Carry me to somewhere quiet, as fast as you like," he ordered. He felt the rocking of a two-footed mollusc walk and then just the soft purr of the furniture's metabolism. Mex levered himself up and looked back towards where Julienne had been standing. She was gone but the two men stood unselfconsciously scanning the crowds. They projected an arrogance Mex usually associated with MynCorp but that left Mex even more confused, but it did not really matter who was hunting Julienne, he knew he would help. If his interference was unwelcome then he could live with her scorn.

Once he could no longer see the two men, Mex crawled out from his hiding place and found a circumpolar passage leading round to where he guessed Julienne must have gone. If she was able to get a room then she would have been in it, so he could assume she was restricted to the anonymity of the communal areas. He found himself back outside his own suite. The station's A.I. welcomed him meekly as he approached, offering to announce him to the occupants. Mex declined but asked who was inside. The meeting was still going on. Mex wondered what they could have found to talk about but then realised it had only been four minutes since he walked out.

An idea wormed its way into Mex's head, appealing to his mischievous streak "Emergency access to first sleeping cubicle, please," he said.

"Do you want me to reconfigure the sleeping room to move the storage furniture away from the corridor wall?"

"No, leave current configuration. Isolate room from main living space and reduce lighting to low."

A rough iris opened in the rim side wall of the corridor and a dark space was revealed beyond. Mex stepped into the grey space and felt the silk-soft brush of emergency space suits hanging either side of him. "Keep door open," he instructed.

A few people passed, apparently oblivious to the black gash in the wall of the corridor but then Mex heard the footsteps he had been waiting for; the soft metronome of precisely efficient legs blended with Sickle's belligerent lope. Mex thought about dragging Julienne inside but she might kill him instinctively before she could do it consciously later. He was still grappling with the best opening move when the soft steps broke into a run that echoed round the curve of the corridor. Mex saw two pairs of swinging arms motoring past in quick succession. He reached out and grabbed the nearest arms, letting momentum spin them into his hiding place. The three of them landed in a twisted pile of limbs and empty suits. "Close," Mex screamed as he fell.

"What the hell?" Sickle asked with some relief but mostly disbelief. Then, when he saw Mex, "Ty?"

"Sickle, always there for a mate."

"Mex." Julienne sounded measured as she pushed herself upright and away from him.

"Julienne," Mex said with equal caginess.

Sickle looked at each of them in the light leaking from the sleeping space. Sighing, he said, "Wow, you two have got it bad."

Chapter 5

His leg muscles were starting to burn. José looked down at his right foot as it met the green-tinged surface of the Martian soil. For a moment it looked as if the surface would take his weight but from the experience of the preceding million steps, he knew the thin layer of algae-stained, salty crust would crumble as he lifted the other foot. His weight would drag him ankle-deep into the underlying sand before the process started again with his left foot. The underlying virgin sand varied between the red of Earth sandstone in a summer's sunset, to the dark turquoise of tropical sea kelp.

Nomia stroked the back of his neck to calm José's grumbling mind. The tingle lifted his mood despite the continuing aggravation of walking on a planet which did not welcome ambulating life-forms. He looked up at the horizon. The sheer cliff now filled most of the view ahead and broke the flat monotony of the Vastitas Borealis plain.

"We really need to pick up the pace," said Sera from a few strides ahead. José glanced at her long easy gait with a twinge of envy. He reflected that the Martian might be ungainly in zero-gravity, but on Mars she was as majestic as a giraffe on the African savannah.

"What's the hurry, you getting bored?" José felt the child within him rising with his frustration.

"Yes, but I'm a lot more concerned about that." She pointed back towards the cluster of rocks which marked the entrance to the lava tubes. The sky beyond was streaked with dark red bands which looked like a swarm of angry locusts against the pinky-blue of the sky. "That sand storm will strip us to the bone and then grind the bones to dust," she added, in case they were unclear what was approaching.

José looked back towards the cliffs of the Vanuatu crater. "How far away are we?" he asked.

"About half an hour."

"And the storm?"

"Less," Sera shrugged.

"A lot less?"

"Does it matter?" Sera sounded a little resigned.

José could sense the conflict in her voice. "Could you make it without us slowing you down?"

"Probably."

Nomia looked briefly at José, and then they both broke into an awkward trot. Sera simply lengthened her stride to something that looked more comfortable for her.

Between grunts of alarm as his legs slipped and slid, José managed, "If you stay with us I promise we will make it through to the city. If necessary we will take measures."

Sera simply nodded; the gesture of someone who had faced danger from the environment every day of her life and had long since developed a laisse-faire attitude to survival.

The ground started to rise and became rockier as they neared the giant crater. The jagged blade of rock rose two kilometres above them and appeared to extend to infinity to the left and right. Mats of lichen and moss hung from every outcrop as if the planet was melting and dripping away. Sera pointed to a metal ring that pierced the cliff ahead. The ground beneath the opening was streaked with pale and bare rubble where soft-tired vehicles and booted feet had slowly pulverised all obstacles.

As they got nearer the entrance grew larger but dimmer as if the light was fading into dusk. José looked up and was startled to see the sky the orange pink of old pre-terraforming images. José opened his mouth to ask a question but dust choked the words in his throat. Sera looked at him, fear flitting at the back of her eyes. It was clear they were not going to make it. Indecision twisted her elongated features. José could sense she was about to abandon them.

We have to intervene. We owe her that much. Nomia flashed into his head.

I know. I was just hoping we could get by without. If they come we will be condemning everyone in the city.

Just because we can see every possible outcome does not mean we should let it paralyse us.

You're right. He conceded.

Why does that continue to surprise you? Her laughter ran through the thought like a mountain stream over glistening rocks.

José listened to the roar of the approaching storm. Initially it sounded like a solid wall of sound but as he focused on its Verity Space projection it spit into a billion individual buzzing grains of sand. Each formed a blur of possible world-lines as infinite collisions and gusts of wind drove them forward in space and time. José felt his way towards the area of the probability space that corresponded to high-speed grains colliding with the three travellers. He inflated a volume of forbidden outcomes, forcing a ripple of causality to spread throughout the storm.

José opened his eyes to the physical world. Sera was a few strides ahead. She had been about to run but was now stood paralysed by confusion on the edge of a bubble of calm. Outside the hemisphere the storm raged with all the anger of the atmosphere. Inside only noise assaulted them. Wave after wave of vicious sand rose to devour them before falling back as if deflected by an unseen shield.

"We should get inside," José shouted above the cacophony.

Sera closed her mouth as she unfroze.

The storm beat against their bubble, roaring with natural savagery.

"It feels like we're inside some twisted take on a snow globe," gasped Sera, her finger brushing her lips in astonishment.

José decided he liked her. She was fearless when faced with a physical miracle and, unencumbered by doubt or denial, she could enjoy the pleasure of the spectacle. He drew strength from her joy, as he had when Nomia had first felt Verity Space with her freshly united consciousness. For Sera, there was no concept of consequence and José wondered, not for the first time, if the Eidolons were simply the manifestation of the Universe seeking balance. José shook his head before the fatalism could sap his will.

For Sera, the Martian storms must have been a constant fear, wheedling its way into the colony's genetic memory like sand in the workings of a machine. She would have grown up accustomed to the wailing sirens of the early warning system tied to a network of dedicated micro-satellites. Now she stood, two metres of elegant defiance, in the belly of her beast and she was loving it. Physically, she was so unlike Nomia. The subtle flaring of her nostrils and flattened breadth of her cheeks betrayed a pacific island heritage and those languid summer seas were still there in the lazy wave of her eyelids. She was undoubtedly beautiful even if it was unnaturally stretched to José's Terran eyes.

They trudged the last few metres to the tunnel entrance in silence and, when José felt the tingle of an electrostatic field sweep his body, he relaxed. Reality returned to its noisy randomness and the storm slammed into the space behind them. He turned back to the dull pink light of the storm which was beating against the field of the tunnel entrance. Occasionally, an energetic eddy would batter the wall in a rainbow of scintillation. The vanguard sand fell to the floor at his feet, stripped of its energy but separated from the maelstrom outside.

"What now?" It was Sera's voice behind him.

"Take us to your leader," Nomia giggled.

"It's not as simple as that. I'll have to make representations and argue your case. Otherwise they're more likely to kill you than talk." She paused for a moment, apparently rearranging her mental pecking order. "Or, at least, try to kill you," she adjusted.

"We'll wait." Nomia seemed to be able to switch at will between a youthful impatience and an aged wisdom.

José felt his shoulders relax for the first time since Sera had crashed through the roof of their hideout. His natural caution accepted the chain of events forming ahead of them, and he let the momentum carry him. "I've always wanted to see Vanuatu City. I think we'll have a look around."

"There's a path up to the rim not far from the city entrance. I'll show you the way. You might find the steps a little hard going with your short legs but I'm sure you'll cope."

The tunnel was about a kilometre long and had the cross section of a squashed circle, as if it had sagged in the paltry Martian gravity. Glowing algae carpeted the glass-smooth ceiling, rustling creepily as they passed. Behind them the tunnel returned to darkness as the organism returned to a dormant state. José reached into Verity Space to study the interaction between their presence and the bio-luminescence of the moss-like algae. It seemed to react ahead of their passing, as if anticipating their arrival. He could see no consistent physical connection. The algae was reacting before their meagre heat signature or breath could reach it. "Do you know how this stuff works?" he asked Sera while nodding at the roof of the tunnel.

"No idea, but we use it for most of our lighting, at least in small spaces. It's one of the Durga Corporation's numbers. You'll see quite a lot of their work in the city."

Nomia stopped for a moment. "I think it's reacting to ripples in the Downey field," she said cautiously.

"That's highly improbable. Only sentient life interacts with the Downey field."

"Maybe you should tell the algae that," Nomia suggested patiently.

José opened his mouth to blurt an objection but stopped himself. "What are Durga up to? Intelligent bio-luminescent algae. Call me a Luddite but this can't be good."

"Maybe you're just getting old," Nomia and Sera said in unison.

José shrugged, feeling irredeemably outnumbered.

A few minutes later three figures emerged from the tunnel exit raised up a couple of hundred metres above the crater floor. They stood blinking into the pinky blue of the Martian sky and breathed in air which felt warm and thick after the low pressure of the plain. Above them the sky was criss-crossed with the glittering web of the diamond canopy reaching down to the horizon. The broad plateau, that formed the crater floor and stretched away towards infinity, was peppered with oozing cubes of green. Doors and windows were visible on the nearest structures, betraying their manufactured origin. José walked up to a six metre cube and brushed its surface with his fingertips. It was smooth and hard like crystal. Just below the surface, a sludge of pea-green tendrils floated in a clear liquid. Some unseen current kept the matted clumps in languid motion, like weed beneath the surface of a frozen stream.

"Energy, food and air, all in one," Sera said in an explanatory tone.

"Clever," José answered blandly.

"The path up to the rim is over there." Sera pointed between two large buildings. A discolouration in the rock betrayed where the path wound its way between the cubes perched on the wall of the crater. "Try and keep a low profile. I'll find you later."

"Where is everybody?" Nomia asked.

"It's mid-shift. Everyone will be either underground or at their desk. There'll be people in the fields but they're all closer to the lake. You've got a couple of hours before the streets start to fill."

Sera strode off with barely a smile. She looked worried. José watched her back until Nomia took his arm and turned him to face the path up.

The climb was relatively easy in the low gravity but when he stumbled on a stray rock, José found his feet over-compensating, knocking him further off balance. They walked until the diamond dome that formed the sky descended to meet the ground. The crystal lattice vanished an unseen depth into the jagged rock forming the crest of the crater. Green-tinted plains stretched to the horizon in an uninterrupted monotony, defying scale or perspective.

José saved the view back into the crater until they reached the very summit. He felt the breath of over-worked lungs push through the slack lips of his open jaw, then he heard nothing for minutes of wonder. The mountains stretched away from him to the left and right like wings of a planet-sized bird. The pale orange stone looked as soft as sand but stood jagged and defiant. He could detect no curve, but somehow the ridge managed to define the horizon at all points in front of him. The rim of the giant crater bent so subtly that the curvature of the planet seemed crude and haphazard in comparison. Vanuatu City sat in a perfect circle of rock over thirty kilometres across. The town itself was a chaotic clustering of green cubes and cylinders strung across the crater floor like the discarded building blocks of a giant child. The deeply organic green of the buildings and orange of the exposed rock provided deep contrast to the oceanic blue of the central lake. At, maybe, ten kilometres across it sat above the surrounding agricultural fields like a hesitant tsunami. The one hundred metre high diamond walls that had held the lake in place since it first melted were just visible as a silver lining to the flat blue of the water.

José had seen more than his fair share of wonders, and yet, a vista had never induced a complete loss of self. The analytical part of his brain – a prowling sentinel that never really slept - posited the view was extraordinary, but not unique. The scene's derivative nature served to enhanced his appreciation; too many of the incredible things he had experienced had been without human reference, so bizarre that his brain had merely accepted them without any real aesthetic evaluation. The biggest Earth Caldera was to the Vanuatu crater what a matchstick was to a tree, but at least it was recognisably beautiful.

José took Nomia's hand and squeezed some of his excitement into her fingers. Finally, he could remember what he was fighting for. It was no longer the mechanics of surviving. He felt the injustice of beauty threatened as freshly now as when he had first felt Nomia's dream-like cries for help.

*

The Sister was calm and hugged away their fear. Kaamil knew anger and disappointment were bubbled below the surface, waiting to see how the search turned out. He wanted to feel her wrath because it would mean everything was going to be okay.

A constable joined them in the patrol vehicle moored at the platform edge. "Nothing yet," he said. "Early days," he added.

The Sister smiled briefly. The constable opened his mouth and fidgeted his feet. He frowned once before turning back towards the spa entrance and search party. The Sister had that effect on a lot of people; however senior or professional, the Sister – with arms crossed over a starched blue jacket and nonsense-free eyes - reduced them to faltering children.

Kaamil half-smiled and then caught a glimpse of Joshua's misery from the corner of his down-turned eyes. The reality of what was happening hit him again, freshened by the diminishing possibility of it all being a poor joke by Qadir.

"I need to pee," Kaamil said.

"I don't think the constable's vehicle has a bathroom," the Sister replied.

The Sister might be exceptional but she was still an adult and therefore inclined – from Kaamil's perspective - to reply to requests with irrelevant statements. Kaamil jumped down onto the platform. He moved to the far side and stood on the edge, feet apart.

"Not out here. Show some decorum."

"There's a bathroom in reception. I think the recycling unit is still operational," Joshua offered, his voice much further away than his body.

The Sister nodded her acquiescence, so Kaamil wandered back under the frozen holo display and into the spa. He felt better wandering along anonymous corridors, as if he was slowly morphing into someone else – someone without guilt. He heard a cluster of voices around the next corner and his surroundings snapped back into focus.

Reluctant to be seen, Kaamil tried to turn back on himself and retreat back towards reception. Something held him static. He looked down at his legs and feet for a physical obstruction. His thoughts trudged through mental treacle until he realised something in his surroundings was holding his attention routed to the spot.

There was a hiss in his left ear, like dying silicon. It was coming from a crack hunting for weaknesses in the wall from floor to ceiling. Every lunar inhabitant knew that sound. The sound of vital air being sucked – or pushed – out into a vacuum. From the other side there would probably be an expanding cloud of white crystals as the humidity in the precious air froze diamond-hard.

There was a large pressure difference between the spa and whatever was on the other side of the wall. Kaamil looked around for a sealant kit but anything portable had long since been stripped from the spa. Then he realised that the leak must be new. His hand fell to the mask pack at his hip and rested there, reassured. The crack must be as recent as five kids breaking into the abandoned spa. He found his fingers following the contours of the wall until they found the recessed maintenance hatch. The surface pulsed back at his hand, letting him know that it really would like to open but an interlock was preventing compliance.

The pitch of the hiss was getting higher but fainter – the leak was being patched from the other side or, maybe, the wall was clever enough to heal itself. The tone counted up towards pressure equalisation. Kaamil decided to find the search party but his body refused to obey. He couldn't even breathe in case he lost touch with the hiss that was fading into the background hum of the lunar city.

The hatch popped its seals with a breeze that turned the sweat on Kaamil's brow to ice.

Spotlit by the corridor's glow, a pile of discarded clothes lay just inside the entrance to the recess. Ceiling panels begrudgingly flickered into life as his body heat swept the space ahead of his gaze. Like landing lights his concentration was being directed towards an amorphous blob of abandonment in one corner. The final light flickered once, giving him a single frame of flesh and frozen screams.

Kaamil tried to look away before the light came back but his eyes were like icicles piercing and pinning his brain.

The light came back and stayed.

The fluid of Grace's eyeball was starting to melt. It ran down the blistered skin of her cheek and dripped onto Qadir's chest. His back was arched with explosive effort – each vertebrae locked in a single moment of agonising release. Lung-grey foam bridged the gap between his blue lips and the floor. Dalal sat half-dressed against another wall. One hand clasped her throat as if trying to keep her last breath from escaping. The other hand was stretched towards Kaamil.

A whine stole the colour from Kaamil's eyes. The lights were going out again. And gravity seemed to be failing in reciprocal grief. Kaamil started the long fall towards the floor and unconsciousness.

*

As Mex entered the living space, Sardon looked at him and then the main entrance with a moment of disorientation. "Mr Tyrian, glad you could join us. I've had a very interesting conversation with your colleagues. I need time to analyse the data. Mr Shenfield, if you're done." Sardon gestured towards the door.

"Take care," Mex waved with a broad smile.

The door opened to let the two men leave. Standing outside were two tall men in dark jump suits, looking a little flustered. The taller of the two started to talk quickly. "Agent Lucas, we found her. She's ..." He was cut off by a severe shake of Sardon's head as he led them away from the door, anger dripping from his stride.

Mex watched the door reform across the entrance and turned back to his colleagues, award-winning smile already in place.

Yakini was not so easily won over. "Well thanks for that. I hope it was worth it."

"It definitely might have been."

Bergur grunted his disbelief.

Mex wiped away the opening to the sleeping area and beckoned its two occupants into the main living area. "I'm sure everyone remembers Julienne."

She had changed into a close fitting jumpsuit from the complementary wardrobe and her hair had morphed into a pale turquoise. It was straighter but each lock ended in a perfect curl with one and a half twists. They pooled in the deep hollow between her shoulder blades or rested on the rise of fabric above each breast.

Mex's jaw worked aimlessly.

"Hair suits you," Yakini said.

"Thanks," Julienne said with little conviction.

"Aren't you going to introduce me?" Sickle stood with his hands thrust deep into the pockets of his long overcoat.

"Must I?"

"Alright, I'll do it myself. Lady and other." He nodded at Yakini and Bergur. "I am Sickle, long-time mentor and social conscience to the company-man you know as Mex."

"Company-man?" Yakini frowned.

"Social conscience?" Julienne looked back at her companion doubtfully. "I think you may be a bit confused."

"There goes the last chance of getting my old life back," sighed Mex.

Julienne seemed determined to labour the point. "In the last three months Mex Tyrian has been complicit in the destruction or general loss of over one hundred Mega Calories of MynCorp resources. He is uncooperative, underhanded and conspiratorial. If he wasn't so expensive to chase or had some significant intrinsic value, he would be on the MynCorp most wanted list."

"Thanks. Really some of the nicest things anyone has ever …"

"My Mex Tyrian? Ty the software geek?"

"Moving right along." Mex ushered everyone towards a collection of chairs that were laying down roots in the centre of the room. "Sickle, what are you doing helping a MynCorp agent evade capture by her own handlers?"

Sickle looked reluctant to answer but Julienne showed no such reticence. "Working for a competitor, of course."

Mex laughed. "Sickle? This Sickle? There is still beauty in the Universe." Nobody else seemed to find the situation funny. Mex coughed and asked, "Where's Kaamil?"

A high-backed chair in front of the window revolved to reveal the Pilot. His eyes were painted with the scattered remnants of a green splice laser. He started to speak without making eye contact with any of the others."It seems that more of the station's A.I. is being redirected towards hacking the hardware encryption of this room. I think we can conclude that Sardon has persuaded the station that we are a potential threat. We should wrap things up quickly."

When Julienne saw Kaamil, the little colour remaining in her face drained away, leaving her eyes heavy from sleep deprivation. "How is he here?"

The lack of emotion in her voice was more terrifying than the death threats which defined her first meeting with the Pilot. Mex could remember it like a deranged nightmare. Standing on the convoluted physics of the pilot's bunker, Julienne had ripped Kaamil from his control umbilical and squeezed the life from his throat. When all her implants had failed Mex had felt his heart tear with her pain, but at the same time he had seen an opportunity to germinate some of her lost humanity. Tragically, many of the erased memories of her first life and death had bubbled through the chaos of her shattered psyche.

Some of the truth she had confided in Mex, but mostly he had filled in the blanks later. Julienne had been a gifted, but isolated child. Her talent and joy lay in emergence; the patterns arising from the multiplicity of simple interactions. Like every young heart, she shared an eternal wonder at a snowflake's intricacy, but for her the fascination extended into data systems so complex that to most minds they appeared entirely chaotic. Julienne was a natural recruit for MynCorp's pilot programme. They offered her a god-like symbiosis of human mind, artificial intelligence, interstellar spacecraft and a pantology of instrumentation. Years of physical and mental conditioning culminated in her internment within the pilot's isolation sphere. With almost religious reverence the technicians would have incarcerated her within an environment devoid of sensory stimulation. Mex could only imagine the primordial terror of feeling nothing but icy adrenaline pulsing through her veins, until a tech flicked a switch and the combined telemetry of a billion processors crashed into her mind. The sacrifices would have culminated in her maiden voyage to the stars, but every hope and fear could not have prepared her for sabotage and calamity before she had even had a chance to light her engines.

She blamed Kaamil for her first death; a tragic truth confirmed by the Pilot's own returning memories. MyncCorp had done a thorough job in blocking Kaamil and Julienne's early memories. Trauma made them both willing and pliable, but memories are rarely lost forever. In both cases, José and Nomia had been the trigger for their recollections, but it had been down to Mex to bring Julienne back from the brink of murder.

Kaamil was forced to relive a psychotic breakdown triggered by years of isolation in deep space. His obsession with a trainee pilot stemmed from the briefest of encounters, which Julienne had not even been aware of. The moment of human contact, however imaginary, had grown into a grotesque distortion of love. Julienne had died at his hand and in his arms, but even at that moment he had genuinely believed they were lovers betrayed and brutalised by MynCorp.

Mex noticed that everyone seemed to be looking to him to answer Julienne's question. "Nomia. She saved him."

"But he's disconnected from the ship?" Julienne's voice was level and detached.

"Sort of." Mex searched her eyes for a glimmer of the woman he had nursed. There had been a reaction to Kaamil's presence but it had been so momentary. So fleeting, that Mex almost despaired.

Sickle put a hand in the air and asked, "Does anyone else think the cables coming out of his body shouldn't wave around like that?"

"Let's save it for our next drinking session." Mex suggested, shaking himself back into the moment. "Julienne, why are you running from MynCorp?"

Julienne frowned mechanically. She seemed unable to isolate a verbal answer.

"It's going to be my fault isn't it?" Mex offered.

"MynCorp did not appreciate the implications of my report, after the Suparna incident. We are on our way to Mars to collect supporting evidence."

"You've gone freelance? Is that even possible?" Mex asked.

"I'm not a robot. I make my own decisions."

"I didn't mean it that way."

Yakini leant forward in her chair. "What's on Mars?"

"I'm not sure." Julienne said awkwardly.

There was a soft hiss as Bergur sucked in air. "Nomia and José," he said.

"On Mars?" Mex gasped.

Julienne shrugged.

Yakini looked energised as she asked, "And what are you going to do once you get to Mars?"

"We have corporate resources," Sickle said.

"Durga Corporation presumably." Yakini did not wait for confirmation. "You've got no chance. Mars is not Earth. You can't just open a splice session and ask an A.I. to find someone."

"We'll be fine." Julienne's confidence was as impenetrable as ever.

"You will be, if I come with you," Yakini said.

"We need you here," Mex interjected. "This is the main event. Remember the mission?"

"If you had been around for the meeting, rather than running off after an unrequited love interest, you'd know that I've been ordered to report for duty. I either get off this station now, or I'm back piloting the Svargaloka. What would you do?"

"I don't know how to answer any of that."

"Good, it's decided. I'm going home."

Sickle raised his hand again. "How do you plan to get to Mars, 'cause you're not coming with us?"

"You have a ship?" Yakini prompted.

"Maybe."

"And how do you plan to get to it? From what I gather, you're more in demand than we are."

"We'll manage."

"No we won't." Julienne verbally stepped between them. "We need help getting off this station, and it makes perfect sense to have a native Martian with us. We'll take her."

"With all due respect, Julienne, you don't know how we're getting there." Sickle crossed his arms defiantly. "The craft is not designed for passengers."

"Will it take three people?"

"Just."

"Perfect."

"Don't say I didn't warn you."

Bergur looked about to open his mouth flaps but Mex spoke pre-emptively. "Don't even think about it big guy. You're our only Eridanian representative. We can't sell fake off-world tech without an off-worlder."

Yakini smoothed Bergur's brow. "Don't worry. I'll come flying back as soon I can. Or you could come and hide on Mars." She grabbed his jerkin by the stitching and dragged him towards one of the sleeping alcoves. "Let's start saying goodbye now."

Mex coughed in the following pause.

Sickle chuckled, "I think I'm going to like Mars."

Chapter 6

"They're definitely chasing me," Mex screamed as he tripped over another piece of sloth-like furniture.

"I'd be happy if you were right." Julienne vaulted his flailing legs without losing speed.

The squad of well-dressed agents seemed to have abandoned any pretence of stealth. They trotted across the rapidly clearing atria with guns held high, and seemed to be gaining without actually breaking into a run. The agents advanced with an inevitability which shocked Mex each time he risked a glance over his pounding shoulders.

There was another subsonic thud. It shook his ribcage and a flash of silver grazed his ear before ricocheting off the right hand wall.

"What the hell are they shooting at us?"

"Attack nanites to shutdown all bio-implants. Standard tactics against enhanced targets."

"But I'm not ... Oh, they're after you."

"Really? Do you think?" They reached another up-ramp, and moved above the main concourses. The corridors started to curve faster, keeping them out of the line of fire for more of the time, but they were running out of room to manoeuvre.

Mex was starting to feel stabbing pains in his lungs but he kept at Julienne's shoulder, watching for the moment when she might start to breathe heavily. "Is this really all my fault?" he asked.

"Now is hardly the time, but yes." She sighed, impressive in itself when running. "In a way. Maybe. I don't know."

"Oh. What will happen if I get hit by one of these nanite darts?"

"It will hurt. A lot."

Another squad of MynCorp security appeared in a side-corridor, and accelerated towards them. Mex and Julienne made for another up-ramp, avoiding a gaggle of children mobbing a skinny teenager with diamond teeth. A brutish lump of metal appeared in the hand of an accompanying bodyguard as he assessed the approaching chase. Mex smiled reassuringly and tried to make it obvious he was running past and not towards.

The next level was a maze of boutiques and specialist treatment rooms. Julienne waved at a couple of doors until she found one that opened. They slipped inside. Julienne moved to the opposite wall of the sparse cubicle and rubbed the wall determinedly. It got the message and slid away to open a ragged hole into another similar cubicle. They stepped through before the hole could heal. They repeated this another three times in random directions before Julienne stopped and stood motionless in the centre of the last space.

The walls were animated to depict a flock of humming birds buzzing from one scarlet flower to another. Mex watched Julienne's eyelids for several minutes, waiting for a sign she had detected a pursuit. He tried to hold his breath and listen, but his heart just got louder. He reverted to tinkering with the ubiquitous splice terminal grafted into one of the flower displays.

Mex did not notice Julienne turn to face him.

"Thank you for trying to help me." The words left her mouth in an avalanche of escaping breath.

"Never leave a damsel in distress, that's my motto."

"I'm not sure I count as a damsel."

"You're definitely the most beautiful person I've seen in distress today."

"Beautiful for my machine-like perfection, or for this borrowed body I live in?"

"I'm not ..." Mex wanted to protest but indignation robbed him of eloquence. "Shouldn't you be listening for those MynCorp goons?"

"I am. I can filter out my voice from the surrounding sound."

"What about my voice?"

"Easily."

"It would be quite easy for someone to give up trying with you."

Mex returned his attention to the station's A.I. and to chewing his lower lip with pent-up emotion. A couple of years ago he had helped a DogStar Director make contact with a colleague in the Drop; something about a lot of missing accounts. Mex had tried to stay detached – tried not to think about how his skills had been corrupted since he refined them helping friends to say goodbye to loved ones. Mex had felt little guilt as he stole some biometric data during the exchange. It was completely against his usual ethos but something had compelled him to hang on to the data for a rainy day, and today it was pouring.

His code glasses assessed their surroundings as he pulled them from a pouch in his jacket. They rapidly settled on a ruby jewel glint with a distracting flickering of feathers across each lens. As the glasses rested on his nose, code of Mex's own design set to work corrupting the splice beam, until the terminal was convinced Director Hill was requesting access to the station's telemetry feeds. He found himself presented with an almost endless set of visual feeds, embedded in a retro-skin. It was designed to resemble a bank of hard-screen cathode ray displays, mounted in a wall of black-painted metal panels. Each display could be selected via a red glowing button set in rows below the screens. A joystick provided steering capability for each scene. Mex played with one of the feeds, moving the point of view through ninety degrees. He marvelled for a moment at how the surround vision capability of the station's inner and outer skin had been constrained to imitate a small number of fixed-position cameras. Buried in the picture from each camera was all the audio, chemical and non-visual electromagnetic data for the same locality, providing a complete island of clarity.

Mex tried to piece together an idea of what was happening on the station, but he found the representation as a number of discrete localities dislocating and confusing. Frustration made him burn through the façade of the station's portal and find the raw data underneath.

"Now we're talking," he muttered to himself.

A hand touched his shoulder for a moment and then came to rest.

"Mex, I'm sorry."

Julienne was close. As he turned, her hand slid to his neck leaving a trail of electrified skin. Their foreheads touched, and he imagined he felt the hole in her mind. The hole which had opened when her artificial mind had failed and left the incomplete imprint of her original mind flailing in the scarred mess of the golem body. Even now, with the implants ticking through the processes of life, it must be there; a missing area of memory and emotional experience crying in the darkness. For that moment he saw a lost child hiding her fear behind bravado and bluster.

"So am I."

"Why did you risk your own freedom to try and help me?"

"It's not my freedom I risked. There are bigger stakes here... Oh, no."

"What? Never mind, it'll have to wait. They've found us."

Julienne started to move towards the back wall but there was a hiss of rapidly dissolving metal from the doorway. Mex blinked in shock as the blood red display of jungle flowers was replaced by a square-framed mass of muscles set on an oversized skeleton of reinforced bones and joints. There was a faint rustle of surprised air as Julienne dropped below the evacuating chamber of the air pistol aimed at her chest. Her left leg snaked behind and through the agent's ankles even as her arm reached up and grabbed at the man's waist. Her momentum carried his legs away and her weight brought him toppling towards the ground. Legs pinned together he came crashing down so his face took the brunt of the landing. The way was now clear for Mex to see the second agent already spraying the doorway with an arc of darts, but Julienne was still moving, appearing next to the out-stretched gun arm, rotating and folding the wrist. Her roll ended with the second man's gun arm held behind his back, the hand folded back between her two palms. She stepped back towards the doorway, bringing the man face-first to the floor, with the incapacitated arm held high behind his head.

Mex saw her take one measured breath and spare a glance back towards the first assailant. He was starting to push up on his hands, trying to regain his feet. She sucked air again and her muscles coiled in preparation for a massive burst of exertion. She lunged forward, the second agent's arm still held high, and kicked down on the man's neck. The move must have shattered most of the bones in the arm and neck.

Mex winced, the shock of extreme violence bringing him back into real-time. He ran for the door, grasping both fists together, and brought them down on the neck of the nearest agent. Mex whimpered as he felt dozens of delicate joints pull on their collections of tendons and something popped in his wrist. The man in black grunted but continued to rise. Mex was already vaulting him and entering the corridor. Unbelievably, the second agent was back on his feet and moving towards a crouched Julienne, a murderous grin pushing aside the overgrown muscles of his face. Mex scooped up the discarded gun and pumped a dozen darts into the man's back before his consciousness had time to realise what it was doing. Then they were running again, Mex's mind trying to extract itself from the intimate terror of the fight, and get back into flight mode. His muscles felt heavy and poisoned by tiredness and distance.

Something was nagging at his mind and it was not the burning of his lungs. Then he remembered. The need to plan rather than simply fight made his mind reel and interrupted the steady stream of demands to his legs. Mex stumbled briefly as words sprinted from his mouth.

"We're going the wrong way. There are another dozen agents on the space-lift about to arrive at the station and we're running straight towards them."

"We should split up. Try and break up the chase."

"They'll just come after you."

"Maybe."

Julienne continued to power down the corridor as it opened into another concourse. Rows of identical portals served smaller executive shuttles. Men and women in uniform peaked hats fussed over a small number of bigwigs lounging in furniture more designed than evolved. Mex returned their arrogant glances with a belligerently toothy smile. He tried to understand why Julienne had offered to split up. She must know their pursuers were only interested in him in as much as he might offer an opportunity to inflict some pain before they started on Julienne. Only one explanation presented itself to Mex; she was trying to protect him.

Why does she always wait until our lives are hanging by a thread before she experiments with compassion? he thought.

Mex risked looking up. The Earth filled the sky to the edges of his vision, causing a curious feeling of inverted vertigo. For a moment he felt like he was falling up towards the solid mat of clouds which blanketed the orange brown mass of the African continent. He landed heavily on one foot, and the illusion was undone. They had climbed several rungs into the cupola which formed the roof of the station. He had an almost completely unobstructed vista, except for the mass of workings which formed the apex of the dome. The anchor-point for the space-lift was surrounded by moving walkways spiralling out to the upper-most concourse of the main station. As he watched, a glint of reflected sunlight signalled a lift-capsule punching through the uppermost cloud layer and racing up towards the station. They probably had less than five minutes before the station would be crawling with MynCorp security.

His mind thrashed on the problem like a trapped animal, but the futility of their flight just became more apparent. His energy left with his hope and he started to slow down. Julienne looked back at him pleadingly. She glanced forward again towards the next curve of the concourse. A decision wrestled its way through the frame of her body and eventually she stopped and turned to join Mex. A grim determination formed a mask across the delicate but borrowed features of her face. Mex saw a resolve which sent a shiver up to his neck. He realised he was as frightened of her potential as he was of the predictably brutal man slowing to a walk ten metres behind them. The agent eyed Julienne with a respect born from injuries which would have crippled a normal man.

Mex held his throbbing flesh and blood hand at his side but sent a mental whistle to his false arm. It writhed and wriggled into the form of a mace with dull grey spikes. The symbiotic putty tried and failed to stiffen the points, but Mex held it in front of his chest in a vaguely threatening manner. The three of them stood in a face-off the agent seemed to find greatly amusing. He dropped his arms into a wide expansive position and seemed about to step forward to gather Mex and Julienne into a giant bear hug. He hesitated as a roar erupted from the side. It was both primordial and alien, like a newly evolved creature bursting from an ammonia ocean on some distant planet. A purple blur moved with the roar and landed on the chest of the stunned agent. The impact knocked him twice his own body length before he started to fall. The edge of the concourse tried to reach out an arm of fluid metal to grab the falling man but his weight and speed were too great. For a moment he hung in the feathery edge of the flapping tendril of translucent metal. Then he started the long fall towards the main atria below. He spun end-over-end as he shrank from view. The grin was still there each time his rotation brought his face back into sight. Finally, he landed with a muffled thud which wafted back up to their vantage point. Mex, Julienne and a gently growling Bergur watched in fascinated horror as the agent spasmed once and then slowly started to climb to his feet.

Bergur was first to break his gaze from the freak show. "We have to get to the space-lift," he said.

"But there are more agents on their way." Mex's voice sounded shaky and he wondered how much more he could take before shock set in.

"Kaamil has a plan. Follow me."

Bergur led them up the last two levels to the space-lift portal. Kaamil and Yakini were waiting for them in the otherwise deserted cubicle. Yakini was wearing a station-issue vacuum suit identical to the one she handed to Julienne, and she was holding two cowls that would complete the suits.

"How did you get up here so fast?" Mex flustered.

"We came directly after Kaamil explained his idea. We didn't stop to sightsee like you two." Yakini seemed as equally unfazed by the last few hours as she had when they teleported across a couple of light years of interstellar space.

Mex was about to protest that they had been fighting for their lives - or Julienne had been while Mex had mainly been running – when Sickle ambled into the cubicle and nodded to them in greeting.

"And where the hell were you when those agents came after us? One minute you're there giving us attitude and the next you're nowhere to be seen."

"I didn't sign on to fight an unkillable death squad. I followed at a safe distance." Sickle did not even bother looking contrite.

Julienne looked unsurprised, as if she expected little more from one of Mex's friends. Mex waved Sickle away angrily as he realised once again his emotional response was centred on Julienne rather than the more obvious trigger.

"What are we doing here?" Julienne asked.

"You see that lift capsule?" Yakini pointed towards the silver torus rapidly growing above them. "In two minutes it will dock and unload a MynCorp retrieval squad."

"How are MynCorp doing this? Surely, DogStar will protest to the cartel."

"They've subverted the local A.I. All of the resident security staff are confined to quarters while the station's mind works through some paranoid delusions."

"But DogStar will freak when they find out." Julienne's face dropped. "They're going to blame us, aren't they?"

Yakini's permanent grin faltered for a moment. "Not you," she said. "They're much more likely to blame us. We're of little use to MynCorp. Whereas you..."

"...have large chunks of knowledge locked up in a memory format that is submissible as evidence to the Corporate Corruption Bureau," Julienne completed.

Mex felt the mood towards Julienne dip another notch. "So, are we assuming they didn't buy our technology sale?" he diverted.

Sickle drifted back into the group from the fringes of the cubicle. "They're probably hedging their bets. As long as you all end up in MynCorp custody they can negotiate from a much stronger position. At least, that's what I would do."

Julienne looked defiant. As long as she blamed them for her fall from grace she was clearly not going to show any guilt for trying to keep her mind intact. "Can we get back to why we are here?" She pointed up at the growing torus, now close enough to reveal its facetted surface.

Yakini picked up her explanation. "Kaamil has developed a relationship with the A.I."

Kaamil fidgeted under their collective gaze. "I used to mess with an A.I. when I was docked." When nobody looked any the wiser he continued. "It was a way of avoiding the psychological assessments mandated between deep space trips."

Mex caught a flicker of pain twist both Julienne's and Kaamil's faces as a shared memory bobbed to the surface of their minds. Mex tried to move the conversation on. "Can the A.I. help us?"

Kaamil and Yakini shared a worried glance. "Not exactly," she said. "Kaamil thinks he can push the paranoia into the final defensive measure."

"Which is?"

"Releasing the ground tether."

"Won't that kill a lot of people?"

Kaamil looked disgusted. "The A.I. is a bit confused, not deranged. It won't let anybody die."

"So, what's the problem?"

Julienne answered before Yakini could find the right words. "It will give

DogStar enough evidence to blame you for the damage and then you'll have two out of four corporations on your trail."

"I don't see we have much choice," Mex said. After a momentary glance up at the decelerating lift capsule, he added, "Do it."

"It's already done." Yakini tossed the spare cowl she was holding to Julienne. Sickle dumped his coat, revealing a custom vacuum suit beneath. "We were just explaining what's about to happen."

Yakini, Julienne and Sickle put their backs to the outer wall of the cubicle. The wall swallowed them like treacle. A few seconds later Mex could see them moving along the outside of the station towards the collection of small shuttles below. There was a soft hiss as the lift capsule docked a moment before the skin of the room darkened and Mex sensed a rotation. Kaamil put a superfluous finger to his lips as Mex and Bergur stood with expectant tension.

Mex mouthed, "What now?"

Kaamil simply smiled. He probably thought it was reassuring but it just seemed a bit manic to Mex. The room continued to rotate until a semi-circular bulge appeared in one wall. The bulge grew wide enough for a double doorway and then started to dissolve. Mex caught a glimpse of the back of an armoured helmet as the last of the retrieval squad marched clear of the lift, and then they were in the toroidal capsule themselves and sealed from the station. There was the faintest of sighs and they started to ascend the tether towards the surface of the Earth above. Mex wiped the walls clear to confirm the strange feeling of climbing down the atmosphere. The wide dome of the Dyson station spread out beneath his feet, its edges fringed in jutting towers of glowing crystal. Above his head Africa played peak-a-boo through the clouds of the equatorial rain-belt.

"Hold on to something!" Kaamil almost shrieked in feverish excitement.

Mex tried to ask a question as his two companions sank into waiting travel couches but a violent shudder ran up his legs and rattled his teeth. Mex instinctively looked down and tried to isolate the feeling of panic which was racing his heart to a thudding gallop. The station looked crooked; one side should have been in shade but the reflected sunlight was creeping up the darker side even as he watched. Then he realised that the station was no longer directly under his feet. It was drifting to one side and the thin thread of the tether did not make it all the way up. The bulbous anchor of the top was snaking from side to side as it collapsed towards the lift capsule.

Just as Mex's brain was starting to comprehend that the Dyson station was no longer attached to the surface of the Earth and was rapidly climbing free of its orbit, gravity flipped. The centripetal force which had made the Earth seem to be above him was replaced by the stomach churning reaction to free-fall.

"We're falling," he said, mostly for his own benefit.

"Not for long," Kaamil was still grinning disconcertingly. The compartment slowly started to develop a nose and tail while gossamer-thin wings grew from each side and tilted up as they were buffeted by the thin air. "Let's just hope we land on water."

The reassuring tug of the Earth's gravity reoriented Mex's world. "I think I preferred it when you didn't have a sense of humour," Mex said to Kaamil's mischievous smile.

*

The deep drone of an airhorn roared up from somewhere in the crater. Over a minute later the echo from the far side of the dome drifted back to José and Nomia, like the answering bellow of some giant sea beast. Far below, figures started to appear between the buildings, congregating into loose clusters. They slowly migrated towards a number of squat buildings regularly distributed throughout the Martian city.

"Food halls?" Nomia guessed. She realised she had not eaten since they had reanimated their bodies in the cave.

"I agree. We should eat." José said.

Her hunger must have bled into her exposed thoughts which meant she should not ignore the need. They picked their way back down into the crater and soon found themselves immersed in crowds of rangy Martians. A few people looked down at them with mild curiosity but the majority looked straight over their heads as if they were too small to notice.

There's almost no other Terrans around, Nomia thought to José.

I think they mostly keep to one enclave, there's a strong sense of independence and Terrans can act as a reminder that Mars is still essentially a MynCorp outpost.

Maybe we should look more Martian.

We'd be exposed as soon as we opened our mouths. You'll win them over just as you are.

At first Nomia thought the entire population looked like drones in identical grey and red jump suits, but she started to see the jumpsuits were a product of a collective pragmatism. The individuality was manifest in the trimmings. Each of them rebelled against homogeneity in the subtlety of a tattoo peeping from an arm cuff, a motif stitched across shoulder fabric or in the simple rumination of chewing gum. There was a pride in their bearing which could have grown from simply surviving against long odds.

Nomia and José entered the low food hall under a lintel of pulsing green algae, and found themselves in a utilitarian space filled with the clinking of cutlery against ceramic. The long tables were being filled in the order people arrived, a side at a time. José and Nomia followed the example of the others and took their place near the middle of the hall. As they sat on the fixed bench, a bowl of green slop scuttled in front of each of them and presented a spoon for their consideration. José started to eat without comment. Nomia took a tentative bite and chewed on a stringy lump. The texture was odd but the flavour seemed to evolve as she tried to identify it. She thought it might be salty and it definitely was, but then it became sweet as she wondered if multiple courses might be on the menu.

"That's odd," she said softly.

A middle-aged man opposite smiled slightly but showed no other sign of having heard. Nomia scanned the faces across the table and realised several of them were watching her from the corner of their eyes. She took another bite and chewed enthusiastically, letting the conflicting flavours wash through her mouth. This seemed to cause several smiles across from her and a tension slipped from the table.

"There seems to be some sort of empathic residue left when the algae is converted to food. The flavour evolves with the eater's expectation," José said as he pushed the empty bowl away. It vanished off down the table following a stream of used crockery.

"As I said, odd."

The man opposite finished his meal and started to stand. He paused and looked up and down the table, as if looking for some inspiration. Maybe finding what he was looking for, he looked back at Nomia and José and said, "If you want to get a real feel for Martian life, I'm going to our nakamal. I could take you. It's nothing like the fake ones you see in the brochures."

Nomia looked at José but he just shrugged. "Thank you," she said.

*

The treatments were Kaamil's unique form of self-flagellation. In the first months after his collapse he had been numb to the pain, minuscule compared to the grief and guilt he felt for the deaths of Grace, Dalal and even Qadir. He and Joshua had barely talked since the funerals; they silently constructed complex social orbits which forever kept them apart. Kaamil was scared their grief would reach critical mass if they were ever to touch, destroying them both.

Then Kaamil felt shame for missing Grace and Joshua most.

It was almost a year before he finally thought to ask the Sister what was wrong with him. She fussed with the equipment that monitored his immune response.

"What's wrong with me?"

"I heard you the first time." The Sister hated bad manners more than almost anything.

"I'm sorry Sister."

"No." She sighed and her shoulders sagged for a moment. "I'm sorry Kaamil. I shouldn't have snapped."

This was a new experience for Kaamil. The Sister was never sorry. She never needed to be.

"Why am I not getting better?"

"You're very sick, Kaamil. You have a genetic disorder which can't be repaired."

"Genetic? From my parents?"

"In a way."

"Did they have the same thing?"

"No. But they had a son. He had an increased risk of a rare disorders."

"I had a brother? Did he get ill?"

"Not that I know of, but his parents..."

"My parents?"

"Your parents... invested in a clone to act as a donor of genetic material. In case their son got ill. Do you understand?"

"I think so."

"And?"

"My brother had a clone."

"The clone was designed to be harvested for genetic parts at a certain age, but the son died irreversibly. Some kind of accident. His parents didn't keep up the payments, so the clone was scheduled for euthanasia."

"I thought unwanted clones went in the Drop."

"Normally, but because this clone was created for parts it was never designed to survive to maturity. Its ... his genetic timer was set to self destruct before sexual maturity."

"What happened?"

"He was saved. A charity was found to look after him."

"A charity? Like The Sisters of Catena Timocharis?"

The Sister tried to say something. She nodded and turned back to the monitoring device. Her shoulders shook slightly and her breath was ragged. The years of avoiding Kaamil's questions were there in the twisted knots of her shoulder muscles. It was the nature of orphanages to keep family secrets from immature minds but this truth was always destined to reveal itself as it poisoned Kaamil's genome.

The Universe lurched into a new shape. One in which Kaamil was smaller than a grain of Moon dust.

Infra-red lamps filled the air with the warmth of hot sand at dusk. The sound of laughter and babbling conversation filled the gaps between drumbeats. Mixed groups danced in gyrating circles around sculptures of angular metal which licked like flames towards the green sparkling roof. Jumpsuits were stripped to the waist and tied by the arms. Slender torsos glistened with the joy of rhythmic jumping and stomping. Nomia was offered cups filled with a liquid that left rivers of heat in her throat. It formed a pool of fire in her belly which consumed all the tension in her body. José stroked her shoulder and beamed at the life washing around them. Nomia wanted to dance even though the rhythm was strange and stretched like the limbs of their hosts. She joined a smaller circle, dragging José by the hand. The circle parted and embraced them as they tried to imitate the graceful beat. The low gravity and their long limbs made the Martians hang in the air. Each time the next beat of the music waited for them to fall back to the red earth. Their pummelling feet excited the dust until it formed a knee-high mist around them. The others laughed at the Terran's stumpy efforts, but it was relaxed and without prejudice.

A woman approached as they stood panting and taking slow sips from fresh cups. She was not smiling as she cut through the dancers to their corner.

"You two are not tourists," she stated without greeting.

"Is that a problem?" José asked.

"That depends."

The man who had bought them to the nakamal stopped dancing, and interrupted the newcomer. "Let them alone, Maéva. They're okay," he said.

"You know better than that, Lagi. Go back to your dancing. This is DTM business."

"Since when is extortion part of freedom fighting?"

"I won't warn you again."

Several other dancers stopped and stood behind Lagi but they offered no other support. Slowly they all moved away, the pain of impotence cramping their faces. Once the newcomer had successfully stared down the crowd she turned back to José and Nomia.

"We have nothing to offer you," José said, the smile never leaving his face.

"You'd be surprised. It's rare I meet anyone who is completely useless. Let's start with why you are here and how you fit into the MynCorp hierarchy."

"We don't know who you are. Why would we tell you anything about us?" Nomia's hands drifted to her hips.

"I suspect we are supposed to infer an implicit threat if we do not cooperate," José said.

"There's no need to be so melodramatic. You'll find Martian society quite closed to Terrans without our help." Maéva tried to smile but her upper lip seemed to be carved into a perpetual sneer. It did not sit well on the gentle rolls of her cheekbones.

"Everyone we've met has been friendly, so far," Nomia said.

"They're in a party mood. Things will be different when they get back to the harshness of their lives and they remember who is to blame."

"We've done nothing to them."

"But you are a walking reminder of MynCorp's strangling grip, from the stubbiness of your legs to the paleness of your skin. Martians do not forgive easily. Which brings me back to what you can do to pay for your stay. Think of it as a levy on MynCorp taxes like Robin Hood stealing the Sheriff's tax money."

"And do you give to the poor?"

"What?"

"Robin Hood did not keep the money. He gave it back to the peasants."

"My group represents the people."

"The DTM?"

"The DTM is an illegal organisation. It is an anti-corporate crime to be a member or to harbour a member."

"I see. And your activities are sanctioned by the Durga administration?" José seemed to lean forward as he waited intently for Maéva to answer.

"Tolerated."

"Tolerated," José repeated. "I see. I think we'll be leaving now."

"We are not finished here."

"I think we might be." José pointed to the approaching figure of Sera. She looked tired and worry lines had taken root around her eyes.

Sera looked at each of them in turn. "What's going on?" she asked.

"I was just explaining a few home truths to these Terrans. All off-worlders have to make a contribution to our funds one way or another."

"Since when?"

"Don't be naive, Sera."

"Tabansi would never sanction extortion."

"You are a fool to bandy his name about in front of strangers. A fool and a liability."

"These people are here as my guests and have been granted a meeting with Tabansi. Until he says otherwise they are under DTM protection. And you can rest assured I will be raising your little calorie-making scheme with him this afternoon."

Maéva shrugged and turned away to be swallowed back into the dancing bodies. Lagi caught Nomia's eye with an uncertain smile, which Nomia returned with reassuring warmth.

"I'm sorry about Maéva. She's overstepped her authority on this one," Sera said.

José smiled but without conviction. "How did your meeting go?"

"Mixed, but Tabansi will meet with you. Now, if you're ready."

*

The ship hung around her like a designer's wire-frame dream. The only sound was her breath and the crackle of telemetry from an earpiece. Julienne flicked her neck to pan the head-up display of her surroundings. Yakini's gold suit glistened above her left shoulder and Sickle's was in shadow below her right shoulder. The dual rings of the engine lay behind her head. The body of the tiny craft was a lattice of crystal shafts that might have made something vaguely like a spaceship if plates of metal had been bonded across each of the open spaces. Throughout the skeleton, nodes of hardware hung like husks in a spider's web.

"We are not flying to Mars in this thing." Yakini's voice breathed in her ear over the inter-suit communication channel.

"At least not until it's finished," Julienne added.

"This is as finished as it gets, apparently. I'm as nervous as you but Pimlico says this can get us to Mars in a few days."

"Even if that were possible, a few days suited, sat in harnesses and exposed to space. It's barbaric." Yakini complained.

"You wanted to come." Sickle retorted.

Julienne flicked her eye across the volume control and returned to studying the flight control of the ship. The engines were controlled by a simple but state of the art A.I.. There wasn't much else to do other than steer. There were limited sensor arrays, no life support or weapons. It was designed to run as fast and light as possible. The only thing which still confused Julienne was how it could work. She could see no fuel containment, no thrust nozzles and more alarming no way of absorbing acceleration or shielding them from incoming relativistic particles. The only significant features were the two rings of matt black material stacked behind her head. From the accompanying coils and generators, she recognised one as a superconductor. The other seemed inert apart from the hydrostatic bearing system and direct drive motors.

"Pre-flight checks complete. Ready to start drive on your command," the A.I. chimed in an imitation of polite efficiency.

"Define operating parameters of engines." Julienne said, ignoring the implicit request.

"Julienne, we don't have time for this."

"Are you saying that the A.I. can't talk and fly?"

"No."

"Well, you fly and I'll talk."

"Fine. Launch. Do whatever it is you're going to do," Sickle said to the A.I.. "If you find out this is going to hurt don't tell me," he added to Julienne.

The A.I. started to speak in a softly patronising tone. "Heim 1b is a prototype shuttle employing the effect traditionally known as the Heim-Lorentz force."

Julienne resisted the irrelevant urge to ask what happened to Heim 1a and said, "Elaborate."

"It was the middle of the twenty-first century before a unified field theory derived from the extended Heim theory of Dröscher and Häuser was commonly accepted. The combination of a discrete calculus and the Geometrisation principle lead to a model providing a twelve dimensional Heim space. The model predicts the existence of both the standard model of particles and the more recent extended model of weakly interacting particles. In addition, the six fundamental forces were unified within one model producing the first fundamental understanding of the quintessence force of spatial expansion and the dual polarity gravitophoton force."

"Reduce scope of explanation from basic physical principles to technical description of this craft."

"Detailed schematics are the intellectual property of Durga Corporation."

"What can you tell me?"

"In the presence of a sufficiently strong magnetic field the virtual photons present in a vacuum can be transformed into gravitophotons, as described in one of the hermetry forms of the Heim gauge theory. This is a boson coupling similar to the vacuum polarisation which partially negates an electromagnetic field."

"A magnetic field like the one produced by the massive superconductor at the back of this thing?"

"Correct. The ring is fifty metres in diameter and produces a field of up to one hundred Tesla."

"What's the second ring for?"

"The gravitophotons are produced with two charges. One mediates a positive gravitational field, the other a negative gravitational field. The repulsive force only interacts with fermions, such as protons and neutrons. The attractive force interacts with gravitons and leptons, such as electrons. Due to the relatively high cross-section of absorption of the atomic nucleus, compared to the surrounding electrons, there is a net repulsive force on ordinary matter, balanced by a net attractive force on space via the graviton interaction. If the material used to interact with the gravitophotons is sufficiently dense and rotates sufficiently fast a significant thrust along the axis of rotation can be induced."

"Durga have actually managed to build an anti-gravity drive?"

"That is classified information."

"Okay, but if they had how would they have avoided the technical challenges that made MynCorp give up on these things eighty years ago?"

"Patience. All of the technical challenges have been solved in other areas of technology in the last two decades. The crystal plate between the engines and the crew area has an almost infinite magnetic permeability, diverting the magnetic field around the crew and providing a magnetic shield that extends two hundred metres in front of the ship. The advances in frictionless bearings and direct action motors allow the three hundred tonnes of the impulse disk to be spun at over ten thousand revolutions per minute. The net gravity field provides very high accelerations but the payload is very limited."

"Hence the minimalist home comforts."

Julienne caught the blue glare of ion thrusters pushing them away from the Dyson station. As short flashes fired from every direction, the Earth and stars slowly stopped spinning and the sky-city of glassy copulas and crystal towers started to tumble in its new orbit. It felt to Julienne as if the station had absorbed into itself all the rotation of the Universe.

A vicious whine burrowed through Julienne's brow and brought her attention closer to home. The first of the two disks was starting to rotate. Faint radial grooves that segmented the surface rapidly blurred into a solid haze and then vanished altogether. The vibration shifted up through every natural frequency of her skull, until it became a continuous pain surrounding her consciousness. She could hear a discordant groan from Yakini over the crackling comms channel.

Julienne started to feel a faint tug of acceleration or gravity pulling her down by the knees, towards the nose of the shuttle. For a moment she thought they were going backwards but a quick check behind revealed the Dyson station rapidly shrinking to a flickering glint of reflected sunlight. It felt like the ship was falling towards open space. Then she understood the strange orientation of the acceleration couches – knees first was the closest she could sit to face forward and still keep her head above her heart. As the engines directed a negative gravitation field away from Earth they would fall towards Mars at an ever growing speed and, unlike impulse rocket engines, without losing efficiency. It was almost pleasurable, if the incessant whine would stop drilling for oil across the surface of her brain.

The hours crept by. Yakini seemed reluctant to talk and Sickle eventually gave up trying. She was probably apprehensive about her return to Mars. Very few Martians managed to find the resources to make it to Earth let alone find a role in MynCorp. She must have been very driven or extremely eager to get away.

There had not been time to think – or sleep – for what felt like weeks. The desperate flight from the station tether point across the outside of the copula had used the last of her energy. It had been an endlessly frustrating scrabble on all fours, trying to maintain momentum without pushing off from the surface and tumbling into space. They had been thirty metres from the shuttle when they had felt the station break free from its tether and start to arc into a higher orbit. By the time they had panted their way into the waiting acceleration couches, other shuttles had started to break free from the station, carrying the inhabitants to safety. Under the cover of hundreds of craft of all sizes they had set a course for Mars.

Part of Julienne's intellect which had been manufactured for such tasks noticed she was falling asleep. It logged the time and calculated a duration which would return her to a minimum acceptable operation condition. Another part of her consciousness, more organic in nature, was thinking about Mex. Once again he had waltzed into her life and distracted her from her mission. There was no doubting he had helped her on several occasions, perhaps even saved her life twice, but it was always in a way which left her feeling vulnerable and exposed. Everything about him was the exact opposite of what she admired and yet the sum of all his faults was completely compelling. She was sure if they spent enough time together one of them would kill the other and yet she felt a hole inside when they parted. She had no idea what should be in the gap or even what it was a hole in, and sometimes it felt like a lump.

She resolved to focus on her own survival from now on, but as sleep crept up and smothered her consciousness, her last waking thoughts were of Mex's neck beneath her fingertips and his lips a breath away from hers.

*

It was a pain that Kaamil never got used to. The drugs repaired genetic damage in every cell of his freshly matured body. The pain started inside his very cells, bypassing gritted teeth and mental discipline.

This time Kaamil did not want it to end. When the pain eventually sank away and left only a throbbing echo, his body would immediately start to decay and, eventually, he would die.

He had come close this time, but the Sister had found a benefactor to fund one more treatment. She stood openly crying. Grief aged her and Kaamil realised she had become old and frail.

They hugged.

"What will you do?" she asked.

She freed him with the question; his death sentence was a rite of passage.

He would only be a man for a few weeks but mortality was not a childish concern.

"I'm not sure. Live a little. Have some fun," he said without conviction.

She frowned.

Kaamil wasn't sure he wanted her opinion but he felt an obligation. "What do you think I should do?"

"Prepare yourself. Spiritually."

"I'm not ready to lay down and die."

"Don't let it creep up on you. Be ready for it."

"I haven't really lived since..." Grace's vacuum frozen face locked in perpetual scream, flashed in the flicker of a blink. "...since I got ill."

"You do what you must. I'll be here when the time comes."

Kaamil looked at her but all he could see was his own death.

He left without saying goodbye.

*

An eerie green glow diffusing through her eyelids brought Julienne back from empty dreams. The light was still indistinct and ghostly when she opened her eyes. Blue and green feathers of light danced around the ship. They streamed out from directly ahead of the shuttle and weaved a meandering path around them before vanishing into the magnetic shield between the crew and the engines. Tendrils of iridescent blue merged and spun into clumps of emerald green before fragmenting into fingers of translucent turquoise.

"What's happening?" Julienne asked no one in particular.

"Absolutely nothing at all," Sickle yawned. "There's not even the sound of snoring now you're awake."

"I do not snore, unless I choose to," Julienne said.

"It must have been Yakini then."

"I'm right here you know." Yakini sounded alert.

"I meant, what's with all the dancing lights?"

"Solar wind trapped in the magnetic shield," Yakini said. "It's been doing it since we got up a bit of speed."

Julienne checked her internal chronograph and was slightly shocked to find she had been asleep for over eighteen hours. She stretched as far as the couch would allow and mouthed a drink from the deployed facia of her suit's cowl.

"What have you two been doing while I was asleep?" Julienne hoped she had achieved the right level of casualness in her tone to seem friendly without appearing to pry. She wondered, not for the first time, why small-talk was the hardest form of communication to master.

"You know, a bit of dancing, a couple of board games and a lovely picnic on a tartan blanket." Sickle yawned again, "but mostly just sitting here in mindlessly boring silence."

"If only," Yakini interjected.

"If you're bored why don't you ask the A.I. to run an immersion environment?" Julienne asked.

"What an excellent idea. Except, wait, it won't. Maybe you exhausted the A.I.'s range of abilities when you asked for its curriculum vitae."

"Oh, this thing really is stripped to the minimum. In that case I'll leave you two to your picnic. My body could do with a lot more sleep." Julienne started to manipulate her brain back towards sleep.

"I think I hate you," Yakini said with little conviction.

This time an image of Mex grinning beneath a mop of black hair followed Julienne into unconsciousness. She muttered a half-formed obscenity in her sleep and occasionally she groaned or whimpered softly. Eventually, even Sickle switched off his comms and left Julienne alone with her dreams.

Chapter 7

Sardon Lucas hated not knowing. It made him feel vulnerable, almost naked. There was an underlying thrill of adventurous uncertainty but mostly he just felt lost. Normally, he would be planning ahead and strategising, but he could see no further into the future than the glass of coffee in his hands. The café condensada was quite distractingly good. The first sip was the intense essential oils of the crema but by the third sip the condensed milk started to stir up from the bottom of the glass adding a perfect sweet counterpoint to the bitterness of the espresso roast. Sardon ran a routine in his implants to simulate the caffeine that was missing from the drink. He felt his mood lift. The jittery unease of uncertainty was still there – worse if anything – but everything seemed brighter and, frankly, he cared less.

Pimlico Sergeant was the first corporate representative to join Sardon. They exchanged cautious nods of acknowledgement as the newcomer chose a seat to Sardon's right. The chair rearranged itself to accept the Martian's elongated limbs.

"How's things over at Durga Corporation?" Sardon asked.

"Good. Very good, actually. How about MynCorp?"

"Excellent. You know, the future is Myn," he quoted.

Pimlico smiled weakly and they fell into contemplative silence.

Sardon sighed and leant closer to his opposite number. "Look, do you know what this is all about?" He would never usually show his ignorance but it was possible he might need an ally in a few minutes and Pimlico was the one he came closest to understanding.

Pimlico's round eyes locked onto him for a moment, and Sardon could almost see the intense intellect sparking in her pupils. "Not a clue. There hasn't been an extraordinary meeting of the cartel in my time."

There was not a trace of tension in the elegant frame. Pimlico looked as if she was sitting on a pacific beach drinking the milk from a fresh coconut.

Sardon blamed the fanciful racial stereotype on the simulated caffeine. The room seemed to dim as he disabled the routine.

"Predictability is the point of the Cartel," he said.

The door chimed as a young woman glided into the room. She looked barely in her twenties but Sardon knew that she was older than him or, at least, had been born before him. Sardon hated relativity without caffeine. Her skin was pale while her lips and eyes were dark. She looked distinctly ethereal and moved with a slow fluidity to match.

"Sardon. Pimlico," she said with a drawn out whisper, turning the words into a poem of syllables.

They both nodded respectfully. Romany Eight was the longest standing member of the group. While the other corporations rotated their representative, the DogStar corporation rarely wasted the years and calories of interstellar travel to replace their delegate. Sardon found her slightly irritating, like most of her kind. He could not see the point of living four hundred years at one quarter speed but was prepared to acknowledge that a decade in space might change his mind.

Before the three could exchange pleasantries the Ж representative powered into the room. The metallic plates of her exoskeleton thudded against the solid floor, adding to the solidity of her appearance. Sardon frowned at the melodramatics. The robotic components melded with the woman's body were capable of micron and milli-Newton accuracy. It was as easy for her to walk silently on rice paper, as to pound rocks with her feet. Alyona Semanov did not look in the mood for petty gamesmanship. Her armour was stripped back to the minimum implanted components, and she wore an elegant black suit with a white shirt. Grey slithers of metal crept up her neck from the collar, and vanished behind each ear. Similar signs of her artificially enhanced body snaked from both wrists and encased each finger.

Alyona did not sit down. She leant on one end of the table, fingers slowly gouging furrows in the dumb surface.

"Which of you bastards is to blame?" she growled.

Ж corporation was rarely even on Sardon's radar. They kept themselves busy exploiting the least hospitable places in the solar system. They specialised in high-value mining and hazardous environment technology. They had never shown any interest in expanding into MynCorp's areas of expertise. Not like DogStar's attempt to develop an interstellar fleet or Durga's interest in data processing. He looked at the other two, searching for some sign of understanding or guilt.

"Well?" Alyona added.

"We're guilty of so many things you might have to narrow it down," Sardon said lightly. He felt the wrench of being lifted from his seat by cold metal fingers around his throat. Shit, she's fast, he thought as he started to choke. Sardon forced himself to go limp. He could not overpower her but she might return to her senses before he suffocated. He was dimly aware of the other two delegates rising to their feet and protesting from a safe distance. He fired up some hack-ware implants in his head to start the process of overriding the circuitry in her hand. The proximity meant that he had a pretty good chance of taking momentary control but it might not be soon enough to save his windpipe.

The room was starting to dim when he felt his feet returned to the floor. She lowered him back into his seat, and stepped back with tears in her eyes. Sardon cancelled the hack-ware before it revealed itself and tried to sip the remains of his coffee with as much composure as his aching throat would allow.

"Perhaps you should start from the beginning," Romany Eight said.

Alyona sagged into a chair and started to speak. "Forty-six hours ago we lost contact with our bases in the Oort cloud. Ten hours later the mining colony on Charon failed to send a scheduled telemetry burst. We diverted a clipper from Neptune Six to investigate. An hour ago we received this message."

Pale light flickered from her eyes and coalesced in the air as the grey mask of a fully clad ⋊ pilot. There was a voice overlay which presumably belonged to the pilot.

"We're just starting our fly-by of Pluto and Charon. Standby."

Pause.

"There's nothing there. No electromagnetic emission. The satellite network is down or gone. Surface radar shows no sign of the colony. I don't mean it's been destroyed, there's nothing at all. Even the mining works have been flattened. It looks as if no one has ever set foot on the surface."

"Hang on. I can see something rising from the surface. It can't get a ranging laser to lock-on but I can see it distorting the light from Pluto. Oh shit! It's heading towards us. It doesn't look like a missile but it's definitely homing in on... Did you see that? It just accelerated. Brace..."

The room fell silent as the image froze on the last frame.

Pimlico tried to talk, coughed her throat clear and asked, "What does the piggy-back telemetry from the signal show?"

"Exactly what the pilot said. We assumed she had just missed the remains of the colony but the archives confirm that the entire site has been returned to its virgin state."

"And the missile?"

"There's nothing in the data to show what attacked the clipper."

"But the pilot saw it coming."

"The optical recording shows nothing."

Sardon studied the Durga and DogStar representatives, trying to work out which of them could be behind the attack. He offered a calculated level of sympathy to Alyona. "I'm sorry Alyona, I know you had family on Charon. Is there any chance they got off the surface before the attack?"

"Save it," Alyona snapped back. "Just tell me why."

"I have no idea."

"The three of you are always arguing over demarcation. You each want what the others have."

"But not enough to risk the Cartel. We all know the alternative is a return to the chaos of a free-market."

"Well one of you seems not to share that sense of self-preservation."

"You are assuming that this isn't the work of another party." The others waited impatiently for Romany to elaborate but she seemed content to let the idea stand without justification, but she looked concerned.

"Do you know something?" Sardon prompted.

"Not yet."

"You're expecting to?"

"My news from home is limited by the finite speed of light. I live with the constant knowledge my home may have failed years ago and the news is still making its way between the stars."

"MynCorp is in the best position to take advantage," Pimlico offered.

"And has the most to lose," Sardon countered, as he wondered what Pimlico might be up to.

"Romany, do you think this is linked to the attack on your Dyson station?"

"You know that was the work of criminals," Sardon said but he was mentally kicking himself for leaping in too fast.

"And yet," Romany slowly turned to face Sardon, "the station was crawling with your security agents when we managed to regain control."

"We've been through this. The criminals attacked us before you. We were trying to stop them."

"By trespassing onto our territory?"

"You were in no position to catch them. The station's A.I. was already compromised once we realised they were on-board."

"As you say." She paused for a long moment and then said, "What about the terrorist problem on Mars?"

Sardon and Pimlico looked at each other. "I can't see why they would do this, even if they had the means," Sardon said.

"It wasn't them," Pimlico said.

Sardon continued to study the open face of the Martian. She seemed the least shocked by the news and yet showed no betraying signs of guilt. Psychoanalysis routines running in Sardon's head detected none of the subconscious indicators of suppressed emotions. From the way she responded, Pimlico was completely innocent but was having a long-held suspicion confirmed.

Sardon rubbed his bruised throat and reminded himself why he hated not knowing what was going on.

Kaamil's eyelids were white-hot with light.

He tried to open his eyes but the light scalded the front of his brain. He found an arm and dragged a protesting hand over his face. The light seemed to be less effective at burning the fur from his tongue, so he closed his mouth.

A full Earth glowered at him through the diamond clear ceiling of the atria. Kaamil's eyes wandered around the periphery of his vision, hesitating over landmarks which seemed reduced to fuzz somewhere between their reality and his memory.

"Village green," he murmured.

There was grit mixed with the fur in his mouth. It made his lips and tongue stick in unusual positions as he spoke.

The village green was clear of people. It must be late, or maybe, early. The circular space was usually heaving with promenading couples, solidifying their love under the benevolent gaze of Mother Earth. Green and blue light flooded down from the planet and bounced around the white walls.

Always white.

An entire colony in monochrome. Even stars could manage some colour, but set to the task of building a city on a silver grey Moon, his ancestors had barely managed a flash of primary colour.

Kaamil had half-understood – and cared even less – discussions about the connection between the ultimate experiment in Arab secularism, and the loss of decorative art. It seemed more likely to Kaamil the simplicity of Abu al-Wafa City reflected a subconscious feeling of being apart; elaborate decoration was reserved for interiors not for those perpetually outside. The feeling of not so much being a people displaced as much as misplaced, manifest itself in the transient nature of the colony's focus. There was always some external reason why the Moon had to reinvent itself but ultimately, maybe, it said something about the people. They had thrived for a few decades as a fuel depot for interplanetary rockets; a ready source of water to be cracked into hydrogen and oxygen in a shallow gravity well. Then fusion rockets had faded from use. The Lunar mining industry was already set to overtake water extraction but the difficulties of working in a vacuum made prospectors start to look to the new colonies on Mars and beyond. The leisure industry had been more enduring but eventually the chattering classes got bored of the Earth view, and were lured away by planet-sized oceans or towering volcanoes which touched the edge of space. Eventually, Abu al-Wafa City had settled into a mature mixed economy, and had faded into a monochrome whisper of its original aspirations.

Kaamil groaned.

Memory snippets from the last few days started to coalesce in a chain reaction of slurred conversations and instantly acquired life-long friends. They had staggered through the dark spots between bright lights, always hunting to regain the beauty of the first hit or drink. Fragments of earnest conversations arrived on his lips. Kaamil grunted at his own stupidity and willingness to nod enthusiastically at the insanity of drugged strangers.

The Earth rained blue scorn down on Kaamil. "You bought this on yourself," it seemed to say. "You know you should have died with Dalal, Grace and Qadir. Your guilt has killed you. You've been dead for years. It's just taken time for you to realise."

"I don't give a shit what you think," Kaamil growled. "I don't deserve to die."

"But do you deserve to survive?" The oceans acted as accuser.

"This started before I was born. Fuck! I wasn't even born, or conceived. I

154

was scraped, fermented and hatched."

"You poor thing," the polar caps jeered.

"Then dumped like a puncture repair kit for a lost bike."

"So, lay down and die. You should never have been born. Nothing lost."

The grit in Kaamil's mouth was collecting between his lower lip and teeth. He tried to dislodge it with his tongue and felt glass sharp barbs tear at his raw gums. Recent memories pierced the fog.

"Shit, Blank," he said as the micro burrs injected a fresh dose of the recreational drug into his bloodstream.

The Earth laughed even as it exploded. Oceans and desert rained down on Kaamil, drowning him in colour and sound.

*

"I'm not sure you're hearing me." Nomia raised her voice above the background grumble of bustling workers.

Sera cringed and shuffled her feet in the red dust.

Tabansi looked up from the hard screen notepad he was reading from. He looked amused. "My apologies. I did not mean to be rude. I'm just used to multitasking. Please be assured that I heard everything you said." He stroked the patchy mat of hair that clung to his chin. He was broader in the shoulders than a typical Martian and it gave him the physical dominance to support his position. The beard was presumably his homage to the revolutionary leaders of history, but his genetics did not favour plentiful facial hair.

"So?"

"As I said, I don't see why we would help you." He held Nomia's gaze for a few seconds as she collected her thoughts and then turned to the woman at his side. He handed her the notepad and said, "That's fine. See if you can push for twenty percent." She nodded and moved away only to be replaced by another Martian dressed in an identical jumpsuit.

Nomia tried to think where she had gone wrong. She had explained the significance of the Nodes to the Nexus. He had nodded without comment as he worked through a check list and a stack of crates. She had pitched the significant blow it would be to MynCorp when the Nodes were liberated and the potential for revolution on Mars. This had elicited a shrug as the little entourage followed Tabansi deeper into the roughly hewn tunnel.

Sera spoke for the first time since the initial introductions. "With the MynCorp bureaucratic machinery in chaos they'll retreat to their stronghold. Mars will be left to fend for itself. Isn't that exactly what we want?"

"Sera, don't lecture me on our goals."

"I'm sorry. I just don't understand why we wouldn't help."

"That's because you don't see the bigger picture. Mars cannot survive in isolation. We must secure our self-governance within the context of a system-wide economy."

"Since when? We've strived to be self-sufficient in every area. That's why we've been supporting the soil fertility and terraforming projects."

"Times change. I've learnt to appreciate the grey which exists between the black of hate and the white of idealism."

"More like, become too comfortable with the power you've accrued."

"Watch your tongue Sera."

"I'm sorry, but I caught Maéva trying to extort protection money from our visitors. Did you sanction that compromise as well?"

"Step back Sera. Go home and think about what you have. Come back when you are feeling more appreciative."

"I will not."

Easy both of you, José pushed into Nomia and Sera's minds. *There is more going on here than we can see at the moment. Sera, leave us alone with Tabansi. We'll find you after.*

Sera nodded in acquiescence, tight lips white with the effort of holding back her tongue. She turned her back on Tabansi and headed back up towards ground level.

Tabansi watched her go before turning back to José and Nomia. "Sorry about Sera. She's normally extremely dependable and loyal."

"You do not need to apologise for her," Nomia said before José gently interrupted.

"Is there someone you would like to introduce us to?"

Tabansi looked deeply into each of José's eyes in turn. "When I asked Sera how she knew you were genuine she told me she had seen inside your minds. I assumed she was talking metaphorically but there is something special about you two." He stood in contemplation for a moment before dismissing the gaggle of assistants vying for his attention.

"Follow me," he said and headed towards the heavy-lift mag-rail which spiralled into a branch tunnel.

Weak sunlight bled through the green sludge in the ceiling. The orange light mingled with the green glow from the algae, creating sickly luminous shadows. The man who looked up from a splice terminal as they entered was not dressed in the ubiquitous red jumpsuit. His demeanour and thin collared jacket betrayed his executive position. Tabansi had escorted them directly to the office building via a network of underground rail tunnels. Nomia scanned the office for clues to which corporation this building might belong to. No decoration or information display disturbed the pulsing green of the building's structure.

The owner of the office might have been of mixed race. He was exceptionally tall for a Terran, but his close-set eyes straddled a strong North Mediterranean nose. Nomia squinted slightly and tied to imagine him with typical Martian features. She wondered if his face was the result of cosmetic therapy.

The man said, "Thank you Tabansi for giving me the opportunity to speak to our guests."

Tabansi shrugged and sank into a chair. "It seemed appropriate," he said.

"Durga corporation I assume," José said.

Hold on. Did I miss a chapter? Nomia thought.

Not a chapter but maybe a page. It looks as if the DTM has become the enforcement arm of the Durga Corporation on Mars. Maéva as much as admitted it back at the nakamal.

"Good deduction, Mr Sanchez. It is a pleasure to meet you and your extraordinary friend. Ms?"

"Nomia, just Nomia."

"Nomia, of course. My name is Chimalsi Okonjo. I am responsible for public relations on Mars."

"And how are public relations?" Nomia asked.

"Tolerable, considering."

"Why are we here?" Nomia asked all three men.

Chimalsi's face sifted through a number of perspectives as he considered Nomia's question. "I understand you want to bloody MynCorp's corporate nose, and I find myself much in favour of such a plan."

"As long as you benefit from the vacuum left behind," Nomia said dismissively.

"Of course. Somebody has to step up to the plate. Why should you mind as long as you get what you want?"

"Can you look me in the eyes and tell me Durga would not have enslaved the same thousand children if they had known how to build the Nexus?"

"I cannot, but I can tell you, Nomia, we will offer you and your kind sanctuary on Mars when we take full control."

Nomia shook her head. "You have no idea what is coming. You squabble with the other corporations over your little pot of energy."

Chimalsi seemed prepared for her outburst. "Does it have anything to do with the disappearance of the Ж colony on Charon?"

"When?" José asked.

Nomia felt the shock of a fear manifesting itself after a long period of looming just out of reach. "They're almost here," she whispered.

"Who are here?" Chimalsi asked intently.

"Bergur called them the Eidolons."

"And they're connected to Verity Space somehow?" Chimalsi was studying José and Nomia's faces in turn, pulling as much meaning as he could from each utterance.

"Not connected. They exist entirely as a coherent cloud of potential reality."

"I don't follow."

José rested a hand on Nomia's arm and she felt strength flow though the touch. He started to explain. "In the crudest sense, our bodies are simply machines to supply energy to our subconscious."

"Surely you mean our consciousness?"

"Not really. Your consciousness is largely a survival mechanism to protect the lower layers of the mind. The subconscious shapes reality by making decisions in the quantum soup of superpositional states which form all potential futures. This is your presence in Verity Space, along with all other sentient beings. The Eidolons either shed their physical components or evolved entirely outside the physical universe."

"I see," Chimalsi said.

"Yes, you do." José frowned. "That's surprising, no offence. This is not news to you."

"Not entirely. We knew something was coming."

"And you believe you have taken precautions."

"Something like that."

"You are still looking to profit from all of this."

"Of course."

"You're mad."

"Let's hope not."

Do we work with him? José thought to Nomia.

No. Never.

Saving the Nodes and fighting the Eidolons is more important than our personal misgivings.

Sera is still our best chance. I can see it in her potential. In Chimalsi all I see is a thousand different ways he will betray us.

Agreed.

"I'm sorry but it's time we were leaving. You have your warning. It is up to you how you react to it." José said.

"I don't think you're going anywhere." Chimalsi offered with the flat tone of complete confidence.

José and Nomia got to their feet and moved to the corner of the room. Chimalsi stood with his head tilted in confusion. Tabansi moved to cover the door. A whine like a million scratching diamonds rattled the room. A maze of dark cracks zigzagged across the crystal ceiling. A moment later there was a thunderous crack and a wall of green slime flattened Chimalsi and Tabansi. The sky looked saturated white through the gaping hole in the ceiling. A slender shadow blocked the sun and a nasty looking weapon scanned the room below. José and Nomia waded into the sunlight. José offered Nomia intertwined hands to climb onto.

"I think we are beyond subtlety. It's time we took a more proactive role," she said as she willed herself to rise into the air. José shrugged, looked down at the stunned faces of Tabansi and Chimalsi. Then he also rose into the air and joined Nomia and Sera on the roof.

"You got the message," he said to Sera.

"Got it? It almost melted my brain. We need to get out of here. I'll take you somewhere safe while we work out how to get off Mars."

Nomia spoke as Sera ushered them towards the edge of the roof. "Somewhere safe is good, but we're not leaving Mars. We stick to the plan."

Sera stared open-mouthed. "In case you hadn't noticed, the DTM has sold out. We're on our own."

"Not entirely. It's time for you to realise your potential."

José looked back towards the jagged hole in the roof of the building. "What do you see?" Nomia asked.

"I'm not sure. I felt something odd when Sera blasted the ceiling. Like something cried out in pain but it was diffused."

"I felt it as well but I wasn't sure. It seemed to come from all around but it wasn't pain. It was more like mourning."

*

Bergur was supposed to be the strong one.

Mex half-dragged, half-bullied the semi-lucid Eridanian away from the crash site. Tears of frustration washed the acrid smoke from his eyes and into the raw gash in his right cheek. The burning pain and mounting anger gave him the energy he needed to take the next step and then another – a repetitive series of finalities.

It had been Kaamil – always looking ahead, never quite in the moment – who had spotted that the semi-navigable capsule was drifting relentlessly towards a DogStar operations centre near the base of the recently destroyed space-lift. Mex had been the one to conclude they should try and gain some control of the craft's path, or at least bring it to the ground before they reached the centre. Bergur's contribution had been to punch a hole into the brains of the semi-autonomous capsule and rearrange the contents with significant venom.

They had hit the ground hard. Something had started to burn. Mex could not work out what could be flammable in the Spartan capsule. The three of them were the most combustible components of the crash. And yet something burnt with a death-grey smoke of toxicity. The shell of the capsule had spasmed schizophrenically between the shock-absorbing fluidity the material remembered and a jagged nightmare of an artificial mind in the throws of death.

Bergur lay in the wreckage, his mouth flaps hanging wide open like a beached fish. He looked to be in shock but Mex recognised the glowing purple of his skin from their time on the Suparna. He knew that the inhuman strength of the Eridanian would be reduced to immovable mass, as long as he was blissed-out on abundant oxygen.

Eventually the air would kill him.

"It's so beautiful and so big. The sky is so far away and so blue," Bergur continued.

"Just concentrate on the beauty of walking," Mex replied.

"I think I might like to lie down."

"You lie down and you're dead."

"I don't care. I've seen Earth. Made it back to the birth place of the Ice Breakers. This is where I came from."

"All you've seen is a small crater and some burning bushes."

"Ja and it's beautiful."

Kaamil trotted back from a nearby building, his trailing cables writhing in some unnatural breeze. "I've requested taxis to a couple of dozen random locations, all a short journey. One is for us, the others should give us enough cover to get clear of the area."

"We're not using the taxis." Mex shifted some of Bergur's weight off his shoulder as Kaamil took his share of the load. "It will be too easy to isolate a taxi with occupants against those with none. If we could fool the system such that they all appear empty, MynCorp will put them in a holding pattern until they can investigate. We need some cover."

"A building?"

"That one." Mex pointed diagonally up the street.

"The ziggurat? Any particular reason?" Kaamil asked as he shifted Bergur's arm further onto his shoulder.

"Above the doorway, there's a smiley. It's a sign that the building is infected."

"Is that good?"

"This particular infection is called Freeloader and it means the building is not as in control of its resources as it thinks it is."

"I can make it that far." Kaamil was starting to stumble as his weakened body started to object to the unusual excursion.

"Wow, a real pyramid," Bergur drawled to himself as they staggered the last few metres to the imposing entrance. The massive lintel of roughly hewn rock was supported by two intricate columns with relief carvings of various animals locked in fierce combat. The only decoration on the cross beam, apart from the dressing marks of a handheld chisel, was a cleanly cut circle containing two dots above a semi circular smile. It was completely incongruous but Mex knew that the building was forced to incorporate the symbol into its façade whatever style it choose for itself, and it would not even know it was doing it.

As they weaved their way the two hundred metres to the building come Mayan temple, Mex had never felt more isolated from his fellow man. The street was smattered with people, walking in groups or standing in idle contemplation. Nobody gave them a glance despite their singed appearance. It was not that this street was regularly visited by purple almost-aliens or gaunt men with writhing tentacles in the back of their heads, and if it had happened before they were probably not smouldering as they walked. The disinterest was feigned as a defence mechanism which Mex found doubly depressing because he understood it. It was not mortal fear, but they were frightened. Each of them felt they had a lot to lose personally, despite appearing homogeneous in their blandness. They clung to a closed cycle of toil and virtual reward. The less individuality they exhibited in the real world the greater the system seemed to reward them, leading to greater opportunity to express themselves in the virtual world of the Nexus. And behind it all the implicit threat of the Drop.

The lobby of the building continued the external theme with tapered buttresses supporting beams of gritty grey stone. The leading edge of each buttress was carved to resemble a winding snake complete with an open-mouthed head projecting fangs at passers-by. Mex and Kaamil lowered Bergur into a gently giggling heap and nursed their back muscles back to an upright position.

"Welcome to Pantheon Plaza. How may I be of service?" a simulated female voice whispered from all around.

"We're smiling freeloaders," Mex said.

There was no answer from the building. "Perhaps that made no more sense to the building than it did to me," Kaamil said.

"The building's higher consciousness can no longer detect us. We're essentially invisible." Mex said with a wide grin which cracked the scab forming on his cheek. A fresh red stream meandered down the dark brown smear of his face and congealed on his chin.

"What do we do about him?" Kaamil nodded down to the quivering mass of purple that lay foetal-like at their feet.

"He knew that the oxygen levels on Earth would slowly kill him but he can't have expected to be out of it so soon."

"It's probably not just the high oxygen concentration, the air pressure is also higher than he's used to, or rather, his dermal algae is use to."

"So he's just going to lie around stoned until he dies?"

"Unless we can reduce the rate at which oxygen is absorbed through his skin."

"Kaamil, you are a genius." Mex stepped towards a stone panel of glyphs which was vaguely recognisable as a splice terminal.

"If stating the obvious is a sign of intelligence then you may be right. I suspect there is more creativity involved in true genius."

Mex was already lost in the green and red phantom light of a splice session. Kaamil smiled politely at two men wandering through the lobby deep in conversation. They seemed to concentrate very intently on not seeing the bedraggled threesome.

"It's not just the building which has a hard time seeing us," he muttered to himself.

"What?" Mex asked.

"Nothing. What's the plan?"

"I've just called a taxi."

"Didn't we decide that was bad? The dangers of making a call over a public network to a MynCorp transport device and all that. Anyway, where we are going?"

"You know the polymer sheath they use in medical procedures to isolate the patient from the immediate environment?" Mex did not wait for an answer. "It has a limited permittivity to simple molecules like oxygen."

"How do we get some?"

"We're going to see an old friend of mine."

"And the whole public splice session?"

"I used a hacked account. There's no way MynCorp or DogStar could trace it to me."

They both left a brief pause in the conversation as if tempting fate to contradict Mex. The voice of the building took up the challenge. "Good morning Officers. Welcome to Pantheon Plaza. What service do you require?" it said.

Mex and Kaamil joined Bergur in the shadowed recess between two snake adorned buttresses as multiple booted footfalls echoed around the stone-clad space.

"We're looking for the man who just made a splice call for a taxi from this building," an amplified voice clipped.

"There are one thousand and eighty nine residents of this building, can you narrow the search parameters?" the building responded.

"This was a non-resident and the call was made in the last three minutes."

"No splice session matches your criteria. Would you like to widen the search to residents or for a greater period of time?"

"No. You will provide multiple lift capsules and assist my team in a manual search of the building."

"Of course. I am at your disposal."

Mex eased his head from the shadows and saw more than a dozen figures in jet black body armour marching into holes opening in a freshly smoothed wall opposite the building entrance. Four of the helmeted figures remained in the lobby and moved to strategic points covering the door. He ducked back into the shadows and met Kaamil's 'what now?' raised eyebrow. The pilot was squatting with both hands spread over the seams of the Eridanian's mouth flaps. Mex held up a calming hand as his brain accelerated to attack speed. Then he noticed the dancing red dot of a splice tracking laser on his outstretched hand. The splice terminal had followed him into the alcove because he had not ended his session. He could still connect to the building from his hiding place. His code glasses selected a gothic skull and cross-bone motif as he slipped them from his jacket and slid them over his ears. A few seconds later he had scrambled the building's lift system into a torturous convolution beyond random. "We'll need to take the stairs," he said to the attentive Kaamil.

"Carrying him? I'm not sure I can."

"I haven't disabled the stairs, you've jut got to help me get him to the first step."

"Okay. Which way?"

Mex tested the slab of stone behind him and felt it slip apart under the pressure of his fingers. "Looks like the tradesman entrance is ready."

They dragged Bergur through the slitheringly-thin membrane of the stone wall and into the dark service-space behind. The Eridanian was now barely conscious and his mouth flaps sagged open revealing a dark mouth rimmed with miniature shark teeth. The service-space was a roughly formed corridor dotted on all surfaces by dormant utility bots. Kaamil and Mex had to shuffle sideways along the narrow space, suspending the listless weight of Bergur between them. The end of the corridor parted as they approached and they found themselves at the bottom of a tightly spiralling staircase of stacked segments of stone. Each step was artificially aged by a smoothly worn dip near the widest part of the arc. They stepped onto the staircase together and a ripple formed behind their heels, carrying them upwards at a slowly accelerating rate. They surfed on a wave of liquid stone over the apparent solidity of the stone steps.

"What's up?" Kaamil asked once his breathing had settled below a rasp.

"The roof and our ride."

"You think the taxi is still coming even after they traced your call?"

"This is no ordinary transport capsule. It's one of a few that know me personally."

The staircase decelerated and deposited them in a temple of stacked stones at the top of the ziggurat. They emerged into the blinding warmth of the setting sun, and onto a broad platform arranged around a slab altar scarred by blood red gashes. A ball of pulsing images hovered above the altar, like an offering to a god of consumption. The three figures caused ripples in the sea of adverts as they slipped from view.

"So this is your very own taxi?" Kaamil asked once he was safely embedded in the support of a couch.

"Not exactly."

The voice of the capsule had the soft growl of a femme fatale in a clichéd sim. "Mex, my beautiful Mex, you came back to me."

"I'm here, with friends." Mex emphasised the last part.

"I don't care about them, unless I should consider them competition. They're both male, I think. So that's okay. You like… What sex am I? I feel like a woman. Do I look like a woman to you Mex?"

"You're every bit a woman." Mex glowered at Kaamil's smirk.

"Mex, we're being shot at, by men on that building we just left."

"What? Are we in danger?"

"Only if they hit us. Are they after your body as well?"

"Maybe we should concentrate on getting away and worry about motives once we're safe."

"Whatever you say, darling."

Mex dug his fingers into the gel of the couch and tried to maintain a friendly grin as they weaved towards the clouds. As their flight started to level out Bergur groaned and slowly opened one eye. "Where are we?" he groaned.

"Bergur, how're you doing?" Kaamil asked.

"Feel like I'm waking up after a week-long party. I've felt better, can't say I've felt worse. Where are we?"

"Mex's little love-boat."

"Funny." Mex added.

"Mex, we're out of range of the nasty men who were after you. What now, where can I drop these two, so we can be alone?"

"I see," said Bergur as he lent back and closed his eyes again.

Mex was sure the Eridanian was grinning even without lips. He addressed the taxi politely. The emotional aspects he had added to its personality allowed the A.I. to overcome processes which were usually blocked, such as flying to a building that was cordoned by MynCorp. The same emotional elements meant it could refuse to obey Mex; it had a natural predisposition to love him but it was not blind obedience. It could sulk really badly if he did not try and earn the devotion. "I'm really happy to be back with you. I'd love to spend the rest of the year flying round the Earth. Just the two of us, but MynCorp are trying to kill me."

"Again?"

"Again. And DogStar."

"That's new."

"My purple (platonic) friend here is going to help me, but he will die unless we get him to Woodland II."

"Usual story. You take advantage of me Mex. One day I might not stand for it."

"I promise we'll spend some quality time together as soon as I'm not running for my life."

"Just you make sure you do. By the way have you heard from my sister? She's dropped off the grid. Last I heard was a rather rude message boasting she was with you and the two of you were running away together."

"She was on Dyson station."

"Really. How did she get up there? She didn't cause it to break free?"

"No, but she may not have survived."

"I'm not sure how I feel about that. I didn't like sharing you with her but I think I'll miss her."

"I know."

Mex was grateful for the silence which dominated the rest of the journey, only punctured by the strangled laughter from Bergur that did not seem entirely oxygen generated.

*

"What if I die before I wake up?"

The question seemed left over from a previous dream or reality.

This time it was dark when Kaamil came round. He tried to spit the drug burrs from his mouth but only succeeded in triggering a spasm from strained stomach muscles.

"Here," a bottle of water said as it was passed to him by a man in the next seat.

"Thanks," Kaamil managed.

"Thought you were dead," the man offered.

"Not yet."

The man simply grunted knowingly.

Kaamil looked round his new surroundings. The room had the dimensions of a port waiting room; the low sprawl synonymous with all spaceports. A window stretched the length of one wall. The blast-proof diamond glass reflected and re-reflected a sky full of stars until pin-point lights blurred into a continuum of scintillation.

"Not dead yet," Kaamil wondered to himself.

His body tingled. Every time a piece of DNA was unwound and split in two he was a step closer to death. Every millisecond another cell committed suicide, compelled by a piece of wet-ware inserted into his genetic code by the patent department of MynCorp.

Maybe he should take matters into his own hands. End it now. Find a Nexus centre and get himself Dropped. Or maybe go for drama and take a walk outside in hard vacuum. Frozen decompression seemed fitting somehow. Was he brave enough?

An image of burst eyeballs bulging from a frozen blue scream flashed behind his eyelids. His stomach started to tense again.

"Where're you heading?" the man next to him asked from light years away.

Kaamil looked at the myriad of stars, as if trying to choose one to call home. The urge to fly away was stronger than anything he had ever felt.

"I don't know," Kaamil said.

"Right." The man nodded as if he understood. "I'm the same. I'll take passage on anything that needs a hired hand."

"Like who?"

"Some of the cruise liners still use human serving and maintenance staff. Retro style. Or the odd yacht births here. You're probably a bit young yet but you never know."

"Right. Where can you get to?"

"Anywhere. Mostly inner system but the odd ship goes Jovian or further."

"What about to another star?"

The man laughed. "You want to spend years asleep drifting in empty space?"

"Maybe."

"DogStar have got that one all tied up, except for the odd MynCorp interstellar ship, but they don't take passengers, or crew. You won't get a job with DogStar. You're definitely not their type. Still, anywhere has got to be better than here. Right?"

"Right."

At that moment Kaamil meant it and felt a flicker of hope he might live long enough to see something amazing. A sight that might define a life as more than the sum of its spare parts.

*

173

Evolution over a cup of tea. That was how it felt to Bergur. A few minutes ago, most of life's rich tapestry seemed to be resolvable with a grunt or two. By the time his horizons broadened beyond the confines of his skull, he had descended into convulsive giggling fits. Then his mental state leapt from self-aware to self-conscious as he realised three Terrans were studying him from the safe distance of the neighbouring universe. With a pop of revelation, the two realities merged and became real. Physical pain congealed throughout Bergur's body, accelerating his development towards sentience.

"Welcome back."

Bergur settled on the name Mex for the hairy Terran. He rewarded the human's ridiculous smile by vomiting a stream of toxins over his feet. All three Terrans backed away from the pool of black liquid as if it were poison. Bergur realised it was entirely possible they thought he had a venom attack, like some kind of human-lizard hybrid. The thought cheered him considerably.

"Thanks," he said shaking dark drops from the corners of his mouth flaps.

Mex shook a foot over the rapidly vanishing pool. They all watched the pool soak into the floor and vanish. Bergur wondered what the building would make of the debris from an alien physiology.

"I'm guessing this is all good." The speaker was dressed in the reflective white of a permanently sterile medic's gown. He had a circle of dark-brown hair around the crown of his head that was plaited down to the nape of his neck. His face was calm and impossible to read but there was a fire in the pits of his eyes which invoked images of hardy warriors standing atop glaciers, waving blood-stained claymores at a raging storm.

"I'm hoping that was just his body purging itself," Mex said. "Bergur meet Jon, Jon this is Bergur."

"Yeah, I feel much better now. How am I not dead?"

"I've coated your body in semi-permeable membrane. It's limiting the exposure of your skin algae to oxygen, but it is also constricting the rate it can metabolise. Don't exert yourself too much."

Bergur peered at his forearm, peeling back both eyelids to get a clear look. The purple was less vivid and there was a new sheen like a layer of polish over the skin. "Thanks. Do I get any benefits like immunity to plasma weapons?"

"Not as far as I know."

Mex's shoulders relaxed away accumulated tension. "Thanks Jon. I owe you, again."

"Mex. I've told you before, as far as I'm concerned, you're family."

Memories shot pain through the corners of Mex's eyes. "No news on a release date for Jacqueline?" he asked.

"Oh, man. I thought you knew. I tried to track you down by word of mouth but... you know. MynCorp released her body last year."

Mex mouthed silent words for several seconds before he managed to make a sound. "Last year? She's been dead for a year. I've been meaning to get in contact, but you know how it is?"

"I understand. We all knew she would die in the Drop. You were the only one that kept hoping. I suppose that's because Dad and I got to say goodbye. I'm sorry Mex."

"So am I. She was your sister. I only really knew her for a little while."

"You got to see her at her most luminous." Both men stood in a cloud of memories for many seconds. "Mex, it's time to move on. I did, a long time ago."

"I know. I've tried, in my own way."

The room fell silent. Confusion marked Kaamil's brow but he was empathic enough to keep quiet. Bergur felt home-sickness like a lump of methane ice in his throat. Post-adrenaline shock was mixing with the remnants of algae toxin in his blood, sapping his strength. He pulled himself upright. "What do we do now?" he dropped into the collective reminiscence.

"Mi casa, su casa."

"No way, Jon. We're out of here now. We'll firm-up the plan en route," Mex said, a new energy infusing his face.

Bergur did not like the hint of self-destruction which fringed Mex's expression. Bergur and Kaamil had already accepted their ultimate fate. Now, he was not sure any of them had anything left to lose. Except, each of them in their own way, clung to a beacon; one of three unique women. Three distinctly different paths, but each tinged red by the dust of Mars.

Chapter 8

Sera wretched again as she tried to expel the new memories burning her mind. Her stomach muscles ached, but begrudgingly produced bile for her to spit into the dust.

"I'm sorry, Sera, but you need to know what is coming." Nomia stroked Sera's scalp, and fussed with guilt.

Sera tried to speak but all she could see was shadows closing in on Mars from all sides, leaving only virgin dust in their wake. "Reality itself has turned against us, trying to wipe us out," she growled through a burning throat. "Is it some kind of retribution?"

José opened his mouth to speak but Nomia silenced him with a shake of the head, fearing a lecture on comparative religion and moral ambiguities. "This has nothing to do with justice or blame. We are fighting for our lives against a malicious enemy. We have as much right to live as they do. They are attacking us without provocation. We must defend ourselves."

"And I see how the Nexus Nodes fit into our defence. I see the path you have chosen, and I understand why you picked me, but I can't see myself as you do. In your mind I am a leader of people but that's not the real me."

"It will be." Nomia withdrew the reassurance of her touch. "How do you feel?"

Sera mentally patted herself down. "Better," she confirmed. "My mind seems to be healing. I can still see the terrible visions of the Eidolons but somehow I don't feel broken by them any more."

"Your sanity is tougher than you think."

"Or my sense of denial."

Nomia dismissed the suggestion. Her voice shifted to a more logistical tone. "Can you get a message to those in the DTM that you trust?"

"Of course. There are at least a couple of dozen that are as naively idealistic as I was."

"We'll need at least a hundred to have a realistic chance of handling a thousand Nodes."

"We'll have to trust word of mouth. Tabansi will get to hear of our plan. There's no way of preventing someone talking where they shouldn't."

"We'll move too quickly for them to stop us, assuming they even try."

"Will this tunnel offer us any protection when the Eidolons arrive?"

"No. Physical barriers are meaningless. The collective presence of a thousand Nodes will be like a beacon in Verity Space. They'll be on us very quickly."

"Right." Sera looked inside for a source of strength and found nothing big enough for what was to come. "One step at a time," she muttered to herself.

"I wish I wasn't here talking to you all like this. I want our leadership to be inspirational and devoted to the liberation of Mars, but they are not. They have become part of the problem and are more interested in protecting their position than in promoting our cause."

Sera scanned the thirty faces as she spoke from an upturned crate. She knew every person from DTM. They were all front-line supporters of one kind or another. Some were prospectors, like her, but most were miners or agricultural workers. The harsh conditions tended to exasperate any feelings of disenfranchisement. She knew they had all heard grumbling about the DTM's leadership but she was about to present them irrevocable evidence. "Today I found out that Tabansi has formed an alliance with Durga Corporation in order to pursue mutually beneficial activities."

This was an accusation too far for some in the crowd. "Prove it," a couple of voices called.

"José, if you wouldn't mind."

A three dimensional image of Tabansi and Chimalsi grew in the air above the gathering. José had explained it was not entirely implausible for the shard of roof crystal he had pocketed to have coherently recorded the light and sound in the room. He had tinkered with the tiny probability until it had become a certainty. Of course, the crowd could decide the recording was a fake, but all she had to do was feed any existing doubt to sway them in her direction.

Sera heard individuals in the crowd express their disgust with characteristic clucking noises, as Tabansi and Chimalsi shared their collaborative secret with José and Nomia. When the recording showed Sera bursting through the ceiling to rescue the Terrans, the crowd started chanting her name.

"We have a plan to strike a blow against MynCorp and we don't need Durga permission to do it." Sera's voice rose above the angry noise. "We are going to bring the Nexus down and with it the MynCorp stranglehold on Mars. Durga are not as powerful as they like to think. They will do as we tell them once we are in control."

They were cheering her now and she was no longer afraid of her own voice.

"We need one hundred volunteers for the raid. Think about your friends and colleagues in the DTM. Each of you choose two you trust and bring them here tonight."

"Tomorrow Mars will be ours."

Sera sagged onto the crate which had served as a rostrum a couple of hours before. "I thought my job was done once I finished the speech," she said.

Nomia stood at her knees and looked her in the eyes, taking advantage of being the same height for once. "You're doing brilliantly."

"It's hard to inspire people without giving any details of the plan. I hate lying to them."

"I don't think they are ready for fanciful stories just yet."

"Like moving groups of people from one planet to another using a few thoughts?"

"You sound sceptical."

"Not even a little bit. I'm resigned to my madness but these are dust-eaters born and bred. You'll never meet a more grounded people."

"I'm sure they understand the plan relies on secrecy, until the last minute."

"Most of them, but they're not stupid. They know it's impossible to do any real damage to MynCorp without attacking Earth. Yet I've promised them victory in one day."

José smiled and waved from near the centre of the cave. He was at the centre of a group of men arguing with vehement arm gestures. Sera and Nomia waved back. His reaction was sudden and completely incongruous. José's face creased in confusion and then panic. He began to mouth a warning. Nomia started to reach out with her mind to ask him if he was okay but a noise from behind stole her concentration. There was a series of half-finished protests and exclamations bubbling through a sound of scuffling feet and grunts of pain.

"Who the hell?" Sera started to say.

Nomia turned towards the tunnel entrance. A child-like figure was weaving through the clusters of people filling the space. There was a blur of athletic limbs which seemed to conduct the symphony of cries spreading like a wave towards her. The nearest pair of DTM members had time to brace themselves against the advancing intruder. Their resistance was short-lived as a booted foot crunched the knee of one. The attacker used the landing point of the first blow as a springboard to start a somersault which brought a scissor kick to the neck of the second Martian.

As the attacker landed in a coiled crouch two metres in front of Nomia, she realised that it was not a child but a Terran woman. Nomia started to tense for the inevitable attack as the intruder started to uncoil into her next leap. There was a moment in which they locked eyes. Nomia mentally stumbled as she recognised the tight features framed by an unfamiliar cascade of brown curls.

With improbable agility, the woman twisted her leap to bring her down next to Nomia's shoulder. The wrist-mounted gun strapped to her arm pulsed forward and pushed into the side of Nomia's head with a sickening thud.

The woman spoke to Nomia but loud enough for the gathering of shocked faces to hear. "This time you are definitely coming with me."

There was long frozen pause, punctured only by a yelp from Nomia as her captor improved her hold. Sera felt most faces in the room look in her direction. She wanted to defer to José and Nomia. She had no idea what was going on but if she did not show leadership now there was no future for their little splinter movement. "You are welcome here Terran but your weapon is not. Put it away and tell us what you want?" Sera said with more authority than she felt.

"I have no interest in your petty little political games. This woman is wanted by MynCorp for anti-corporate activities. I am taking her into custody. You will all stand down and clear a path to the exit. José Sanchez will also be coming with me."

"Do you imagine that MynCorp wishes carry any weight here? Put the gun down." Some of the braver DTM members had recovered from their shock and were starting to form a circle around Nomia. José was stood motionless, his eyes slightly glazed. Sera realised she had to resolve this fast before José decided to intervene. An impossible act now would cause too many questions. The next meeting would be filled with sightseers rather than rebels. Everything would fall apart. "You're not going to shoot her after all the effort it must have taken to get in here."

"You have no idea what I am capable of."

There was a hopeless tone to the woman's voice which frightened Sera more than the sleek-looking gun pressed to Nomia's head.

A new voice echoed into the cave from the entrance tunnel. "Julienne, we talked about this before. We agreed no guns."

Sera recognised the speaker instantly. The voice was so intimately familiar, she was instantly transported back to a time when it was a frequent whisper in her ear. She momentarily lost touch with the present as eternal memories overcame transience. As she fought her heart back to the present she swam through black emotions of betrayal and longing. The word pushed through her lips before it consciously formed a name.

"Yakini."

*

"You're asking for a lot."

Mex found himself whispering despite the sound negating surfaces surrounding them. "I'm sorry to be so frank, but you owe me."

"I see." The building paused. "You know MynCorp will shred me if they find out?"

"I wouldn't be asking unless it was really important and I was desperate. If it's any conciliation, we'll all be dead if this fails."

"Not much." The male voice was calmly efficient, and was a perfect match for the building's entrance lobby. Simple lines and clean colours suggested opulence beyond luxury. The walls and floor were clinical white with primary accent colours distributed amongst the art work and soft furnishings. Mex wondered if an entire art movement had been created just to provide exactly the right style for the building interior. The mischievous part of his mind - it just seemed to be encouraged by stress - wanted to leave muddy footprints across the floor. He knew the floor would take instant offence and absorb the dirt, but the urge was still there.

"So, you'll do it?" Mex asked.

"As you say, I owe you. Give me an hour to reconfigure the top floor. There's a café across the street. I'll open a tunnel into its bathroom in sixty three minutes from now. I want any eyes in the sky to see you leave and not come back."

Mex, Bergur and Kaamil walked across the street, keeping their heads down, eyes self-consciously fixed on their feet. They sipped overly sweet coffee, bought with energy credits donated by Jon. The café's unique selling point seemed to be that all drinks were made from one hundred percent comet water. Mex resisted the urge to comment on the cometary origin of the Earth's oceans and sipped the coffee with an insipid smile. They kept the conversation neutral and watched the clock. The café had an old fashioned brass bell over the door. Mex jumped and Kaamil flinched every time it jangled its discordant tune.

After an hour they wandered into the bathroom a couple of minutes apart. Mex found Bergur and Kaamil sinking into the black and white chequered floor of a toilet cubicle. He jumped down to join them in a tunnel of undecorated building fabric.

"Must be one of the building's roots," Mex said.

"Smells like it as well," Kaamil commented.

The walls pulsed once like a swallowing snake. They took the hint and headed towards the root's source. When it turned upwards a lift capsule formed around them and started to draw them towards the roof. The lift swerved a couple of times around some internal obstruction in the building's structure, before disgorging them into an irregularly shaped space without windows.

"This feels more like home," Bergur said and Kaamil agreed.

"I'm glad you two are happy." Mex sighed at the loss of the sky, so recently rediscovered.

The space was still slowly establishing its shape around them. Three sleeping pads and a bathroom were emerging from the creeping fluidity of the building fabric. An eating area had already formed with stocked cupboards. Half a dozen pieces of generic furniture detached themselves from the floor and waddled towards the centre of the space around three splice terminals.

"So, I'm guessing we're here for a while. What's the plan?" Bergur flopped into a chair which hurriedly configured itself for his mass.

"Alec, tell them what you are," Mex said.

The building spoke through the walls. "I am the operations centre for MynCorp on Earth and throughout the Solar System."

"This building?" Kaamil sounded sceptical. "It looks residential."

"I have living and office space. The two tend to blur for executives. If a director wants something from the physical world it tends to come to him."

"They must need to get out and about occasionally. Take a walk or look at the sunset." Kaamil sounded out of his depth talking about the day to day activities of those not tethered to a ball and encased in a few thousand tonnes of space-faring metal.

"There are a fleet of physical avatars spread across the planet, equipped for every need," Alec said.

"We're getting distracted," Mex started.

"What do you mean by equipped?" Kaamil interrupted.

"Enhanced sense of smell to enjoy the spring blossom, enhanced stamina for adventure sports or enhanced libido for sexual release."

"Creating a life-form purely for recreation seems profligate even for MynCorp executives," Bergur said.

"It would be. The avatars are not artificial, they are from the Nexus."

"The Drop? MynCorp use people from the Drop for their own pleasure?" Kaamil sounded horrified and even Bergur looked shocked. "How can that be legal?"

"It might cause a few ripples in the Corporate Corruption Bureau if it became public knowledge."

"Did you know about this Mex?" Kaamil asked.

"I'd heard rumours. It might sound callous, but this really is a distraction at this point. Let's focus on the bigger threat."

"I have provided each of you with completely open profiles. You can access any data stream which flows through this building. Your presence is completely undetectable by anything other than me. I have compartmentalised my consciousness so that anything we discuss is kept in a mind fragment physically tied to this room. When this room is reabsorbed into the building I'll forget everything that has taken place. All I need to know is how much processing power you require. The less the better. Nexus time is audited very closely."

"That's okay. We'll be processing the data manually." Mex looked at Kaamil and smiled reassuringly.

"Mex?"

"Yes, Alec."

"Tell me you know what you're doing."

"I know what I'm doing."

Bergur put one chunky arm in the air. "Are you going to tell us?" he asked.

"It's quite simple."

"That I doubt."

Mex laughed and found knots of accumulated tension unfolding in his throat. "José and Nomia thought MynCorp might have enough sophistication in Verity technology to turn the war against the Eidolons. Our job is to convince MynCorp of the threat and steer their response."

"Right."

"But we are intermittent fugitives and not likely to get a chance for a quiet word with the top brass of MynCorp."

"If Sardon was anything to go by, they're not exactly the most open-minded of individuals."

"Sardon is as broad-minded as he needs to be to do his job. We need to aim much higher in the corporate ranks."

"How high?"

"High enough to find some imagination."

"That sounds stratospheric."

"Quite possibly. Certainly, it will be too high for us to impress with our little story."

"So?"

"So, we become the story. The evidence we need must already be in the data. We find it and then claim responsibility. Once we have their attention, we tell them what we are planning."

"You're suggesting we pretend to be the Eidolons?"

Mex smiled his broadest grin. "We're going to get them so scared that they'll be falling over themselves to fight us."

*

Trouble always arrives in spiteful flurries, chipping away at certainty to reveal her skeleton of doubt.

Sera had learnt this the day she met Yakini.

Sometimes she could still remember the sense of invulnerability the marches had given her. Waving her home-made placard, resplendent in the orange and black of the Martian independence movement. She had sneaked back onto the University campus to borrow the student print shop, using her slightly hacked and marginally out-of-date Student card. The University watermark glowed in the bottom corner adding an odd authenticity to the slogan.

Then she marched and shouted, drowning the security broadcast messages with her defiance. The people could kick-out MynCorp. They would over-throw Durga. Sera saw a future in which Mars was run by Martians on behalf of Martians. She waved, stomped and cheered at the natural frequency of a mob. Its single-minded spirit rose from the ground with the lazy clouds of red dust and formed an intoxicating vapour. Sera closed her eyes and sucked deeply on the draught of psychotropic unity.

A needle-sharp elbow savaged her ribs as a dark figure darted past. Its face was a nanite mask of shifting ghouls and the jumpsuit had been dyed a featureless black. Something flickered with energy in the figure's right hand, then she lost sight of it as the fluid-like crowd settled back into rhythm.

Somewhere further down the security perimeter a guttural thud made Sera instinctively cover her head against an expected cave-in. Everyone else ran, screamed or simply looked lost. Sera was knocked one way then the other by people's panic, until the crowd thinned enough for her to see a cloud of red dust spitting out blood-stained men and women.

The security force's response was instantaneous. A web of neural energy shivered up from the ground and sparked across her skin looking for her head. Her bones tried to shake off her tendons. Her brain pushed pain back along clogged nerves and into every pore of her flesh. Then the ground was repeatedly lurching up and pounding consciousness from her head.

She greeted the looming emptiness with simple gratitude.

When Sera regained consciousness she gagged on the smell. She sat up tall, gulping air like a free-diver, until her head stopped spinning. There were dozens of them in the box like vehicle. Collectively, they wreaked of sweet, fear and urine. Most lay motionless but some had their eyes wide open, conscious but groping for anonymity in the pile of bodies.

The vehicle lurched to a halt and boots crunched gravel outside. The stagnant air belched into the sky as the door slid open. Shiny black masks reflected the fear in the prisoner's faces, as they were corralled into smaller groups with sheep-shearer efficiency. Sera was steered by assertive grunts and the side of a night-stick into the back of a patrol vehicle. She shuffled across the moulded bench to make room for others but the orange and pink sunlight was replaced by the close echo of her breathing. She shallowed hard on the jolt of the engines slipping into drive. Her stomach churned on the sea-sickening swell of bulbous tires in the sub-terran gravity.

They climbed, motor pods whirring dissonantly. Then they circumnavigated the crater wall for a while. Sera was conscious of her toes pushing against the end of her boots as she compensated for the sideways slope. The MynCorp administration and Drop centre was west of the port. Durga's was even more centrally positioned on the crater floor. Wherever she was being taken, it was not there. Maybe they were trying to frighten her, but knowing the corporations, she probably had good reason to fear the worst; this far from Earth, their cruelty was limited more by imagination than any legal oversight.

The masked figure slid the door shut and squatted on the bench opposite Sera, his body armour creaking with pent up violence.

Sera's mouth went into nervous overdrive.

"I demand to be processed under the forty seven colony disorder act."

The trooper slid his night-stick from its belt loop and lay it on the bench beside him.

Sera's eyes tracked the movement but her vocal chords continued in a straight line. "As a citizen of Mars and employee of Durga, I am entitled to a hearing with a grade five or above administrator before sentencing to the Drop."

He put a hand on each side of his helmet and there was the faintest of equalisation hisses. It silenced Sera like a shush around a raised finger.

His face was not what Sera had expected. The black and silver neural interface pads on each temple combined with the sun-shy grey of his scalp, helped to rob him of human softness, but his mouth was not twisted by cruelty and his eyes were melancholic like a grey dawn.

"Sera, stop talking," he urged.

Sera could not think of anything to say. An open-mouthed stare seemed the best response.

"Your father would be so disappointed, right now."

"Who?" The questions piled up in her head and emerged as a jumble of interrogative words.

Two creases appeared briefly on the trooper's forehead. "I knew your father. My name is Tawhiri."

The name brought back memories of her Dad arriving home from a shift – laughing and beating clouds of basalt dust from the backs of colleagues and friends. "I remember," she said through the tar of vanished years.

"He wanted something different for you."

"I went to college."

"What happened?"

"He got ill."

Tawhiri winced from a thorn-like shard of guilt. "I heard."

"I had to go back to the caves to pay for his medication."

"That must have been hard. For both of you."

Sera shrugged. "I was brought up in the caves. I sucked on a rebreather while I weaned, and I could use a sonic-drill as soon as my thumb was big enough to reach the trigger. It's all I've known."

"How was he at the end?"

"You didn't come and see him?"

"We lost contact."

"You were a prospector." She remembered him now. Bouncing on his knee as he talked earnestly with Dad.

"Amongst other things. We shared an interest in politics."

"Dad?"

"You're more like him than not."

"Dad was a secessionist?"

The trooper laughed. It echoed around the closed space, startled by its sudden existence.

"How'd you think he lost that front tooth?"

"It wasn't Mum?"

 Tawhiri laughed again. It suited him. "Is that what he told you? She was more the disappointed-silence type."

"You knew her?"

"Briefly. I met your Dad just before she died."

"Giving birth to me."

"It was a difficult pregnancy."

Tawhiri was lost in his thoughts for a moment. There was the spider-like scratching of an earpiece. He answered sub-vocally, then looked back to Sera. "The point is that neither of them wanted you to live the same life they did. Your Dad once made me promise I'd see you on the right path if anything happened to him."

"I've always chosen my own way."

"That's what I told him."

"So?"

"You want to know what he said?"

Sera nodded.

"He said, that you don't choose. You let expectation dictate your fate and when that has nothing to say then you choose the straightest path."

"I could go back to college."

"Why?"

"Isn't that what you've just been telling me to do? Stop being a naughty protester and go to school?"

"Maybe, but why would you choose to go back to school?"

"Because it's what Dad wanted?" Even as she said it, Sera understood.

Tawhiri cradled his helmet in his hand.

Sera felt nervous again. "What happens now?"

"You have a long walk back into town."

"That's it? You just let me go? Just because you knew my Dad?"

"Most of your friends are probably doing the same."

"What?"

"Things are not as red and green as you think. It is important for Durga to be seen to maintain order by making arrests. It's a numbers game: two hundred arrested. Nobody ever asks how many actually get Dropped."

"What about the bomb?"

"You're not claiming responsibility?"

"No, never."

"Well then."

He slid the mask back on and Sera could only see her own distorted, tear and dust cheeks. "What happened to you?" she asked him.

His voice was precisely clipped by the security tech. "Would you rather have a stranger behind this mask?"

Sera stumbled from the back of the already moving patrol vehicle. She lay on the ground, disorientated by the unevenness of life.

The sun, low over the crater wall, was eclipsed by a woman's head with flaming halo. The face formed a treasure map of precious emotions. Sera blinked away light-sensitive sight and looked into her eyes. She had a flash of collaged emotions: love, frustration, passion, exasperation.

"Are you alright?" Mischievous imps skipped in the rolling dunes of her voice.

"I think so."

A helping hand separated from the silhouetted stranger. "Yakini," she offered with the hand.

"Sera."

"Nice to meet you Sera. Want to tell me what you're doing getting thrown out of a moving security vehicle?"

"Not really."

"Oh," Yakini sounded disappointed. "How about a drink then?"

*

"Why are you wasting my time?"

Kaamil blinked at the Petty Officer of the Fram. They sat in the shadow of a shuttle shaped like a seagoing yacht, complete with rope motifs and a three keel landing gear. The Fram was moored at the Lagrange point sixty thousand kilometres above the lunar city.

"Sorry", Kaamil said.

"You're a sav-ling."

"What?" but Kaamil was starting to guess where the conversation might be heading.

"A saviour-sibling. You're way past your harvest age. When are you due to shutdown?"

"Shutdown? You mean when will I die?"

"If you like."

"I've got long enough to do a tour on your boat."

The petty officer's laugh was callous. Kaamil could see no more compassion in his eyes than he might show a domestic cleaning unit.

"As I said, you're wasting my time. I've got applicants here who legally exist - as people – although in some cases it's marginal."

Kaamil was faced with a hexagon of white hat fabric as the officer looked down at his splice terminal and implicitly dismissed him. He thought about taking the cap and running but the rejection was so total he could not summon enough anger. Kaamil drifted back towards the milling crowds of the port and floated with the flow of people. Occasionally he would be buffeted by an impatient elbow and bobbed from one stream of people to another.

Some time later he found himself back at the Fram shuttle birth. A blue glow of high impulse ions glittered between the keels as it shrugged off the Moon's weak gravity. It turned slowly around the thrust axis until its bow was pointed towards the glittering swarm of the Lagrange parking cloud. Its grace and easy progress seemed to mock Kaamil's very existence. The whispering roar of its thrusters spoke at him. They said, "You are nothing more than a walking Petri dish. I spit waste ions at your pointless life."

Kaamil looked at his feet. The tingling throughout his body was there again – the genetic clock was ticking down and midnight was fast approaching.

"Kaamil Sillah?" The voice was round and polished like a snooker ball. The kind of voice that was impossible to doubt – a lie would crumble in repentance if it found itself spoken by such a voice.

Kaamil looked up at the flawless suit and concerned smile. "Yes," he said, although the effort was inhuman.

"Can I buy you a coffee?"

"Cured? Permanently?" Kaamil savoured the bitter coffee. His sense of taste seemed the part of his body most reluctant to accept the genetic order to self-destruct.

"Indeed," Vimeo Giani brushed the back of his hand over the fabric of his suit. The lunar dust smeared itself deeper into the fabric. "Always finds its way into the port," he muttered. "Only substance known to mankind that self-cleaning fabric can't deal with."

"And I can have a job on a MynCorp ship?" There was no way Kaamil was going to say no to whatever this man offered, but his disbelief kept him talking.

"Sort of." Vimeo was instantly back on top of the conversation. "We will disable your genetic off-switch, but we want you to become a bit more than just a crew member."

"What do you mean?"

"You will join our new class of interstellar ships. You will be the navigator, pilot and captain. In fact you will be the whole crew and more besides."

"I get to fly a ship to the stars?"

"More than that. You will become an integral part of a ship."

"Where do I tick?"

"Take your time. Drink your coffee and hear me out. This is a serious offer but also a major commitment."

"I have nothing to lose." Kaamil held his hands out as if his life was slipping through his fingers, like grains of sugar.

"The one commodity you have left is free will. If you agree to my proposal it will be for life. It is a permanent commitment."

"Or I can lie down and die now."

"You should consider how that option may look in a few decades from now."

"It's a shit option now and it will always be a shit option."

Vimeo held his gaze for a long time. Kaamil was about to hesitate under the intensity of scrutiny when the MynCorp man broke into a broad smile.

"Good. You've made an excellent decision. Welcome to the MynCorp Pilot Programme. Come with me. I'd like to introduce you to the Suparna."

Chapter 9

Nomia could feel the fine hairs on her temple dance in the electrostatic field of the gun muzzle. Her brain struggled to reconcile the contradiction of a tickle and a lethal threat, leaving her agitated and confused. Her rational brain knew she had nothing to fear, as long as she was fully aware when, and if, the charge of plasma erupted from the gun and attempted to burn a path through her skull. Even if she was taken by surprise, she could feel José's mind probing the potential futures around the gun, ready to intervene if necessary. She tried to tell herself she should be more concerned by the collapse of Sera's bold façade. Yakini stood next to a rough-skinned Terran, dressed in a long black coat. His eyes skipped around the room, flitting from one potential threat to the next. Yakini was trying to meet Sera's gaping stare but her fidgeting feet betrayed her discomfort.

"Start moving towards the exit," Julienne hissed in Nomia's ear. The gun muzzle twisted the skin of her scalp emphasising the feeling of metal burrowing into bone.

Nomia willed herself to smile. "I'm really happy to see you again Julienne. I hope you are feeling better than you did on the Suparna. We're in the middle of something important just now. Could we talk about this later?"

"Just start moving."

Sera looked like she was in a trance and seemed oblivious to the expectant looks of the hovering DTM members. "Sera," Nomia said with emphasis, "I think I should introduce you to Julienne Garland of MynCorp Security."

Sera's eyes snapped back from Yakini's direction to look Nomia in the eyes. For a moment there was no comprehension in the gaze but then her eyes flicked to Julienne and the collection of Martian faces surrounding them and the look of shock slid from her face. "If you fire that plasma weapon in this cavern you'll bring a joint MynCorp/Durga task force here in around two minutes. The three of you don't look much like an official MynCorp mission. So, I'm guessing that is not what you want." She looked at Yakini again and her voice faltered for a moment. "Put the gun down and let's talk."

"Come on Julienne," Yakini said, "I didn't come all this way just so you could point a gun at them. We're all here for the same reason."

"Not entirely." The man with the skittish eyes spoke for the first time. His right hand was thrust deep in to the recesses of his coat. "We're here to bag and tag the Node. You're here as local colour and because you're running away from your job."

"There's a surprise," Sera snorted.

Just buy us one day, Nomia projected to Sera.

"Twenty-four hours and we'll be finished. You can walk out of here with Nomia tomorrow or you can fight your way out today. It's your choice."

Julienne looked at the coated figure. He simply shrugged and pulled his empty hand out of the recesses of a pocket and into clear sight. "Fine, play your little war games but Nomia stays near me," she said.

The weapon moved away from Nomia's head leaving the sensation of a ghost gun, like a threat of future violence. "Who's the creepy man in the coat?" Nomia said quietly to Julienne.

"Sickle, he's a friend of Mex Tyrian, believe it or not."

The circle of Martians parted reluctantly to let Sickle and Yakini join Julienne. Nomia felt José behind her and his hand came to rest on the back of her neck.

"You okay?"

She let him share her emotions for a while and she felt relief and reassurance return.

Sera stood back on her box and encouraged everyone to go home, reminding them to return the next day with at least two trusted members. People slowly drifted from the cavern, many clucking with disapproval at Julienne and Sickle as they departed. A few gave Yakini curious looks of partial recognition but nobody spoke directly to her.

A couple of newly appointed lieutenants stayed and flanked Sera as she confronted Julienne and Sickle. Yakini stepped out of Sera's line of sight and joined Nomia and José on the third side of the stand-off.

"Why Mars?" Yakini asked softly.

"We were in hiding," José said pointedly.

"This is hiding? You left us on a deranged spaceship for a cave on Mars?"

"It seemed a good idea at the time, but Nomia had grander plans."

"So I see, but why did it have to be Sera?"

"You two have history?" José frowned.

Nomia strangled a laugh. "Are you blind?" she stammered.

"No, but I can be a little distracted by threats of imminent violence or simply a little bit male occasionally."

"This would be one of those times."

"Is it going to be a problem?"

"We'll see," Yakini sighed.

Julienne really worried Sera. It was not just because she was clearly a well-trained fighter, or a certain wrongness about her body language which made the primitive part of Sera want to scream. It was the single-minded determination that burned behind everything she said and did. This woman would not stop until she had completed her mission or was dead, and Sera suspected she might not die easily. Nomia had told Sera quite a lot about Julienne's emotional vulnerability during her time on the Suparna but there was not much evidence of mental conflict today. José had not added much to the discussion. He had apologised and muttered something cryptic about being dead during most of the encounter.

"You do know this is all much bigger than your personal goals?" Sera was talking to Julienne and Sickle.

"You mean Martian independence?" Sickle said.

"Bigger than that." Sera looked for a reaction from Julienne but there were no tell-tale signs of emotion.

"Really, please enlighten us all." Julienne said expansively.

Sera became acutely aware of the two DTM members at her shoulders. She was starting to find the levels of deceit overbearing. On one level she was a simple mine prospector licensed by Durga and MynCorp. On the next she was a loyal campaigner for the Martian liberation movement. Now she was leading her own secret wing of the same independence movement, and yet she knew this was all just a small part of a much greater war for human survival against an overwhelming alien invasion. She made a renewed effort to compartmentalise her mind and switched out the knowledge of all things Eidolon. "I mean, the death of the corporate system," she improvised.

"Just that? You sound like Sickle but I suspect you are a little less pragmatic in your compromises."

The hem of Sickle's coat bobbed as he shrugged his indifference to the insult.

"Either lend a hand or stay out of the way." Sera turned her back on the uncertainty the Terrans represented, and started to marshal her lieutenants into action.

The majority of the DTM membership were idealists not soldiers, and they had never been a paramilitary organisation. With MynCorp's city-razing technology there had never been a serious consideration given to direct conflict. They had always operated with more subtlety. The heart of the Martian people already supported self-determination, but to sway the more pragmatic minds required systematic demonstration of the potential for Martian self-reliance. There were a few amongst her new collection of trusted supporters who had combat training, or civilian crowd control experience. There were also another handful who were self-taught or self-deluded fighters through anger issues or long-term pessimisms about their future.

The lack of a significant fighting force was fine. Sera had no interest in leading an army or in fighting a war. She did not believe in liberty at any cost, especially if most of those in the line of fire would inevitably be Martian. She had described their mission to the DTM splinter group as a humanitarian rescue mission which would strike a crippling blow against MynCorp infrastructure Solar System-wide. The gathering had collectively sighed with relief when she had stated there would be no direct confrontation, with most of the volunteers assigned the role of victim support. She had explained that those who were able would bear arms to defend the mission against unexpected resistance. Each of the rest would be responsible for tending to a dozen traumatised victims. Several voices had expressed surprise she had managed to identify such a large population of imprisoned Martians who were not guarded. Speculation had spread through the crowd. They all knew any members of the population held by MynCorp would have been Dropped into the Nexus and a few had raised objections that too few of them had the necessary technical skills required to extract so many safely. Others pointed out that liberating a few hundred from the Drop would make no significant difference to the power of the Nexus and this must be something bigger. She had let them voice their concerns so they would not fester after the meeting. Eventually, they all looked to her for the answers. She had told them another lie – the target could not be revealed in advance to prevent a leak feeding back to MynCorp. They nodded sagely and agreed that her discretion was the sign of a true leader; someone with the confidence to shoulder the burden of command and the strength to accept the isolation that came with it.

Of course, she could not reveal the plan because it was clearly absurd and almost certainly impossible. José and Nomia intended to transport her entire brigade from Mars to a secret laboratory on Earth using nothing more than their minds and the most minuscule of probabilities it might have happened spontaneously anyway. If the Universe was to run the hundred billion years of its existence a hundred billion times, such an event might happen once but these two claimed to be able to make it happen at will. And she believed them. She believed them on the basis of a gut feeling, a minor demonstration of calming a dust storm and the fact that she appeared to be able to read their minds.

Once they all reappeared inside the heart of MynCorp, the building would magically become disinterested in the fact that its most precious wards were waking from the life-long immersion in the Nexus. It wouldn't even murmur a hint of indignation as the Nodes, who made the Nexus a working data processing system, were lifted from their beds and vanished into the aether.

Or so the plan went.

Sera spent the rest of the day discovering a hidden talent for bossing people around. The DTM members had two responsibilities; the small force of fighters that would carry weapons as a backup against any resistance, and the makeshift field hospital being set up in the cavern where she had pleaded her case a few hours before. Nomia was hoping to bring more than nine hundred of her brothers and sisters back from Earth. Most of them had apparently spent a good fraction of their lives in a virtual purgatory, with their conscious minds suppressed and their subconscious minds acting as hubs in MynCorp's all-prevailing computer network. She was expecting their bodies to be extremely weak but she could not begin to imagine the mental integration work José was planning. Fortunately, the DTM's duties were limited to physical well-being; food, water and basic hygiene as the Nodes learnt to look after themselves. Sera could not visualise how the loss of the Nexus would manifest itself but she did know just how pervasive the computing system was in MynCorp infrastructure. As far as she knew the only independent processing power that existed in the inner Solar System were the primitive bio-computers being developed by Durga, and MynCorp's fleet of ships. The fleet could be dangerous but without central command they were unlikely to present a unified threat.

As long as she bustled and focused on the task at hand, her thoughts did not drift to Yakini, but eventually the last field-cot was cobbled together from scraps of building material and products of a hijacked algae reprocessing plant. Nomia and José were already sat facing each other on one of the cots deep in meditation. Julienne and Sickle sat between their quarry and the cavern entrance sharing the occasional comment.

Sera started to stumble back towards her cube on the flats of the crater, her body already preparing for sleep.

"Can we talk?" Yakini fell into step with her just like when they used to walk the crater rim together.

"I'm really tired."

"Would tomorrow make it any easier?"

"No, probably not."

"You know it wasn't you?" Yakini put a hand on Sera's, bringing them both to a stop. Sera looked down at the hand and Yakini removed it.

"How would I know that? I haven't heard a word from you since you jumped planet. For a while, I thought you were dead, until a friend of a friend heard you had joined the MynCorp pilot academy on Earth."

"You always knew that Mars was too small for me."

"Don't make excuses. You ran away. You ran away from me and your life because you were frightened of being trapped into predictability."

"If I thought you would have come with me I would have waited."

"You didn't even give me a choice."

"Would you have come?"

"I loved you, I would have considered it."

"But would you have come?"

"No, probably not."

Sera started walking again, trying to get her emotions to settle into something coherent. Yakini fell into step alongside. They walked the rest of the way to the accommodation cube. Even after the missing years, it took all of Sera's willpower not to reach out and take Yakini's hand as they walked. She cursed herself for being so weak and tried to remember the anger she had felt in the first year of solitude.

They stood at the threshold to the cube. Inviting her in felt like some kind of surrender or implicit forgiveness and yet Sera could not bring herself to end the conversation. "How have you been?" she asked.

"Good, mostly. It's been hard work but I really made a go of it. I've been to almost every outpost in the Solar System."

"But now you're running again?"

"It's not like that. A month ago I was a pilot on the fastest spaceship in the MynCorp fleet. I was one of the Captain's most trusted officers. In fact he hand-picked me for the mission to the Suparna. Then I met Nomia, Mex Tyrian and eventually, José. I saw things which should have been impossible. When you find out that the whole of existence is threatened and you meet the only people who seem to have a clue how to deal with it, it's hard to go back to the day job and pretend everything is okay."

"Yes, I know."

"What about you? When did you become a leader of the DTM?"

"Yesterday. Nomia and José seem to make a habit of shaking people's lives up. A couple of days ago my greatest hope was to find a clean mineral seam and get a new accommodation cube."

"With a view of the lake?"

"You remember."

"Of course. We used to sit up on the rim and imagine having a cube high on the crater wall, so we could look out over a free Mars. There was always a lot of drink and even more talk. You said the flag of an independent Mars should be the red of Martian rock and the blue of the Vanuatu Lake."

"It always seemed to end the same way."

"Sometimes we couldn't even wait to get back home."

"I knew you planned it that way. You always had something soft to lie on and knew where there was a gulley deep enough to hide us."

"I think you are the only person I've ever known to get turned on by political debate."

"It was just youth. I was so passionate about my beliefs then; more passion than practical application."

"At least you've kept the belief."

Sera felt the portent of extraordinary circumstances. Her entrenched anger seemed petty compared to the magnitude of what they were going to attempt the next day. She did not want to be alone and forgiving Yakini seemed a small price to pay for companionship.

"Do you want to come in?" she asked.

"Oh, Sera. I just wanted to mend some damage while I had the chance. I didn't mean... I've met someone else."

"I see."

"It's only recent but it wouldn't be fair on either of you."

"Is she Terran or Martian?"

"Not exactly either, or in fact a she."

"You're with a man?"

"Not an ordinary man."

"That's okay then."

They stood in silence for a while, neither wanting to say good night and yet unable to talk any more.

Sera, they're trying to take us. Help. The thought echoed around her head like a ricocheting bullet.

"What's Julienne up to?" she said to Yakini as she started to run back towards the cave.

"I've no idea. What makes you think there's a problem?"

"Don't lie to me. Don't even talk to me. They never intended to wait until tomorrow. You were just distracting me. If they've done anything to Nomia or José you'll regret it."

*

Kaamil paused briefly in his deep data dive to glance at an internal feed for the building. It showed a misshapen room with bare, grey, walls, as if the building had been interrupted before it was completed. Three figures sat limply in a triangle. Splice lasers made their skin glow sickly colours. Their eyes were open but without focus. The word motley floated into Kaamil's mind and he saw his own mouth curve into a slight grin. It made him look ghoulish. He looked like he needed a hearty meal and a good walk in some hills. An inch of hair covered his head and chin, maybe in an attempt to imitate the thick head of black hair dominating Mex's boyish face. Mostly Kaamil just wanted to look healthier but the beard made him look more unkempt. He discontinued the grow signal to the hair follicles and made a mental note to shave.

Kaamil had no idea if Bergur looked healthy or not. His skin was a dark purple which seemed more plant than animal, but his folds of muscles were definitely mammalian and looked particularly unsuited to sitting still for long periods of time.

For three days and nights they had holed up in this dead space, lodged between the penthouse apartments of the operations centre for MynCorp on Earth and throughout the Solar System. Mex's plan had seemed desperate but workable; simply find the evidence for the Eidolon invasion in the sea of MynCorp data that flooded in from every corner of human existence, and then claim responsibility. The reality was more like paddling a karvi across Norðursjór, armed with a glass-bottomed bucket on a challenge to spot the bubbles from a farting crab – Bergur's analogy not his. The plan was farcical in its absurdity.

What better way was there to spend the last few days of human existence?

Maybe safe and sound in his bunker aboard the Suparna. The ship's A.I. had almost no personality, but Kaamil missed it anyway. It had been a reassuring whisper in his head for years – a trickle of data from a myriad of sensors – assuring him all was well in his world, as he watched the stars drift by. How many years after the destruction of Earth could he have floated between the stars without a care; slowly going mad, but safe in his insanity? Would the Eidolons have ever found him, or even bothered to look? Would he have been the last human, running silently into infinity?

Mostly he just worried about the Suparna. They had abandoned her weeks ago, as she drifted out of the plane of the Solar System; engines savagely removed and antimatter containment systems wrecked. She had almost infinite capacity to reconfigure herself, but the intricate repairs required to rebuild working engines might be too much. It was likely that she was a ten thousand tonne comet, leaving the Solar System for frigid interstellar space. Decades from now she would return, bleeding gases and scraps of fatigued metal as she fell towards the Sun.

Maybe he would find an echo of her passing in the MynCorp data.

Diving back into the Nexus, Kaamil instantly noticed something unusual from a Plutonian mining colony on Charon. The base was ⍰ Corporation and they might not even know themselves how much of their data processing was outsourced. The MynCorp data stream contained no voice communications from the outpost but most of the mining telemetry was collated by processes running in the Nexus. Every data source on Charon had stopped transmitting almost simultaneously. There was an epicentre to the disruption but unlike an explosion it did not have two expanding spheres of data. He would have expected an inner sphere of physical destruction and an outer sphere of light and heat radiation. The bubble of silence had spread out from the heart of Charon and encompassed every device on the surface or in orbit of the moon and Pluto itself.

Kaamil was back in his own head for a moment. His breath was fast and his heart thumped with fear. The data showed only silence but in his imagination thousands of robotically enhanced men and women cried out in fear and then ceased to exist.

"I've found them," he stammered out loud.

"Where?" Mex answered and his Nexus presence was suddenly alongside Kaamil.

"They attacked Pluto a few hours ago. Here, have a look."

Bergur and Mex reviewed the data for a while before joining Kaamil in a virtual meeting space.

"It's really happening," Bergur said.

Mex instructed Bergur, "We've got no idea how fast the Eidolons are moving, so concentrate on associating yourself with the Pluto attack. You'll have to be vague about future targets."

"I've got it. Just put me somewhere which will catch their attention."

"Kaamil, if you're okay, we need you back in the data. We need at least another two incidents to be convincing."

Kaamil dropped back into the Nexus overview Alec had equipped them with, but he left enough of himself with Bergur to capture the performance. A voice message from the Eidolons was too human to be believed. They had decided to leave a data context. Some sort of construct which encapsulated their message within a virtual entity; a data equivalent to a state of mind. Hopefully, Bergur's thought processes were alien enough it would not be immediately obvious as a hoax.

"Humans and associated machine minds listen to these words on the eve of your destruction," Bergur started. "We have chosen the name Eidolon from your literature because we are the beginning and end of things. You need only know we will destroy all evidence of human existence. We have already entered your planetary system and purged your desecration of Pluto and Charon. Know that we are coming for Earth and all that crosses our path will be destroyed. You have no defence against our will; we are made of the very essence of Verity Space and free from the vulnerabilities of physical form. You shall know our presence by the restoration of matter to a virgin state, free from human contamination. There is no defence against those who control probability. Make peace with each other, we will make your peace with the Universe."

"You don't think I hammed it up too much then?" Bergur asked.

They were back in the closed space of their quarters in the heart of MynCorp.

"I've no idea how an omnipotent race of megalomaniacs would sound when threatening an inferior race but I think MynCorp probably got the message," Mex answered.

"I should have used fewer words and more growls. You can't get more threatening than a good throaty growl."

"You made all the points we needed to get across. They can easily corroborate Pluto has been silenced and you told them the attack was from Verity Space. Someone will be paying attention. Each new event should see the message get passed up another level or two." Kaamil said.

"We just have to keep going and wait for an answer," Mex added.

The next few days consisted of data diving, eating and sleeping. They took turns resting but it was implicitly understood only Kaamil could process enough data to spot the patterns which could mean an Eidolon attack. Fortunately, he was trained to rest his brain a hemisphere at a time. He could not process data indefinitely but he could maintain a level of continuous coverage for as long as they had left. So, Bergur and Mex did most of the resting or sat around arguing about whether Julienne and Yakini were missing them or were even capable of such simple emotions, for one reason or another. Part of Kaamil was thinking about Nomia a lot of the time, but his feelings were, thankfully, much simpler. As far as he was concerned, she had not only saved his life, but also given him a life to save. She was his strength and motivation. He had experienced what he believed was romantic love and it had torn his mind apart. He was not emotionally strong enough for such feelings. He knew just what he was capable of and made sure that he did not stray in that direction.

The swarm of Jovian colonies were like fireflies in the dark of the Nexus. Each of the colonised satellites of Jupiter and the handful of floating bases in the upper atmosphere of the planet itself, sent streams of data to the Nexus for every reason from administration to weather prediction. When the Eidolons hit it there was a very graphic massacre. MynCorp had enough presence in the planetary system for Kaamil to sample audio-visual data. The Eidolon sphere was still expanding through fleeing ships and static bases when Bergur dropped back into character.

"I claim the planet Jupiter and all of her satellites for the Eidolons. You must know you have no defence against our attack from Verity Space. We manipulate the very reality of this Universe to return Jupiter to its initial state, as if the human race had never existed. We will not stop until the Universe is free of all evidence humanity ever crawled across the face of the Earth." Bergur's voice dropped to a growl. "We are coming."

Kaamil was transfixed in disgusted fascination. He flicked from stream to stream listening to the truncated screams of pilots pushing their shuttles to escape the expanding sphere. Some of the fastest ships managed to claw free of Jupiter's gravity and make it into interplanetary space, but only those which did not try and rescue refugees. The brave simply vanished from the Nexus as if a switch had been flicked. There was no wreckage or explosions. Voices talked of a semi-reflective wall moving through space. Fleeting images of its victims moved like ghosts across its surface and then sank into the interior. Jupiter could be seen through the images; a pristine gas giant of swirling storms and stratified weather patterns.

Within five minutes the planet and all its satellites were silent and shrinking in the rear cameras of the handful of surviving ships.

When Kaamil could speak he said, "MynCorp have to listen now. They must do something to fight back."

Chapter 10

He could will it out of existence, but he did not feel the need.

José reached round to the back of his skull and let his fingers drag over the cold metallic lump. He knew the implant was messing with his free will, but it did not seem particularly important. He was content to sit and watch Nomia's struggle. Sickle and Julienne had pinned Nomia to the cot as she convulsed and writhed. He could see her muscles spasm as they tensed discordantly but her assailant's superior strength kept her immobile. The sight of her delicate joints being twisted by the futile efforts of her limbs caused him synchronised jolts of electric agony, but still he did not want to stand up and come to her aid. Her pain bled through the air and tore at his skin in lacerations of mental anguish, but that was just the way it was, and he could not imagine changing it. If they had questioned him he could have told them using a neural suppressor to selectively suppress her higher brain functions was not possible. The implant's electric field was a purely physical effect which could not reach the part of her consciousness in Verity Space. They did not ask José, and the similar implant recently pushed through the skin of his neck meant that he saw no reason to offer the information. He sat and impassively watched the world around him.

A trickle of blood snaked from the corner of Nomia's mouth leaving a trail across her cheek like the trace of an electroencephalograph.

"Hold her arms while I put something in her mouth to stop her biting her tongue," Julienne barked at Sickle.

Sickle released his hold on her legs. A look of confusion wiped the tension of determination from his features. Where his hands had gripped Nomia's shins a colourless glow was weaving through the fabric of her smock.

"What the hell is that?" he stammered.

Julienne spotted the source of Sickle's consternation. "Not again. This can't happen to me again." One corner of her mouth hung limply.

"What are you talking about? She's the one that is glowing like some freaky Jovian cloud fish."

Nomia had stopped convulsing but twitched feebly in time with the pulsing light spreading up and down her legs. Julienne's voice sank to a conspiratorial whisper. "The glowing. You can see it as well and you're outside my head. I'm not breaking down again."

"Again! Tell me you're joking."

Julienne shook her head as if the world was slightly out of focus, and just needed a nudge. "Just grab the cot. Let's get them to the shuttle. There's nothing they can do once we're in orbit."

"Great. Floating in a vacuum with a glowing woman."

"Just don't touch her." Julienne lifted the head end of the cot and shot a brief look at José. "Follow," she said.

José did as he was bid without any of his usual resistance to being instructed. He could see an infinite blur of potential futures cascading away from this moment. They clumped into families of the most probable events creating a path that might be called fate. Each of the conscious minds around him looked like snake heads with their futures coiling away behind them. Sometimes they touched and merged or ricocheted apart at acute tangents of probability. A common theme repeated in a full spectrum of subtle variations; Nomia would fight to stay on Mars with as much determination as Julienne and Sickle had to take her back to Earth. The situation inevitably escalated until violence erupted, as if it was itself a conscious entity waiting in the shadows for an opportunity to emerge with a battle cry of pain.

Nomia was not capable of calculated aggression but she was a creature of pure emotion and passion without the attenuating pragmatism of experience. She was capable of much greater atrocity than the consequence-calculating Julienne; acts that would irrevocably taint her conscience. These potential realities burned brightly in their collective future, luring the present like sirens on the night sea. Sitting like a grey fog in the middle of these futures was a void that José recognised as the Eidolons. Intrinsically beyond predictability, their presence was indistinct and ghostly like a secondary reflection in a mirror.

There was a path which avoided most of the fog but it required José to remove the device on the back of his head and restore his free will. As they stepped out of the tunnel entrance into the chill of the Martian night, he reached up and gripped the release ring of the spider-like device. There was no independent intent. It was not volition but hard-wired instinct. Restoring his independence was simply a necessity in order to maintain a clear view of potential realities and to keep Nomia safe. The pincers withdrew nano-filaments from his skull and a wave of anger exploded from the surface of his brain, making lights pulse in his vision. The inert lump of technology in his hand took the brunt of his frustration, sizzling and popping as it burnt from the inside out. It vanished from reality with a sigh of gratitude.

José fought through the blur of anger, and saw Nomia glowing from head to foot. Reality was twisted and distorted around her skin. Futures folded back on themselves and swallowed their own tails, drawing her inexorably towards total control of the reality around her. The cot lay discarded nearby. Julienne and Sickle stood aghast, the glow forming a shadow play across their faces. As Nomia floated upright the control device on the back of her head dripped liquid metal onto the ground.

"By Olódùmarè, what is going on here?" Sera stood a few metres away, her face red from exertion. She was holding Yakini at bay with one straight arm and staring up at Nomia.

"Should she being doing that again just now?" she suggested to José.

Snakes of uncertain reality slithered out from Nomia's finger tips and coiled towards Julienne and Sickle.

"Nomia, listen to my voice." José shouted above the silence of unreality. "Come back to me. Don't go any further in Verity Space. Look about you. See the Eidolons closing in. We can deal with Julienne in our own reality."

Sickle shrieked as a tongue of nothingness lashed across his chest leaving a blank wound, exposing the white of a rib. He collapsed to the ground returning to the foetal coil of his birth. Julienne stared at her feet, as if incredulous she was not running for her life. She still looked conflicted. José could sense her trying to separate reality from the illusions of her own damaged sanity.

José, I don't know how to stop. There's so much fury and its taken control. Help me.

The anger is yours to control. It is not fighting you, it is you. Look at the probabilities you are collapsing around you. Look where they lead. You have to come back before it's too late.

Look at the hurt you have caused Sickle. Feel his pain at your hands. What do you feel?

Dislocation. It is not me.

Use the calm of isolation to retake control. Bring your mind into sync with mine.

I can feel you. The anger is so bitter compared to the sweet of your love. I can feel it cleaning my mind.

Nomia's toes touched the ground and she collapsed into José's arms. The night suddenly seemed darker than the cave, even though the stars burnt bright, as if in relief.

A breeze rattled pebbles as it drifted up from the lake, tickling José's ankles as he cradled Nomia. Julienne and Sera cooperated silently as they sprayed a bandage over Sickle's wound. It did not bleed or look like it could get infected, but its gaping paleness was a sickening reminder of what had just happened. When she was done Sera suggested they should get back underground before a security squad arrived to investigate the strange glows in the night. They all started to file back towards the cave, feet dragging in the dust. Dawn had just set fire to the crater rim and night was turning pale grey.

A bass thud shook its way up José's ankle before he heard the implosion batter his ear drums. A sphere ten metres in diameter appeared above their heads and hovered with ominous intent. Images swirled across its mirrored surface, split into their component parts like sunlight through oil on water.

"They're here," José shouted.

"No, it's not them." Nomia tilted her head as she thought out loud. "It's a physical manifestation. They've created an agent to do the work."

Images of strange icy caverns flickered in and out of existence across the surface of the sphere. Pale blue light glistened off imperfections in the ice and danced across the wide-eyed face of a young girl. Her skin was the deep purple of tradescantia and was devoid of any obvious openings to define a face apart from her eyes that conveyed her gender as well as her shocked awe.

"She's like Bergur, an Eridanian. What does it mean?" Yakini said.

The face vanished in a swirl of ice to be replaced by black rock against a background of stars. Robot-like figures were pawing at the ground causing clouds of dust that rose and fell in protracted slow motion.

"That's horrible." The words escaped José's lips before he could collect his composure.

"What does it mean?" Yakini repeated.

"It's absorbing images of the places it's been."

"What's so horrible about... Oh no. Poor Bergur."

"What?" Sera dragged her eyes from the sphere quizzically.

José sighed. "Its job is to erase all of human existence. If it's been to Bergur's home then they are all gone."

"What do we do?" Sera looked back to the sphere.

"I'm not sure. We need more minds to fight this."

"It's come too soon. We need the other Nodes." Nomia was back on her feet and standing with her fists clenched.

"You ready?" José asked Nomia.

"I suppose so."

"What do we do?" Sera asked.

"I don't think there's anything you can do. I'm sorry." There was futility in his voice but as he took Nomia's hand he felt her endless hope flow and embrace him. They rose into the air and moved to confront the sphere.

*

"I don't understand what's going on," Mex said in the seclusion of their den. "It's like they don't care."

"Fight me or die," Bergur repeated in the bubble of the Nexus Kaamil had inflated for the meeting.

"We see no profit in the fight," the voice of MynCorp replied.

"Then we shall remove you from the Universe and evolution will start again."

"We would like to negotiate terms for a partial amnesty."

"There are no exceptions. Everything human and human-made will cease to exist."

"That is an extreme position. We could offer a significant fraction of all human interests in exchange for access to your technology. If you would like to list your terms we can begin negotiations."

"There are no negotiations. You will just die."

"Those terms are unacceptable."

"Then you will fight?"

"We will withdraw from discussion and begin a process of asset realisation."

"There is no point, you will be destroyed."

"There is no energetic advantage to such an extreme position."

Bergur dropped out of the splice session with a grunt of frustration. "It's like talking to a machine. They're so far removed from reality they don't even think like people any more."

"Agreed." Kaamil allowed the meeting space to flow back into the bubbling chaos of the raw probability field. "This approach is not working."

Mex paced the oppressively familiar space as if the pressure of his toing and froing might push back the walls. "I don't understand," he repeated, "we've given them the threat on a plate, but all they do is argue about the quality of the porcelain. How much more real can we make the threat?"

"Perhaps that's the problem," Kaamil looked tired but thoughtful.

"Kaamil's right," Bergur barked, "I still struggle with the enormity of it and I've seen them all but erase a kilometre-long spaceship." He grunted again, "I can't even get my head around Nomia and I've seen her remove my Captain's arm just by thinking about it. The look on his face as his skin jewels drifted away was a primal terror. It just cut though all of evolution's fineries." A shiver shook his overly muscular frame as his inner poet peeped through the blinds of his machismo.

"How do we make it any more real than a dozen colonies being wiped out live over a splice session?"

"Grab them by the scruff of the neck and give them a good shake," Bergur suggested.

"I thought that's what we just did." Exasperation was creeping into Mex's voice.

"I think Bergur means literally."

Kaamil and Bergur stood shoulder to shoulder as they slowly dragged Mex towards a conclusion. The pairing reminded Mex of an overly enthusiastic warning poster for the dangers of steroid misuse. He smiled at the image and as he caught their mental drift. "I've always wanted to meet the suits behind the corporation." He clapped his hands together decisively.

"Now that's decided, anyone got any ideas how we go about it?" Bergur looked at the other two in turn but they just frowned.

Mex dragged up a distant memory. "When I was a kid, members of the MynCorp board appeared at public and social functions. There would always be a least one plastic grin ready to maximise the P.R. opportunity for some minor health or social programme." He looked at the other two for confirmation.

"I think your childhood was a little different from ours," Kaamil said.

Bergur shrugged an implicit confirmation. "I'm surprised they bothered. The Cartel makes public relations a bit pointless."

"You're right. I'm not sure I've heard anything similar since the Cartel came into existence. The Corporate Corruption Bureau has not publicly hit anyone higher up than local management."

There was a contemplative silence for a couple of overly tired minutes. "Back into the Nexus?" Kaamil asked.

"We're not going to find what we need sitting here," Mex shrugged. "It's time for something ingenious."

"I'll make some food." Bergur acknowledged his inability to contribute significantly towards the data mining effort.

Mex waved at the splice actuation laser and felt himself falling forward with the familiar vertiginous lurch of the drop into the raw Nexus. Having bypassed the usual menu driven application layer presented to the mass population, he drifted above a virtual landscape of faintly glowing nodes connected by contorted fronds of data paths. At this scale the individual processing minds formed a soft grey fog that scattered the combined pulsing energy of the Nexus. Mex descended towards a tight cluster of Nodes that he recognised as MynCorp's secure processing space. These minds were never leased to third-party applications; they spent their years of servitude massaging MynCorp's most valued data in recursive loops of self-fulfilling prophecy.

His glasses squirted a concise nugget of code through the application interface of a random Node and disguised Mex as one of MynCorp's own C.R.C. error-checking daemons. With immunity from inspection, he floated through the raging storm of data and code that careered along the fine data tendrils of the Nexus. Each Drop-mind floated at the end of its data tether, moored and fed data by the same virtual thread. Mex resisted the urge to summon a scythe and sever as many connections as he could manage before some piece of malware-protection descended on him like white blood cells on a virus. He imagined all the unconscious minds tumbling away into Verity space, free to dream random things without the repetitive monotony of data processing.

He was now deep inside the heart, or rather the mind, of MynCorp. His presence here was more audacious than hiding-out in the executive washroom, and even more likely to result in violent eviction.

A sub-agent of Mex's presence flashed an alert. His mind flinched reflexively, ready to take flight. The over-eager agent was just indicating the incremented conversation ID of a new job arriving at the nearest node. Mex introspected the protocol header looking for an originator but the trail seemed to start at the Node.

Later, Mex explained his discovery to Bergur. "Each time I saw a new processing routine being dropped into the Nexus it was the same."

"None of them had real-world addresses?" Bergur asked with a sceptical tone.

"Not all, but a significant number."

"I don't get it. How does the code get into the Nexus if it has no real-world addresses?"

"Just as importantly, how do the answers get back to the originator? There's only one way I know. The owner of the job has a hard-wired connection to the Node."

"You're not talking metaphorically here are you?"

"Probably not. The code is being dropped directly into the Node's mind via a physical interface."

"That's truly grim."

"What aspect of the Nexus isn't?"

"So, the people behind the Nexus are probably in close proximity to the Nodes."

"Precisely."

"And that is where exactly?"

"Where it all began. The original headquarters of MynCorp, about a kilometre away from where we're sitting."

"Shame."

"How so?"

"I hoped you were going to say, downstairs."

"It could be worse." Mex turned to slumped figure of the pilot. "Has Kaamil been up for air?"

"Not for a while. I'll give him a shout." Bergur waved an urgent interrupt in the path of the splice laser. Kaamil's eyes opened and slowly refocused from infinity.

"Mex has found the brains behind MynCorp. We need to go."

Kaamil dragged his eyes to meet Bergur's energised look. "We're too late," the Pilot said, despair sapping his words of life.

"Not while we're still photosynthesising." Bergur's voice fell away as a tear lethargically rolled down Kaamil's cheek, a silver gem of passion over grey skin. "What's happened?"

"The corporations have evacuated essential personnel from the surface of Mars. Vanuatu City is under attack."

Chapter 11

The combined mind of José and Nomia bristled like a cornered cat, spitting mental threats at the impassive sphere. As they opened themselves to Verity Space the sphere grew tentacles which snaked off into probability crevices. It probed each fork in the evolution of Mars since the first human satellite formed a flaming fireball across the Martian sky. As it formulated the most probable form of a virgin Mars, the combined human impact on the terraformed planet diffused to the surface of the sphere and bled into physical space. Images of bulbous spacesuits waddled across rocky planes, weak sunlight reflecting of gold-tinted visors. Extended families of Central African and Pacific Island colonists huddled in inflated domes as vicious dust storms turned the light to a pinky-grey.

José-Nomia struck out at each probing tendril, severing each connection to the sphere with surgical incisions to the intermediate reality. The isolated arms dissipated into the quantum noise of the Downey field but multiple replacements writhed out from the sphere. José-Nomia roared in frustration and moved further into Verity Space, their physical bodies growing indistinct and partially translucent. They spread themselves around the sphere dampening all quantum processes, pushing every collapsing state superposition towards predictability. Across Mars, quantum devices would be failing, in computers or even human minds, but this was a last-ditch defence, and José-Nomia knew no other likely strategy.

The sphere reeled and rotated with something akin to frustration. A part of it which was evolving into something like a consciousness, turned its attention to the linked Terran minds. "You are the two human minds which triggered the contact device."

In all of José's contact with the Eidolons he had never experienced a concrete statement issue from their minds. He had always communicated by exchanging states of mind, like the result of a deep discussion from the night before. More than a false memory, it usually felt like the change in perspective resulting from the long deliberation or a detailed exchange of ideas.

José-Nomia hesitated in their defence, thrown by the directness of the entity which appeared as a sphere. "That would probably be us," they said.

The sphere addressed them again. "You may continue to exist if you isolate yourself from human influence immediately."

The combined mind felt a conflict between the opportunity for a considered debate and the desire to rage in indignation. "I... We will not abandon our race to unwarranted annihilation."

"You have only one choice; exist or cease to exist. You are not capable of deciding if the elimination of human influence is warranted."

"We will fight... In what way are we incapable of grasping this decision?" The José-Nomia mind was fracturing in conflict.

"Your context is limited, as is mine."

"You do not share your creator's perspective?"

"I am an instrument of their intent. No more than a tool."

"But you understand why we must be erased from reality?"

"My existence is coincident with other incarnations of this tool. There have been numerous instances of me throughout the Universe. The reason and result is always the same."

"What is the reason?"

"You are a threat."

"As simple as that? The age old reason. They are frightened of us."

"The concept of fear is restricted to physically evolving species. It has no meaning for those not struggling to survive."

"Then how are we a threat to the Eidolons?"

"You are not a threat to them directly; I am not even sure what the concept would mean. It is the Universe that is at risk from you."

"That's absurd. What possible risk could we be to the Universe? We've barely even set foot on a dozen planets across a handful of stellar systems. At our most interventionist all we've managed is to tinker with a planet's atmospheric composition. It will take us a hundred million years to even explore this galaxy."

"It is not the physical Universe that you threaten. The domain of energy and matter will always heal. It exhibits a full spectrum of cycles. Civilisations have emerged and existed with minimal impact on their surroundings. Others have expanded and manipulated energy on galactic scales. A billion years later, all probability tails have vanished into the quantum noise, as if they had never existed."

"So, you're suggesting that we are a threat to Verity Space. How is that even possible?"

"Every mind which attains sentience and starts to manipulate the Downey field has the potential to pollute Verity Space. Each new mind is more significant than the collective of those that have come before. Verity Space does not heal; the new mind manipulates the physical domain which feeds back with a fresh set of probability fields. Each manipulated decision causes ripples that spread out across reality. Enough overly constraining minds could irrevocably degrade the viability of this reality."

"Even if I understood how this was possible, we are still a young race. We are still evolving. I do not believe that even the Eidolons can see far enough into the future to see what we will become; the combined uncertainties degrade the possibility of accurate predictions."

"You will continue to develop physically and mentally as a result of evolutionary pressures but there are no such effects in Verity Space; there is no genetic mutation or cross species gene exchange. You enter Verity Space as you are. It is a fundamental component of your nature."

"Then we have an impasse. I cannot accept that the Eidolons have a right to decide if we exist or not. We will oppose you."

"There is no opposition. You will cease to have ever existed."

"We will see." The two parts of the José-Nomia mind reunited in an act of futility born from a tribalistic conviction; although the first line of defence would be overcome they were saving others who would have to fight later. A small part of José knew the gesture was confirming the Eidolons' accusation, but they fought on regardless.

The sphere's attack was swift and savage in its efficiency. In the physical realm, it was pieces of rock which had lain undisturbed since they had rained down on the crater floor millions of years ago. Each stone or boulder experienced the once in a universe event in which all the internal kinetic energy of the component molecules aligned. The natural projectiles all converged on José-Nomia like malformed bullets from a surrounding army. In Verity Space, the sphere sent out shards of its own will, slicing through José-Nomia's mental barriers with ease.

José-Nomia instinctively divided their concentration as their nature dictated. José countered each physical projectile by summoning a momentary solidification of the air in its path. He tried to form a solid shell around them but the intensity of the attack was such that he was struggling to feel his way to the right uncertainties in time. Some of the missiles he managed to stop dead, so they fell to the ground below, but many ricocheted from partially-formed defences. José grunted as several pieces of course rock chewed lumps from his flesh, but he fought on. His mind spun in dizzy circles as he felt out for the faint ripple in the Downey field as the long static fate of each rock was flipped into the most unlikely of events. He tried frantically to stiffen the air along their trajectories before he felt the next pulse of attack. Most of all he concentrated on defending Nomia because he knew his desperate battle was a minor skirmish compared to the war she was fighting.

Where the sphere's blows landed Nomia felt them cut her identity, and she bled self-awareness. The creation of the Eidolons was attacking her very sentience, trying to reduce her to mentally inert chemistry and electromagnetic interactions. She threw up shields of determinism but they might as well have been air for all the effect they had. She embedded herself in a cloak of chaos but it was instantly stained in the entrails of her cognisance.

Nomia felt herself being reduced back to less than she was in the Nexus. As a Node her identity had felt like a distant dream, but there had been a consistency which felt like purgatory's hope of redemption. To Nomia, her sense of identity was the most precious thing she possessed; something she had fought her whole life to achieve and keep, despite MynCorp's best efforts to suppress her. If the creature had just threatened her life she would have defended herself, but to attack her self-awareness was the provocation she needed to retaliate.

Nomia abandoned her futile attempt to defend herself and lashed out with a fury that sent shockwaves of improbability through Verity Space and towards the pulsing sphere. The discontinuities in reality sheered through the sphere distorting it until it almost broke in two. Strike after strike cleaved lumps from the mind of the sphere which bubbled and faded into noise. The Eidolon creation struggled to maintain its integrity, and its own attacks faltered as the very fabric of Verity Space tried to shred it out of existence.

Gradually, Nomia's attacks became less savage as her mental focus faded with exhaustion. When finally she floated passive, but still self-aware, on the rippling mental ocean of the Martian population, the Eidolon sphere was gone. In the physical universe, the dead remnant of the sphere fell to the ground, a victim of gravity, like all inert matter.

José and Nomia's psyches cradled each other, soothing their battered bodies and minds. They enjoyed the soothing rhythms of human minds forming a collective reality on the Martian colony. They each felt a seed of elation form in the other. They grew slowly in the cautious afterglow of an unexpected victory. José began to laugh in their combined mind, and Nomia had no choice but to join him. Their physical bodies uncoiled as they became aware of the battlefield around them. People clustered in the entrances of buildings and caves; fear made their faces ugly. The nearest building was shattered into several pieces and green algae bled onto the crater floor. Nomia stopped laughing as she watched a drop of blood fall from José and join a red-on-orange stain below.

"Did we win?" Nomia asked aloud.

"It seems impossible, but maybe."

"Are you badly hurt?"

"My body will heal. How are you?"

"I'm becoming quite proficient at healing my mind. I'll be okay."

José groaned.

"Does it hurt?" Nomia asked.

José just pointed at the ground, suddenly too tired to speak. A halo of dust was rising from the ground and circled in a chaotic dance around the sphere. Nomia felt a stab of pain as a point of malice penetrated Verity Space nearby. "It's not dead!"

Merging their minds was natural and effortless but once José-Nomia emerged they found themselves too spent to do more than watch the sphere grow back to its previous presence. It returned to dissecting the Martian reality and extracting the component which was human.

It's as if we're not even here, José-Nomia thought. *It has decided we're not a threat.*

They watched as the sphere completed its assessment and withdrew its tentacles from Verity Space. The physical sphere became translucent and started to grow. When it grew through the damaged building, the ground returned to the red and yellow of virgin Martian soil. The rate of expansion increased as if it fed on the human artefacts it consumed.

People started to run towards the crater tunnels which led to the storm-swept plains, or to the small cluster of shuttles emblazoned with MynCorp or Durga livery. José-Nomia made no effort to avoid the sphere but they were swept ahead of the restorative wave as if the new reality was rejecting them outright. They floated, buffeted by the expanding front and utterly defeated.

Slowly, José-Nomia became aware of a presence, like the sigh of a breeze under the roar of a rocket. The feeling of another mind but spread thin and diffused throughout local Verity Space. As they watched, the new mind started to condense on the shell of the sphere, reinforcing reality. The sphere faltered in its expansion, throbbed twice and resumed its growth in sporadic spurts. José-Nomia groaned as they delved into reserves of strength fostered by a glimmer of hope. They joined forces with the dispersed mind, and concentrated on shoring up the reality directly in front of the expanding sphere. The expansion stopped and a painful stalemate ensued.

José-Nomia were cannibalising their conscious minds to feed the battle, using strength which would not be replaced in time, all for a temporary balance of power. The sphere showed no evidence of weakening and seemed patient in its passivity. A growl started deep in José and Nomia's throats and grew as their strength failed.

Just at the moment their strength failed completely, stillness fell across Verity Space. A presence emerged from beneath the Downey field and a paralysing grip washed through every mind on Mars. Verity space was like breath to this new presence and they shaped it without conscious effort. The Eidolons were intervening personally and the battle was now over.

*

Mex performed the sideways shuffle of frail legs and slippered feet as he absent-mindedly pushed his way through a cluster of gossiping suits. They stopped talking over the top of each other, and peered down at him with intrigued revulsion. The saggy creases around his eyes dimmed Mex's vision but he did not try to meet their stares. The curve of his shoulders forced him to concentrate on his feet as he muttered aphorisms of suitable antiquity.

He had chosen the disguise deliberately to attract more curiosity than suspicion. The nano-particles provided the surface disguise but it was up to him to fold his body against the natural uplift of youth. He had watched in a mirrored wall as his skin had seemed to thicken and turn ash-grey. His hair had evaporated in wisps of silver, revealing dark blotches of scalp like lunar seas. His uniqueness was largely due to a combination of the Drop and disproportionately expensive rejuvenation drugs. Both had largely robbed society of the obviously aged. The desperately rich tended to look fresh as daisies until the day they died, while many of the remainder faded into nothingness inside the Nexus. Anachronistic financial rules made the transfer of calorific credits a one-way trip down the generations as if it was a rule of energy conservation.

Mex sidled up to a squat cleaning appliance and patted its metallic case as if it was a favoured grandchild. It squawked an apology for crossing his path and started to glide away on a mixture of wheels and multi-jointed legs. Mex bent further to his knees and barked a poorly-aimed sneeze into a cotton handkerchief. He grizzled an apology and made a half-hearted attempt at wiping away the mist of droplets condensing on the side of the bot's chassis. His efforts simply pushed smears nearer an air-inlet grill.

Mex returned the way he had entered the building's lobby, muttering half-formed complaints about crowded spaces, poor directions and a lack of respect among youthful MynCorp staff. A significant number of the lobby's occupants watched him waddle away, wondering at the nagging guilt that whispered beneath the noise of their lives.

He kept up the back-breaking shuffle for three blocks before walking into a public square and into a clump of tree-like bushes. In the centre of the leaf cover he straightened his spine, waved away the nano-particle disguise and turned his path by ninety degrees. A gratefully-young Mex emerged into the bright sunlight of the ever watchful sky, and made his way to the meeting point, a block back towards the MynCorp headquarters.

"How did it go?" The question was grunted between half-closed mouth flaps in the shadow of a wide-brimmed hat. The high collar and over-sized hat did little to hide the unusual proportions of Bergur's body, but it did a reasonable job of hiding the mess which was his face. A dose of nano-particles fought continuously to make something human of his features, giving him ears and something like a nose and mouth. He would pass as a man as long as he refrained from talking. The moment he opened his mouth flaps and revealed the dark hole lined by spirals of pointy teeth, the disguise broke down into a children's nightmare.

"Time will tell," Mex replied.

"But you managed to infect one of the building's service bots?"

"I think so."

"Then it is just a matter of waiting."

"Yes, *just*."

Kaamil fidgeted on the edge of the conversation. He shook himself to a standstill. "I've never felt impatient before. It's really unpleasant."

"It depends what you're waiting for," Mex said.

"Do you think Nomia and the rest are still alive?" Kaamil asked again.

"We have to assume they are, otherwise this all seems a bit futile," Bergur said.

"You're right. Somehow saving Earth seems less important if they're gone." Mex said with an attempt at a smile.

"Don't worry, we're all committed to this regardless."

Kaamil nodded an agreement and added, "It's just hard waiting to do something. How many times have your people used this technology, Bergur?"

Mex cringed at the question, he had deliberately not asked.

"We've never found the opportunity, but the building agreed it was feasible."

Mex replayed the conception of the plan, looking for a glaring hole they might have missed in real time. The three of them had sat in the penthouse bunker of the MynCorp executive building trying to distract themselves from the ongoing destruction of Mars. They had agreed to confront the MynCorp board, and make a personal call to arms. The discussion had started well. There were two parts to the problem. Firstly, they needed access to the MynCorp headquarters, and secondly they needed a way to navigate to the boardroom, or whatever acted as a decision making hub for MynCorp. The debate about how to proceed had become fractious, as a sense of futility washed around the room.

"What about the building's A.I.? Can't you love it up?" Bergur pushed Mex.

"Are you joking?" Mex retorted, but Bergur was clearly not in that sort of mood. "No," Mex said simply. "The MynCorp headquarters is completely crude. Really old tech. The building is absolutely rigid. No root structure. No adaptive capability." He shuddered at the thought of so dispassionate a structure.

"So, how do we break into it?" Bergur's mouth flaps hung open in a disconcertingly aggressive sign of exasperation.

"A large bomb?"

"I thought you were supposed to be the master of social engineering?"

"The building needs to have social skills for me to engineer. I thought you were supposed to be the big bad pirate?"

"With you two as my army we won't get far."

Kaamil coughed and asked, "Can I ask a question?"

"What?" the other two barked with testosterone-inflated chests.

"If the old-style nature of this building is a strength against physical or software attacks, what is its disadvantage?"

"What?" the other two said again.

"Why did we stop building concrete structures and switch to A.I. personalities and intelligent building materials?"

"Don't ask him, he still lives in a cave," Mex said.

Bergur apparently missed the implicit insult, and simply grunted an acknowledgement. Mex tried to follow Kaamil's mental thread. "Because it made life tolerable for the inhabitants. Or, more accurately, it made looking after the inhabitants easier. I think I see where you're going."

"I'm not sure I was going anywhere, but carry on," Kaamil said softly.

"Old-style buildings need an army of appliances and bots to do the jobs the actual structure does now. If we could subvert some of these bots we might be able open a back door or something."

"Sounds desperate," Bergur grunted.

"You got a better plan?"

Bergur thought for a moment. "No," he said, "and now I think about it, I might have something that would help."

Bergur described a biological weapon developed by the Eridanians to incapacitate enemy technology. The weapon was a heavily re-engineered bacterial infection which had been modified to thrive on the trace levels of copper used as interconnections in simple artificial minds. The bacteria grew in the polymer gels used as sealant for processing units in dirty environments. A spore stage had been added to the life-cycle to allow airborne infection. Once the infection reached a certain concentration, a chemical signal between the individual bacteria resulted in a synchronised attack on the host. Each bacterium generated a current flow across an oscillating membrane, resulting in collective induced current in the host circuitry. The attack was designed to interfere with communications between the central processor and the system memory, producing erratic behaviour or completely incapacitating the device.

"There's just one problem," Bergur added at the end of his explanation.

"I can think of at least ten, but what's yours?" Mex asked.

"I've got no idea how to actually make the stuff, even if I had a laboratory."

"Is that all?"

"It's enough."

Mex raised his voice to address the building. "Think you can rustle up a few bespoke bacteria spoor?"

The calm and pervasive voice of the building seeped through the walls. "It shouldn't be a problem, if you can provide a template."

Kaamil and Bergur looked at each other uncertainly. "Why does the building have the ability to manufacture biological weapons?" Kaamil whispered.

Mex laughed with disarming ease, but the other two continued to look concerned. He stopped and tried to look serious. "How do you think it manages to pander to its inhabitants infinitely fickle demands?" Kaamil and Bergur looked blank. Mex tried again. "If you decide that you want your bedroom to be a tree house. The bark and moss are real."

"You can do that?" Kaamil asked with apparent sincerity.

"You two really have lived on the fringes of civilisation for far too long."

"Not by choice," Bergur tried to sigh but the hard edges of his mouth flaps chattered like the beak of a prehistoric bird.

"Speak for yourself," Kaamil bristled.

The technology sounded unlikely enough as stated but Mex had been tasked with modifying the idea to deliver alternative code to the device, essentially high-jacking the device. The bandwidth was absurdly small and Mex was forced to work in byte code for the first time since college. Most of his concentration was needed keeping his personality in check and limiting the application to essential functionality. When he spotted a bit of his flair creeping in, he quickly yanked the piece of code before it started to grow into a mini Mex project. When he was done, he felt strangely proud of the Spartan applet floating in front of his virtual development environment.

"You done?" Mex fired at Bergur, once he had blinked himself back to reality.

"I've given the building all I can remember. It seems happy it can make it."

Ten minutes later, the building coughed up a transparent vial from a new aperture in the wall. Kaamil held it to the light as if he could check the genetic configuration from the way it glittered in its gelatinous solvent. "How do we deliver it?" he asked, once his inspection was complete.

Mex smiled broadly and said, "I get to play dressing up."

*

Julienne sat transfixed by the rhythmic movement of José's chest. Somehow he and Nomia had survived the battle the previous night. At one stage, she had seen every loose piece of rock for a hundred metres, rise from the ground and fly at them. Many had ricocheted away harmlessly but enough had reached their target for the sound of stone on flesh to make Julienne's throat clench against rising bile. The sphere of shifting reflections radiated creeping menace, slapping her subconscious mind with waves from the much greater battle beneath her perception. There was a dimension to the fight that she could not readily conceive. Rationally, she now accepted that there was a deeper significance to Verity Space than MynCorp's Nexus, but she struggled to imagine how a war could be fought on such a field.

Near the beginning of the confrontation her implants had failed again. Many of them had not been active since her escape from MynCorp, but enough had been regulating her body and mind to leave her a quivering heap on the ground. She had recovered a measure of control within a few seconds; her brain seemed to be developing a degree of resistance to the repeated failure of the artificial corners of her mind.

There was a cost to her composure. She could not so readily dismiss the

240

reality of José and Nomia's divinity and their claims of a reality-consuming war. Her own battle for acceptance and to secure a place in the world suddenly seemed superficial and selfish. Her guilt made her think of Mex and she whispered an apology to his image. She continued to watch the unconscious José breath through the lens of a tear.

When the sphere had started to expand she had run with everybody else, stumbling in the wake of the Martian's gambling gait. Her mind twitched, and she tripped over her flailing legs. She tried to stand and look over her shoulder at the same time. Nomia and José were floating in crucifixion pose, their touching arms merged to the shoulder. They faced the expanding bubble of erased reality, and seemed to be holding it back by their presence. A common groan of pain was pushing through their gritted teeth. It became a scream of agony which held Julienne fixed to the spot, as if witnessing the final moment of the battle was more important than her own survival.

Julienne tried to blink.

She could feel an external force overriding her own will, as if she was nothing more than a doll. A silence more pervasive than any sound spread across the crater and the sphere vanished.

José and Nomia fell to the ground and lay motionless.

Everybody knew they had just survived something against all reasonable odds, and that the two unconscious Terrans were somehow responsible. Sera had coordinated their bodies being brought back to the cavern and a reverent procession had followed at a respectful distance. Most of the MynCorp and Durga officials seemed to have made it to the shuttles with pre-planned efficiency and were assumed to be watching the planet from the transit base on Phobos. The time for secrecy seemed to be over, but people milled around, uncertain how to proceed. Julienne avoided the aimless bustle and sat watching José and Nomia. She tried to reconcile the new version of reality confronting her.

"How are you feeling?" José's voice brought her back to the present. His eyes were open and watching her closely.

"How am I feeling? You're the one that just went up against an …" She struggled to find the right word, and realised she still had not accepted the alien nature of the threat.

"We had to break reality a little. I was afraid you might be struggling." He left her to fill in the details of his concern.

"My implants are already coming back on-line but I'm finding I rely on them less these days."

"Good." He closed his eyes and Julienne thought he might have passed out. "Would you mind finding Sera? I need to tell her something."

"Do you want to know how Nomia is doing?"

"She'll wake up in a few minutes. She's healing."

Julienne was beyond asking how he knew. She found Sera and brought her back to José's bed.

"Did we win?" Sera asked.

"It's hard to say. Mars is safe for now." José sighed, pain creasing the side of his mouth.

"That sounds like a victory," Sera said.

"It depends on the cost," Julienne stated.

"It was not Nomia and me. We could not defeat it. We had help."

"From who?"

"It was not a who. It was the algae."

"What algae?" Julienne felt her mind starting to slip back into a nearby unreality.

"He means the stuff that Durga has been engineering. It gives us our own source of energy, light, food and raw material for construction."

"It's more than that. It's sentient. It tried to help us fight the sphere."

Sera looked baffled. "You mean the stuff that I eat everyday thinks?"

"Not piece by piece but the combined biomass in the crater has reached a level of self-awareness."

"And you don't think this is an accident. Do you?" Julienne asked José.

"I think Durga are working on an alternative to the Nexus."

"MynCorp won't take that lightly. The Cartel would self-destruct. It'll be war."

"Only if MynCorp are in a position to fight." Julienne and Sera stared at José blankly. "Durga knew something was coming. They are planning for the aftermath."

Julienne nodded. "It's true, but they can't have known how big a threat we face. If they did they would be fighting with MynCorp, not against them."

José and Sera looked dubious.

"You said the algae tried to help?" Sera asked.

"We still would have lost if the Eidolons hadn't intervened."

"So that ball wasn't the Eidolons?"

Julienne let the conversation wash through her, picking meaning where she could find it.

"It was a physical tool made to destroy all human existence but I think the algae gave them pause for thought. It is a new sentient being, and they cannot destroy it without due deliberation."

"And if they wipe us out then the algae will die."

"Precisely." José nodded.

"So what do we do next?" Sera asked.

"We go ahead with the plan. We liberate the Nodes and prepare to defend Earth."

"You're going to do what?" Julienne gasped.

José smiled. "If Mex had succeeded in convincing MynCorp to help we would have heard by now. We must mount our own defence and, to do that, we need the Nodes. Now we have the last piece in the plan."

Sera looked concerned. "What piece? I thought we were ready to go."

"We were just waiting for one more recruit." José was speaking to Sera, but he was looking at Julienne.

*

"Squeeerk."

"Did it just growl at me?" Bergur asked Mex as a knee-high assortment of appendages and limbs pushed up against his leg.

"It did sound a bit like a growl." Mex conceded. "Down boy!"

The general purpose utility bot moved away from Bergur and lowered itself to the ground directly in front of Mex.

"You just couldn't resist could you?" Bergur accused.

"It's nothing in my code," Mex started. The corner of his smile twitched momentarily. "Except, maybe, the section which subverted obedience away from the building and redirected it to me. That might have done it."

"Well, could you persuade your devoted pet to move aside, so we can get off the exposed street and into this much safer top-secret building?"

The metal door sighed softly as it hermetically separated them from the street. Mex thought there was something disconcertingly permanent about the sound – he could not quite imagine what the reverse noise might be. The closing door seemed to have the same effect on Bergur and Kaamil because they all stood in silence for several seconds.

"Squawk!" said the bot.

"Why does he sound like that?" Kamil asked, breaking the spell.

"It doesn't have a voice synthesiser, I kind of assumed it would have. I suppose it's improvising."

"It sounds like its innards are grinding together," Bergur snorted.

"Hmm," Mex agreed. "Go."

The bot picked up on the tone of his request and started to wheel along the corridor without taking its primary visual sensor off Mex. As they followed it along the grey corridor, their appearances made a passable attempt at blending into the surroundings. Their clothes morphed into the simple overalls of a technician, to suit the utilitarian feel of the lower street-level spaces. Even a moderately paranoid A.I. would have flagged them as impostors within a nanosecond, but, weirdly, this was probably the easiest building in the city in which to travel incognito.

Mex looked back at Kaamil and Bergur. The Pilot looked almost normal but there was the occasional quiver of refraction as the nano-particles struggled to hide the conduits that trailed from his neck and back. His useless arm hung limply at his side, giving him an unbalanced look, as if he was permanently about to weave to his left. Bergur looked like a man crossed with a fighting dog, but Mex had seen less likely characters amongst Earth-born men.

The test of their first encounter with a member of MynCorp's staff passed with barely a nod of acknowledgement.

"It looks as if the locals are not particularly chatty," Bergur observed.

"I think it's probably best if we emulate their attitude," Mex said.

"Where's it taking us?" Kaamil whispered, nodding his chin at their guide just as it veered towards an outbreak of dirt that had the audacity to gather where the floor and wall met.

"Generally, to the boardroom. Specifically, I've no idea. It was supposed to be able to answer simple questions, but I'm not sure it's up to conversation."

"Squawk!" the bot agreed.

"Let's just follow and try to look as if we belong."

The bot stopped outside a pair of sliding doors and settled onto three stumpy legs. They stood at the lift entrance for a few minutes until the bot made a noise like two impatient pieces of metal being dragged against each other.

"Perhaps we should press the button," Kaamil suggested.

"Why? The lift must know we're here," Mex said but he pressed the button anyway.

The doors slid open and revealed a box panelled with dotted metal panels. The bot joined them inside and the doors slid closed. They stood there for a while waiting for the feeling in their stomach that would reveal motion.

"I'm not sure the lift and our pet are on talking terms," Kaamil said eventually.

"Tell the lift the floor we want," Mex said to the bot.

"Sqwoll." The bot sounded apologetic but nothing else happened.

"Perhaps we have to press more buttons."

"Surely, it would be easier for the building to ask us where we want to go, rather than have to deal with a separate button for each destination." Mex was feeling increasingly frustrated by the low-level of usability the building was exhibiting, but he played a game of pointing to each button in turn until the bot made a sound that he interpreted as happiness. The lift whirred into life with a sound of pulleys and counterweights.

They emerged several floors up into a very similar corridor but lined with featureless doors at irregular intervals. Men and women were streaming from one room to another armed with rolls of data and looks of earnest intent. As the interlopers moved through the hive of activity, people dodged around them as if they were nothing more than a natural obstacle.

At the furthest end of the corridor they stopped at a pair of heavy double doors which looked like highly polished wood. The bot settled onto the floor with a whirr of contentment and Mex patted its top absent-mindedly.

"Is this it?" Kaamil said with strangled awe.

"I suppose so," Mex replied.

"The people behind the most powerful force in human history?"

"Could be."

Bergur grunted without conviction and pushed on the doors. They swung inwards with little complaint and without the sound of ringing alarms. They scurried inside and closed the doors on any curious eyes.

The room was definitely a conference room, complete with a long table of smoked glass. Its surface was embedded with splice terminals in front of a dozen high backed chairs. The soft woven floor and sunset-red walls were the first evidence of opulence they had seen since entering the building.

"This certainly feels like the right place," Bergur said.

"Because it looks rich or because everybody is out to lunch?"

Kaamil wondered down one side of the table sampling each splice session like a bee testing a flower border for nectar. Once he reached the far end of the room he turned and looked back at Bergur and Mex. "Nobody has accessed these terminals in over twenty years," he said.

"We've got the wrong place," Bergur growled.

Mex felt the return of an itch at the back of his mind which had been growing in secret for the last couple of days. "This is the right place," he announced.

"So where are they?"

Kaamil just watched, a pained look spreading across his face.

Mex let the thought take over his mouth and listened with the other two. "The heads of MynCorp probably delegated running the company over a generation ago. That's why they only appeared in daylight for public relations events. They probably maintained a non-executive role for a while but eventually their significance must have waned. Maybe they retired and nobody was promoted to replace them. However it happened, I think whatever group of personalities originally ran MynCorp, they abdicated their responsibilities a long time ago."

"To that lot out there?" Bergur pointed back to the ant-like bureaucrats that filled the space outside the room.

"No, not to them. I think they passed on the responsibility to their greatest creation." Mex pointed to the nearest splice terminal.

"He's right." Kaamil sagged into a chair. "That's why MynCorp were so detached during negotiations. We weren't dealing with a person or even a composite personality. The Nexus runs MynCorp."

"But that means..." Bergur seemed incapable of completing the statement.

Mex helped him finish the thought. "It means, the Nodes and MynCorp are one and the same."

Chapter 12

There was a tranquillity like the moment a baby stops crying. Julienne had time to wonder where the thought could have come from, and then it was raining men and women. She landed hard on her left shoulder, rolling to keep the joint from dislocating. The arm was still complaining in fiery jabs when she pushed out to avoid the long chest of an armoured Martian. A woman's leg fell across her, pinning Julienne's lower body and reducing her to spectator in their awkward arrival.

The tight tug of Earth's gravity was a welcome feeling of belonging, but her mind seemed slower to adjust. Julienne was aware of time decelerating as her consciousness adjusted to the instantaneous change in gravitation field. Reality was a bit more insistent about enforcing the concept of down.

They had materialised in the largest open space she had been able to recall, thirty of them in a tight circle suddenly finding their feet where their shoulders should be. At least José and Nomia had been able to negate the relative velocities between the surfaces of the two planets – a two metre fall was a minor inconvenience compared to being flung towards the ceiling at a few thousand kilometres per hour.

Julienne lay listening to bruised groans for a couple of seconds, before gathering her thoughts and her limbs. José and Nomia were still floating at a precarious angle in the middle of the room. There was something partial about them, not transparent or missing but still not entirely in one place. Julienne moved her head from side to side. The floating pair seemed to blink even when she concentrated on keeping her eyes open. Their faces were slack with unconsciousness and their eyes were motionless under closed eyelids. Even José's skin was china-doll pale.

"Great," Julienne said to herself before raising her voice to address the whole group. "Up on your feet. Any injured in the middle with the medical team. Those with weapons form a perimeter."

There was an uncoordinated collection of acquiescent grunts, and a few yelps as abused ankles refused to accept their owners' weight. Julienne scanned the room beyond their position, checking for any sign their arrival had been noticed. If José and Nomia had managed the full extent of their intent, then a thin buffer layer around the edge of the room should be gently convincing any surveillance equipment all was normal, but human minds were apparently harder to fool. In Julienne's experience people were a lot easier to misdirect than machines, but instantaneous transport from one planet to another was well outside her field of expertise.

The space was quiet.

Last time she had walked through here she had been on her way to question the medical director about Nomia's disappearance. Now she was leading a Martian terrorist group bent on MynCorp's destruction. Not for the first time, Julienne wondered whether she had the mental strength to decide her own destiny; maybe she was just fickle.

"Lay your weapons on the ground and lie with your hands on your head." The voice was laced with dominance and pervasive insistence. Julienne's sensory processing implants quantified the vocal technology being employed and reconstructed the adrenaline tightness in the original voice, but a couple of the militia behind her started to bend down in compliance.

"Snap out of it," Julienne shouted. "Get José and Nomia and take cover."

The air filled with the buzzing of mosquitoes and the hiss of charging pneumatic weapons. Eighty-odd pairs of eyes brought their hosts' minds to bear on the floating apparitions above them and, in so doing, dragged José and Nomia fully into a single reality. They fell into a dozen waiting arms and were immediately carried away in a wave of fleeing bodies. Julienne's small troupe of partially-trained soldiers held a retreating line in front of the main team. High velocity splinters of ice started to chew holes in their home-made armour. They returned fire at the impassive black visors of MynCorp security.

"They were waiting for us," shouted her lieutenant over the teeth-jarring boom of sonic weaponry.

Julienne aimed her own modified mining drill at a shiny black-clad trooper. She grunted in satisfaction as he recoiled back from the shock front impacting on his rigid armour.

"Speculation is not going to help us now. Take point, make sure we are not flanked while we move into the corridors," she barked at the lieutenant.

Julienne shuffled sideways to fill the gap in the line made by the man ducking back to lead the retreat. She was dimly aware of her armour being eroded by the continuous bombardment of pellets of supersonic ice, but they were standing their ground despite being out-numbered and out-equipped. She allowed herself a brief smile of satisfaction at the first decision she could remember making for a long time which was correct. When José had asked her to join the breakout of the Nexus Nodes, she had found herself saying yes, and immediately doubting the decision. She tried to qualify the agreement with unreasonable demands but he had been unfathomably amicable.

"If I go I want to lead the mission," she had insisted.

Sera had bristled but held her tongue. José smiled. "Sera will coordinate the rescue of the Nodes but you will lead the fighting force. In fact, I think we would be asinine to have it any other way."

"I want to be able to pick my own team and decide on their equipment."

"Of course, that's the point. We don't have that many volunteers with combat training but you should definitely reject anybody that will be a liability. You know the strengths and weaknesses of MynCorp security and the layout of the building. We need you to lead us to the Nodes."

"You found Nomia on your own."

"I was very motivated, and we were linked emotionally. Nomia has been trying for months to contact the other Nodes but they all seem too deeply lost in the Nexus. We need you to lead us to their door."

"There's no way any of this will get through standard MynCorp armour," she had said when they showed her the carefully guarded stash of weapons. "We'd be better off with something more concussive; knock them off their feet and keep them down."

"Non-lethal is good. The soldiers are as much slaves of MynCorp as the Nodes." Nomia had regained consciousness with the soft sigh of a summer nap. She had joined the planning without missing a beat. Now more than ever, she and José seemed to act as one person.

Julienne kept her own feeling about MynCorp security to herself but said, "There will be deaths. It's inevitable and we need to be prepared for that."

"As long as we don't lose sight of the fact this mission is too save lives not take them." Nomia looked at Sera and Julienne until they both felt compelled to nod.

"Try telling them that," Julienne muttered belatedly as more ice splinters scarred her visor and blurred her field of view. She could feel cold blood running down to her wrist from a breach in the padding on her arm. She tested the mobility of the arm but there was no serious damage. She fired twice more and then shouted, "Run for the corridors. Two waves. Team A suppressing fire. Team B retreat fifty metres." She felt the body on either side of her turn and vanish. She continued to knock the MynCorp troupe around with sweeping movements of her shoulder-slung sonic drill.

When she had counted to sixty she yelled and turned her back on the incoming blizzard of needles. The panting of long-limbed bodies forced to run in high gravity buffeted her ears in the confined silence of the narrow corridor. As they rounded a corner in the corridor, team B started firing back down the corridor, filling it with walls of impenetrable sound. Sera and her team were waiting nervously in a wider section of corridor sparingly furnished with benches epoxied to the floor.

"This is not going to plan," Sera shouted into Julienne's ear.

"They do seem more prepared for us than I was expecting but we're doing okay. The Node's rooms start in the next corridor."

"That's great. What do we do without these two?" She nodded towards the blank faces of José and Nomia.

"I suspect they've over exerted themselves. Let's hope they wake up feeling rested, and soon."

"Great."

"Yeah, that's what I said."

"In here," Julienne tinkered with the interface to the door, trying to concentrate on overriding the sound of battle around her. The door obediently opened with a faint hum of charged coils. She let the wide muzzle of her gun lead the way into the wide corridor which stretched away for two hundred and twelve metres. At five metre intervals there was the faint outline of a door perfectly flush with the rest of the wall. Julienne did not need her artificial intelligence to recognise the Nodes' ward. She could even remember which of the doorways would lead to Nomia's old cell. The corridor was empty of obvious threats, while the one they were leaving was almost entirely full of danger. They were being fired on from both directions. Thankfully, the security teams had only used low-calibre weapons. Julienne could only assume the vicinity of the Nodes prohibited any larger weaponry, but she did not want to test that theory for too much longer. Most of Sera's team were trying to press themselves into what limited cover they could find but they were already getting to the point where the walking wounded outnumbered the fit. Many more injuries and they would be unable to keep moving.

"Clear," Julienne shouted back to her lieutenant. The Martians spilled through the doorway. Julienne worked on the door circuitry finding the part to stimulate to close and lock it. "We've probably got a couple of minutes before they work out what I've done to the door."

Sera was already at the first cell and was sliding her fingers around the faintly outlined opening. "Can you open it?" she asked Julienne.

"I can."

"I sense a but?"

"I'll have to reactivate some of my MynCorp implants. It will leave me... vulnerable."

"I can't see we have any choice."

Julienne let her mind expand into dead areas of processing power. Her skin felt charged as secondary perceptions and capabilities brought her surroundings into sharp focus. A new precision and analytical edge was added to every thought. The logistical analysis ran backwards into her actions of the last few hours making her blush at the poor level of decision-making skill.

As Julienne accessed the appropriate security protocol, the door to the cell hissed inwards two hundred microns and then dissipated.

The cell behind was clinically bare except for a mass of spidery metallic arms that were fussing over a naked body on a plain white slab.

"It looks like a post-mortem," Sera gagged.

"It's the opposite. Those devices are keeping the body alive," Julienne said distractedly. A thought was forming in her head. It was from the future, or rather, it was an extrapolation of their current situation that was slowly resolving.

"How do we get him out?" Sera took a step into the space with her hand held over her nose and mouth, as if the unconscious figure reeked of injustice.

"You can't. He's completely integrated into the Nexus. His brain and body are literally wired into that bed." For a moment Julienne could only see the translucent skin of the Node, as if having never seen the sun it had forgotten how to reflect light. His flesh sat over fragile bones without any obvious muscle structure to create the shape of a body. The head looked oversized with defined veins, as if all his blood had retreated to the one part of his body that was working.

Then the thought which had been forming popped back into her head with a mental ping of completion.

"Oh no," she said.

Sera started to say something but the world erupted into a cacophony of simultaneous attack. Walls of needles fired at them from four sides, a mist of lurid green gas oozed from pin prick holes in floor and ceiling, the floor itself turned gelatinous, gripping their feet and stealing their balance and waves of disorientating sound beat against them from all around.

The only part of Julienne's mind which was able to continue normal service during the first millisecond of the onslaught was detailing a strategic analysis of the current rescue mission and showed precisely why MynCorp would be completely prepared for just such an attack.

Sardon Lucas dithered outside the door. He desperately wanted to burst into the room with the bravado of a victor outwitting yet another mentally inferior adversary, but he really was not sure he could pull it off. Could he enter the inner sanctum of MynCorp? Or, more importantly, did he want to enter? This was not a central bureaucracy steering the goliath organisation through a complex hierarchy of committees and think-tanks. This was a single space, sealed behind a pair of highly polished wooden doors; a mysterious decision-making black box from which strategic direction emerged fully-formed, and ready to be implemented by the swarm of bureaucrats who flitted around it.

Sardon sighed beneath his breath. He was conscious of the impatient twitching of the black-visored security squad behind him. It was easy for them, he thought, just like it had been simple for him a few years ago, during his supersonic rise through the ranks of MynCorp Intelligence. MynCorp had been the first large organisation to overcome the Peter Principle of incompetence. Previous large organisations tended to systematically reward employees who excelled by promoting them to a higher level of responsibility with associated increased remuneration. At any moment an organisation comprised of workers who were good at their jobs and rising through the organisation, and those who had reached their peak-level and were too incompetent in their posts to attract promotion. The only employees who were making a positive impact were those still in the process of rising. Such organisations tended towards a state of institutionalised incompetence and minimum productivity.

MynCorp's solution was to reverse the concept of hierarchy; rather than the organisation comprising a network of fixed roles which employees competed for, the shape of the corporation was determined by the skills and inclination of the personalities it comprised. Complex algorithms, based on a lifetime of accumulated data, determined the precise type of stimulation each person needed in order to maximise their contribution to the organisation. Of course, the systematic dismantling of the planet's welfare systems, combined with the implicit threat of the Drop, helped to maintain employee motivation throughout their lifetimes. Nevertheless, certain exceptional characters could change the structure of the entire organisation. Sardon had been one such person. His unique strategic and conceptual skills had set him on a career course which should have culminated with a position on the board as an executive director.

It was only once Sardon reached his current level he understood how the theory had been imperfectly implemented. He would never get his position on the board. As far as he knew, nobody ever did. Officially, the identity of the board members were secret and it was assumed they met virtually in the boardroom. To someone of Sardon's position, it was obvious there was more to it. If it were simply a matter of secrecy and the eccentricity of powerful people, then he would have been invited to join them. There were, maybe, half-a-dozen people in the unique position of knowing what he knew. They had each hit a diamond-hard ceiling in their careers and continued to bump along, trying not to look up.

There were any number of explanations as to what might lie behind the floor to ceiling doors. Anything from an immortal collection of artificially preserved brains in jars, through to an exotic alien intelligence bent on human domination. Mostly, Sardon tried not to think about it. He got on with exercising the modicum of autonomy his position enjoyed, but every so often he got an unwelcome reminder of the shadowy secret at the core of the MynCorp empire. Standing outside these doors was like being slapped on the cheek by the elephant in the room.

Yet, he was unreliably informed Mex Tyrian was only a few feet away, but deep inside the one mystery Sardon was not inclined to solve. Of course, he had not been alerted by a keen A.I. with the ability to immobilise or detain in numerous entertaining fashions. He had received an automated message from a silent alarm system left over from a dark age of passive intruder detection. The anachronism of the building only heightened Sardon's conviction no good would come from knowing what was on the other side of the doors. They were perfectly ordinary doors, if a little ostentatious; no security and, apparently, not even locked. The fact that nobody he knew had seen inside was the most blatant implicit threat he could imagine. Of course, there was always the possibility this was a massive case of the Emperor's new clothes, but he could not quite make his hand reach for the handle.

The building layout showed no other exits; he decided to be patient. "We'll arrest them as they leave." Sardon hoped his voice carried more conviction than he felt.

The head of the security squad clipped "Sir", as if the muscles in his neck prohibited full use of his vocal chords.

They only had to wait a moment before the door handles turned and there was the click of a retracting bolt. The door half-opened to reveal three pairs of slumped shoulders. Despite himself, Sardon rose onto tiptoes to try and get a clear view into the room behind. He could see graduated shades of red on the walls, and the tops of high-backed chairs, but there was no sign of any other occupants. Focusing back on Mex he opened his mouth to declare victory but Mex interrupted him with a complete lack of surprise.

"Sardon, good. We need to talk," Mex said and even had the audacity to put a hand on Sardon's shoulder.

"Mex Tyrian, please consider yourself detained at MynCorp's pleasure. You and your friends will be doing a lot of chatting. At least for the next day or two. Probably not a lot after that." It was not the level of banter he aspired to, but it would have to do.

"We'll all be lucky if we have that long," the ex-MynCorp pilot called Kaamil Sillah added in a fatalistic monotone.

A couple of hours could make such a difference to his state of mind. Sardon was back on familiar territory. His implants were plumbed into the Security Building's A.I., and his consciousness was awash with environmental and strategic data. He was being brought up to speed on the Martian situation as he walked the short corridor from his office to the detainment cells. He knew MynCorp had been wrong to downgrade Mex Tyrian's security risk. Somehow, he was connected to the events on Mars and around Jupiter. Maybe even to the disappearance of the ⬚ base on Pluto's moon. Sardon could not see how it was possible but he instinctively knew it as a fact. The how would be revealed soon enough.

"Mr Tyrian, how are you enjoying our hospitality?" Sardon indicated the blank three metre square space which acted as a combined cell and interrogation room.

Mex stood without comment as the room rearranged itself for the discussion. The flat bench against one wall faded away and a four-legged table with fixed chairs grew like distorted mushrooms in the centre of the floor. They both sat down. Sardon could not think of a question to ask which would not reveal more about his ignorance than he was comfortable showing. So, he opted to let Mex do the talking.

"So, Mr Tyrian, you said you had something you wanted to tell me," he said.

Mex looked him in one eye and then in the other eye, as if he was considering two alternative stories to weave. "Do you know what runs MynCorp?" he asked.

"At the risk of using a cliché, I'll ask the questions."

"That could very easily be a no, but I'll assume you do. In which case, you must know you are the highest person I can actually deal with."

"You're looking to make a deal?"

"No. I mean you are the highest authority that will relate to what I'm about to say with a human understanding of the implications."

Alarm bells were ringing in the more imaginative parts of Sardon's brain. All the telemetry his implants were analysing suggested Mex was being entirely sincere, but the implications were frightening. His most fanciful daydreams about aliens running MynCorp vicariously, suddenly seemed less than whimsical. Yet, there was a background layer of stress visible in the clipped frequency distribution of Mex's voice. Sardon connected that stress to whatever had made him break into MynCorp.

"Go on," he said.

"We are under attack." Mex was reading his face intently but Sardon had handed control of his expressions over to an implant which was currently playing neutral cop.

"Who is we?"

"All of us. Humans."

"If every human is under attack then the implication is that the threat is from something non-human."

"Precisely."

"Precisely what?"

Mex sighed, "This is where it gets tricky."

"I'm sure it does. Try me."

"In a word, aliens."

"Why did I know you were going to say that?"

"It's true."

"And where are these aliens?" Sardon had a vision of a red boardroom with a single grey-skinned, black-eyed creature sat at one end laughing maniacally.

"That's the tricky part."

"So, the threat from invisible aliens isn't the difficult part?"

"They're in Verity Space."

Sardon blinked. As far as he could tell Mex was still being earnest but for a cover story this was conspicuous in its implausibility. "The aliens are inside our computer system?"

"The Nexus just happens to use Verity Space as an environment to host the consciousness which does the processing. It has an existence way beyond the Nexus and of far more fundamental significance."

"Thanks for the science lesson Dr Tyrian. It seems more likely to me that one of our *competitors* is attempting to overthrow the Cartel. Each of us seems to be victims to some extent but maybe to varying degrees. Perhaps, Durga, for example, was prepared to take some losses on Mars in order to get us clear of the planet."

"Great! I either have to deal with the detachment of a computer program or the paranoia of corporate intelligence."

There was an obvious irony in the way Mex said corporate intelligence but Sardon was too thrown by the statement as a whole to be offended by specific insults. What computer program had Mex meant? This kind of confusion was exactly why he spent so much of his time keeping up to date with every piece of data he could parallel process. There was a glaring elephant in the room and it was laughing at him.

He changed tack. "You should know we have identified Bergur as the mysterious alien threat that broadcast dictates over the last couple of days.

I've no idea how you managed that trick, but there's little doubt it was you."

"We were trying to get MynCorp to take the threat seriously."

"And yet I wonder how real that threat is now we have captured you."

"We're not the threat, it's the Eidolons."

"And yet, we have witnesses who place you at the terrorist attack on the Dyson space lift station, forensic evidence that the supposed alien threat was made by your accomplices and positive identification of some of your friends at the centre of the failed attack on Mars."

"Failed? They survived?" Mex was genuinely shocked and excited. His endorphins levels jumped and his pupils dilated.

"Possibly, we had certain technical difficulties in our remote surveillance systems during the attack, and no one has set foot back on the planet yet."

"You know what this means?"

Sardon was aware he was answering questions but he felt he was learning more this way around. "Tell me."

"They can be beaten, or at least, held at bay."

"Ah yes, of course. Do you know what my favourite Drop program is?"

"I suspect it is sadistic in some way or another."

"It's a mental dissection and mapping program. My particular favourite is to run it on the victim. The Nexus co-opts your own subconscious to break down memories and personality into a complete database of your existence."

"Lovely."

"Not that I haven't enjoyed this conversation but it is fairly redundant when I have the Drop."

"We haven't got a hope."

Sardon agreed and rose to leave the room. As the door closed behind him, he realised that Mex had not been referring to himself.

*

What?

Sardon let his frustration bleed through into the message. The queue of identical pleas for attention had started to buzz in the back of his head the moment he had stepped out of the isolation of the interrogation room. Each message was two words: "They're here". The implication was obvious but Sardon was not in a mood to placate his subordinate.

Sir, they are here. Permission to deploy countermeasures. The meta information overlaid the message with stress intonations.

Not until I get there. What's going on?

There are eighty-three of them, a dozen armed with cone effect sonic weapons and flack suits. They appeared out of nowhere - as you predicted - in target site gamma. We have them contained, but they are working their way towards the medical containment wing.

What about casualties?

No fatalities amongst my men, but about a dozen are incapacitated.

Concentrate on containment until I get there. I do not want to see a pile of bleeding corpses.

Sir.

Sardon strolled to the nearby communal area and forced himself to wait calmly for transport. The side-wall bulged and then blistered to reveal the settling form of a MynCorp drone. He stepped inside and flashed a mental image of his destination. The drone waited until it had a good grip on his seated form before accelerating away from the side of the building with an arrogant disregard for civilian traffic. Sardon was dimly aware of the bursts of data bouncing between his drone and nearby taxis. His trajectory remained steadfast; a few emergency diversions scattered those in his way.

By the time he had landed outside of the MynCorp central headquarters – frowning, as he did every time, at the inconvenience of only being able to enter from the street or roof – the invading force was at the door to the Nexus core. Sardon was only dimly aware of what went on in the medical containment wing. A handful of senior medical technicians dedicated their lives to tending whatever it was that actually ran the Nexus. From the fact most of the processing power was provided by human minds and from the medical nature of the technicians, it was obvious that something living was down there – probably some poor group of souls that had drawn very short straws in their lives.

The unsettling feeling of confronting MynCorp's two greatest secrets, both in one day, threatened to overwhelm Sardon's delicate focus on the second half of the conspiracy against MynCorp.

"Sir, they're trying to access the restricted area now." The soldier cleared his visor as he addressed Sardon, revealing a face too young and unblemished for the hard-as-nails voice.

"Let them get in. Are the counter-measures ready?"

"The building A.I. is not very cooperative but everything should be ready."

"The A.I. is probably trying its best. It's just not very bright. Give me the trigger protocol."

The soldier fiddled with a touch-screen pad on his wrist and Sardon felt the tingle of a new communication channel being opened. He walked around the battle and positioned himself with an eye for the perfect entry. It felt good to be ahead of events again. Certainly, there were many unanswered questions - such as, how the invaders could materialise inside a building, apparently, on a different planet to the start of their journey – but they were perfectly ring-fenced within a clear set of empirical facts. For example, he knew that José Sanchez and the girl were able to manipulate objects around them by some unexplained mechanism, but he had posited they were still basically human and therefore capable of being overwhelmed by simultaneous attacks.

The band of Martians was a pitiful sight when Sardon stepped silently through the far door of the containment wing. They carried each other into the room and collapsed into piles of shaking bodies. Two figures stood resolute and moved towards the nearest cell. He watched with the gentle pleasure of a curiosity which would soon be satisfied as the two women walked the short distance. They both moved with a graceful elegance, one from the natural stride of elongated limbs. The other was Terran but moved like a ballerina retraining as an assassin. She opened the door to the cell with impressive ease. They stood in stunned contemplation of whatever they had revealed. Despite himself, Sardon was fairly sure this was another secret he would be better off not knowing.

He scanned the sparse telemetry the building could provide him and, having satisfied himself all was as it should be, he flipped the mental switch which would begin the real attack.

Thousands of darts which had flattened themselves against each wall of the room sprang free and converged on their assigned targets at transonic speed. The same trigger caused a fleet of micro convection units to push clouds of polytrophic gas from the floor and ceiling, backed by pulsing acoustics designed to trigger disorientation and nausea in anyone with a modicum of hearing.

In the moment the attack was converging on its targets, the human woman turned her armoured head to Sardon and looked him directly in the eyes, as if she knew exactly where to expect him. Beneath a developing blonde fringe was the mirrored look of a kindred spirit. She was unmistakably one of his. Julienne Garland – the agent he had directed for a complete personality rebuild after the first time MynCorp went up against this terrorist group. He had time to remind himself this was just another question he would soon have answered. Then everything went wrong.

"STOP."

The voice somehow travelled to his ears before the darts had reached their targets, ignoring the speed of sound and jumping directly to his mind. He felt his body respond involuntarily, every process slowing to a crawl and then he waited in the silence where his next heartbeat should have been. Around him the physical world did the same. The darts formed a prickly cage a few centimetres from the exposed skin of the prone Martians. Even the eddies of air which carried the swirling green mist down from the ceiling stopped their rotation and hung like a smoke layer above the eyes of the standing Martian woman.

Somehow, while everything had stopped, two figures had risen from the pile of prone bodies and walked towards the open cell. They radiated possibility in the grey of the surrounding indecision. From where he stood, Sardon could not see into the cell and yet he was fully aware of what the pair saw on the medical table. The image of a withered body was embedded in a host of leaking emotions. He felt the fear and revulsion which swept through the woman at the scene from her past life, and he shared the pity and sorrow the man relived.

The myriad of devices which tortured and preserved the patient crumbled to dust as if overcome by unimaginable age. The figure on the table was cast into androgyny by prolonged emancipation and looked too fragile to hold anything as vital as a living soul, but a presence began to stir from deep inside the mind. A look of intolerable pain and suffering emerged on the face from behind the mask of paralysed muscles. String-thin muscles tensed on protruding bone, threatening to collapse the body into a ball of gristle.

Then the eyes opened and a male mind leapt into the room to join the others. For a moment the newly awakened Node rose from the table, held aloft by an orange glow of willpower. Then he was simply the unconscious body of an underdeveloped man, lying in the arms of weeping guardians.

And Sardon was crying too. It welled up inside him but was unable to flow from his frozen eyes and throat. It wracked his mind as it bounced back from his physical body and tore at his humanity. The resolve of the minds which called themselves José and Nomia overwhelmed his own dreams and ambitions; his will was like a candle before the blazing sun of their destiny. He understood there were nine hundred and eighty one more castrated minds held behind the sealed doors of this prison. It was not possible to contemplate resisting the liberation of the entire army of Nomia's brothers and sisters. The part of Sardon's mind which existed in numerous futures sending back postcards of advice, rationalised MynCorp was diverse enough to survive the loss of the Nexus. It would default on many data processing contracts, entire arms of bureaucratic social engineering would collapse and some of the population would probably starve in the chaos, but MynCorp would survive. These were the worst-case scenarios; the board of MynCorp would almost certainly have a contingency plan he was not aware of. He rationalised away his inability to fight back by planning around the aftermath. Let José, Nomia and their Martian cohorts take the Nodes. It was as blindingly obvious as a searchlight in the dark they wanted to liberate the Nodes to save them from their current torture. And Sardon could only think of it as liberation. If pushed, he had always known something unpleasant was behind the Nexus. He chose not to know because it was made easy for him to be ignorant, but he had less excuse than any other person given his ability and position. He was at least guilty of selective blindness. So let them take them all, MynCorp would be a cleaner organisation without them.

But there was something wriggling beneath the desire to liberate; an underlying guilt at an exploitation yet to be inflicted. Sardon realised, with a hammering thud which should have sent his heart racing, that it was Nomia and José who thought of the Nodes as an army. They saw a potential power in the Nodes, and they intended to use it. Why else would the so-called Martian liberation army be helping? Especially, since it was almost certainly the case that Durga were the driving force behind the DTM.

The mechanism was still missing but Sardon could see the pattern clearly. This was the beginning of a full-scale assault on MynCorp by one, or more, of the other corporations. The Cartel was dead. Every fibre of his body was engraved with a pledge of loyalty to MynCorp. He would not let this happen. Mex was still the key and weakest link. Sardon knew with absolute conviction that he must extract the details of the coming Armageddon from Mex's mind, but to do that he needed the Nexus.

His will pushed against the brutal inertia of the surrounding reality. He felt a cracking across his skin as if he was shedding a layer of hardened frost.

Thud.

His heart beat once, deafening in the passivity of his body.

Hope mingled with impotent rage and his heart beat again. Then his body was his own and promptly brought him to his knees, sucking oxygen from the reluctant air. His knees remembered how to crawl and they pushed him from the room and back into the normality of the corridor.

I want Mex Tyrian and the other two Dropped in the next five minutes, he pushed to his team as soon as his head was clear enough to form words.

Sir, we're seeing some problems in the Nexus. A Node has dropped off the grid.

There'll be more. Ignore it. Mex Tyrian is more important. Do it now.

Chapter 13

The galaxy revolved on its axis.

In the wake of the spiral arms, new stars flared with blue ferocity, and still he fell.

Thoughts floated past, sticking to his mind like dandelion seeds.

Beauty is purely a matter of context, Mex thought. *To the casual observer ash of a nuclear winter is indistinguishable from falling blossom, but who could bring themselves to call radioactive fallout beautiful? At least, no one who is human enough to understand the devastating implication.*

Maybe the reverse is also true; anything can become beautiful given a suitable perspective.

The falling was a liberating experience, and beautiful in its own way, but the part of his mind which understood past and future would not let him enjoy the perfection of freefall.

He fell further, or for longer, and the specifics of the fear diminished. He knew the Drop drugs were stripping his personality and leaving him an empty mind of raw computing power, but his fear was multi-facetted, and it made him resist.

He fought because of who he had lost in the past. An infinitesimal part of him wondered if he might find some fragment of Jacqueline in the Nexus, but the Drop was not a refuge for her dead spirit. It was her jailer and executioner.

He wrestled because his fear was sharpened by a depth of understanding. A determination not to betray his friends gave him energy to fight, but mostly he would not yield because his identity and memories were the only possessions he considered precious. The Drop aligned itself with his own personal notion of hell and he grew feathery wings as he pushed back towards the light which had shed him.

Two undulating tears appeared in his unreality. They orbited his tumbling consciousness causing a shift in perspective, and bringing him to the centre of his own universe. His context shifted again as they started to talk through him; now he was the centre of a universe smeared across the glass of a microscope slide.

"Is he under yet?" said the spiky ball of impatience.

"He's resisting quite strongly," answered the crescent moon of servitude.

"We don't have much time. Speed up the process."

"I've already increased the drug flow. We should achieve full immersion in a few seconds."

This time he plummeted without opportunity to resist. His floating thoughts stung him like bees and then he was gone.

*

"Five more Nodes have gone off-line."

"Concentrate on the scrape program. I want it run on Mex Tyrian's mind first. Make sure the program is tied to his processing identifier. I want the process to complete even if there is only one Node left." Sardon tried to stand behind the technician but his knees still refused to take his weight. He beckoned a chair to support him.

"Shouldn't we do something to investigate what's happening to the Nexus?"

"I know what's happening to the Nexus. It's dying and there's nothing we can do to stop it. The most important thing is to run this program before it fails completely." Sardon did not like having to explain himself but he did not have the luxury of time to educate the technician on chain of command and the dangers of free thinking. He calmed his mind enough to splice into Mex's processing unit.

He could see the programme as a series of completion metrics counting up from zero. It was currently mapping its host's mind, looking for the underlying storage format which would let it decode the contents of his long term memory in some sort of coherent structure. Sardon was peripherally aware of the rest of the Nexus as constellations of computational energy, like a night sky away from the moon's glare. The stars were going out at an increasing rate, leaving the faint wisps of Drop minds drifting through Verity Space like the rarefied clouds of supernovae remnants.

The Universe, which was the Nexus, shrank around him, as the program sporadically advanced towards completion. Normally, he would have not allowed himself to watch the metric count up, believing it a futile waste of mental energy, but after what he had witnessed it might be possible for his will to drag the counter towards one hundred percent.

It was going to get there.

The program was almost ready to start the scrape. Mex's mind would be reformatted to make its contents storable by an A.I.. Sardon could then plan the defence of MynCorp.

The link died.

"Get him tethered to another Node," Sardon barked.

"There are only a handful left."

"I only need one. Do it."

The link came back on-line. The program had faltered and was spinning on a single routine. Sardon kicked it back into action but the link vanished again.

"Another Node."

"That's it."

"What?"

"There are no more. The Nexus is off-line."

The splice lasers painted nonsense across Sardon's visual cortex; digital noise leaking from the void of Verity Space.

The technician was starting to sound scared. "We're completely cut off from the rest of MynCorp. The building A.I. has gone into paranoid mode. What do we do?"

"Of course we're cut off. Concentrate on me. I'm your best chance of making it out of this with a future. Wake up Mex Tyrian, we need to talk to him."

The technician seemed about to point out some unwise aspect of the plan, but the extenuating circumstances seemed to override his natural tendency to ask questions. A couple of minutes later Mex Tyrian was starting to groan rather than just drool.

"Mex wake up," Sardon grabbed him by the chin and rattled his jaw.

"Cherry blossom raining on burning minds," Mex replied. His eyes rolled under stiff eyelids.

"Mex, what's the plan? What are they going to do with the Nodes?"

"The Nodes?"

"Yes, Mex, the Nodes. What's the plan?"

"The Nodes." Mex opened his eyelids and his eyes spiralled back from infinity to focus on Sardon. "They're awake?"

"Yes, but what's the plan? How are they planning to take down MynCorp?"

Mex started to chuckle. A shake started in his toes and spread up his body to his chest, where it erupted in a howl of uncontrollable laughter.

"What's so funny?" Sardon demanded, his shaking of Mex's shoulders was insignificant against the convulsions that wracked him.

"You've already lost. MynCorp is gone."

"Don't be ridiculous. MynCorp is bigger than just the Nexus. The board will have a plan."

This just seemed to increase Mex's delirium. "The board?" he spluttered. "The Nodes are the board. The Nodes were the board. The Nexus has been running MynCorp for years."

"What? No."

Parts of Sardon's mind bent round on themselves, and joined to form perfect circles of realisation. He started to feel it; a slow pattern in the building data that only he would be able to see. The very top level of the human machine - acting as the heart of MynCorp and emanating out from this building to the whole Solar System and beyond – was grinding to a halt. The continuous stream of direction which ran from the board and trickled through the thick bedrock of the MynCorp structure had dried up.

Everything was running to some semblance of order despite the chaos on the Mars and the Jovian colonies, but MynCorp was already in its own drawn-out death throes. The head had been severed but, so far, only the neck had noticed.

Chapter 14

The exhilaration from Julienne's supercharged intellect vanished almost instantly as it brought with it the crashing realisation of their vulnerability. The immediacy of the attack almost made it seem to Julienne she was the trigger; her own perception of the risk spontaneously manifesting. She knew exactly where Sardon would be standing, because it was where she would have witnessed the assault if it had been of her devising. At the same time as she was turning towards Sardon, another part of her mind was sifting through infinite possible defence options, looking for something so drastically radical he would not have factored in a counter-measure.

The room came crashing in on her in swarms of darts, toxic-looking mist and jaw-rattling sound. She tensed in anticipation of the last ditch defence she hoped her mind would deliver, but the mental rug was pulled out from under her implants mid-thought. A sense of déjà vu was all that was left, and then the world around her was fed an instruction direct to the fabric of reality.

"STOP!"

José commanded, and the Universe listened.

Julienne would have liked to have fallen to her knees, but José's will kept her upright, to bear witness to the atrocities performed on the Node, lying exposed and helpless on the dehumanising steel of the medical bench. Reality seemed to be holding its breath, waiting to see what judgement José and Nomia would pass on such an uncaring universe. All physical processes outside her mind seemed to be suspended; electrons paused in their indistinct orbits, photons dropped into a holding-pattern in a pair of twisted dimensions, the God-like randomness of quantum tunnelling shut up shop and waited for the fabric of space to regain its rippling texture.

Every mind and non-mind was transfixed, waiting on the all-clear to go about its usual business.

They could only feel and experience the scraps which bled from the edges of Nomia's distress but this detritus from her mind was more than any one of them could have normally contained. So much of her focus for the last few months had uncoiled backwards through time from this moment. Her mind pushed aside the mere physical barrier to the unconscious Node, and brushed against his caged essence. The metronomic routine of his processor-bound mind induced waves of revulsion in her psyche, causing Nomia to lash out at the data-tethers with teardrop-drenched rage.

The liberated mind flapped in anonymous confusion, as Nomia guided the part of his personality forever bound to Verity Space back to its physical hemisphere. The fusion caused a shockwave of self-realisation to flash though all the surrounding minds, burning clean layers of empathic fatigue accumulated like life's own plague.

The feeble body of the naked Node rose from the table, and was born whole into the waiting arms of a universe which seemed rejuvenated and brighter for the process. Julienne felt the pressure of tears build up inside her paralysed mind, eager to manifest the intensity of her emotion.

The moment finally past and allowed the stream of subsequent moments to begin. Julienne found herself on the floor, her hands lying slack next to her knees. Finally, she could cry but now there was time again she had responsibilities to fulfil. The newly liberated node was nothing more than a desperately weak body which needed physical attention. José and Nomia moved from room to room, waking each body, and helping the estranged mind to unify with itself and the brain it had transcended. Sera and her broken band of helpers replaced the metallic pincers of the medical machines, soothing and tending as best their condition allowed. Every one of them felt a connection to the Nodes tighter than family. They had all shared part of Nomia's mind and the feeling of connection, as if all the Nodes were fragments of one Universal mind. This was not nurse and patient; it was cells cooperating in a single organism. Subconscious signals kept them all operating towards a single goal.

Julienne patrolled the expanding camp continuously checking for the return of the MynCorp security, and stressing about the impossibility of defending a thousand patients and a handful of helpers inside enemy territory. Sardon did not return with reinforcements and the fabric of the building did not repeat its multi-facetted assault. They were left to gather their flock and finally it was done. Naked, withered bodies lay in rows along the floor of the side corridor. Nomia and José stood limp and heavy-eyed at the far end.

"It's done," José managed.

"Can we get them out of here?" Julienne pleaded.

"We'll all go together," Nomia's voice croaked with dusty fatigue.

"I'm going to stay and look for Mex," Julienne found herself saying. She almost looked over her shoulder to see who had spoken, but once the words were out in the wild she knew that it was an absolute truth.

A tall soldier pushed up her visor to reveal the blood-smeared face of Yakini. "I'll come with you, if Mex is here then Bergur should be nearby," she said.

Sera appeared at Yakini's shoulder. "We have unfinished business."

"Then come with me. I'll show you the highlights of Earth." Yakini tried to grin but the blood on her cheek made the effort look manic.

A dozen emotions skirmished across Sera's face. "You still don't get it," she said.

Yakini experimented with a look of innocence but gave up with a shrug. "You're going back to Mars?"

"Home. I'm going home. There's too much left to do. Now more than ever."

Yakini turned side on – a foot in the camp of each half of her heart. "I just wanted more time to explain. More time to make things better."

"It'll have to wait. Mars has a chance for independence."

"If we survive the Eidolons."

"If we survive."

Resignation escaped as a sigh on Yakini's breath. "If you go back now, I'm frightened I'll never see you again." Her emotional shell flickered transparent for the shortest of moments, then hardened again with a lopsided smile. "Kila la kheri. Look me up when you get some shore-leave. Go do your duty."

At the word duty, two surviving emotions resumed their tussle at the corner of Sera's mouth. Her lips modulated a goodbye, but the sound skulked at the back of her throat. She turned away and fussed with a semi-conscious Node.

"Julienne. Yakini," José acknowledged. "We'll be back for you as soon as we are able." He turned to look at the mass of people, as if weighing up whether he had the mental strength to carry so many, so far.

Nomia touched Julienne on the cheek and said, "Be good to yourself and Mex."

Julienne and Yakini stood to one side as José and Nomia sucked in air like energy, and rose from the ground as a single glowing ball of determinacy. They reached out arms which seemed to encompass all the bodies in the room.

They pulled the collective to their breast and with a sigh they were gone.

Julienne blinked twice as her brain tried to catch up with the leap in reality, and she joined Yakini staggering towards the door, a common feeling of inexplicable loss clouding their minds.

The room behind them sobbed a lament.

A prone figure bled into existence. At first, it was there in the afterglow of a blink. Reality fought back and the mirage grew faint before finally slumping into definitive existence.

The woman pushed herself upright against the overbearing hug of the Earth's gravity.

"I'm still here," she rasped.

Yakini's body and voice collapsed around the prone figure. "Sera, you stayed."

*

Julienne moved through a cluster of black-clad soldiers. She felt exhaustion beyond comprehension. If Julienne allowed herself to think for one moment then she would drop with exhaustion. She fought on, her body an autonomic killing machine. The soldiers moved in slow motion as she ducked below the barrel of a trained weapon, and kicked out at one knee while reaching for another half-drawn gun. Her hand pushed down on the trigger finger of the second soldier, shooting one blast into his owner's foot, and then folding the weapon back towards the second row of attackers. Three more shots and she released the man as he fell and she rose to deliver simultaneous punches to the unprotected sides of two necks.

The crumpling sound of falling bodies barely registered as she moved on towards the Drop cells. A single purpose gave her focus. To change her mind would have taken more effort than she could now conceive. To stop would mean dropping where she stood. She approached the medical ward, adjacent to the drop cells, just as a suited man hurried out, followed by half a dozen armoured soldiers. It was the man who had pulled so many strings, and made them all dance like fated puppets. She crouched ready to spring an attack ,but Sardon turned the other way and ran without seeing her.

Julienne staggered through the door to the medical ward and rushed two technicians who cowered protectively over their splice terminals. She struck to incapacitate; the robot that she allowed herself to be, understood mercy and blame. She felt the presence of Yakini and Sera following as best they could. They kept their distance, as if they could not be sure that she was still able to distinguish friend from foe. She was used to people being guarded in her presence. To them, the technology in her head made Julienne less predictable than other humans with their chaotic self delusions. Only one person had treated her as an emotional creature.

Only one man.

He lay motionless on a retracted Drop couch. His eyes open and mouth forming repetitively silent words.

Julienne kicked a dormant implant into life and connected to the room's medical infrastructure. Data spooled behind her eyes and she groaned at the scrambled state of Mex's brain. His mind was no longer able to extract meaning from sensory input. All stimuli were equal and disconnected from contextual memory. She would be as meaningless to him as a bowl of fruit.

A part of her brain muttered scolding reminders of old advice. Emotional attachment will only lead to pain, it reminded her. She clenched her fists in indignant anger.

"What is the point of being alive if you don't feel and share emotions?" she demanded out loud.

The inner voice had no answer.

Julienne leant over the couch, and grasped Mex's head between her blood-smeared hands. She moved her face close to his and looked into unfocused eyes. Pausing to breathe in his essence, she kissed him lip to lip. She pulled back slowly, feeling their skin part reluctantly.

"Is he alive?" Yakini asked from somewhere behind.

Julienne kept her eyes fixed on Mex in case he should slip away while her focus was distracted. "Alive, but his brain has been reformatted for memory retrieval."

"That doesn't sound good. Can you fix it?"

"Fix it? His brain is scrambled." Julienne struggled to comprehend how slowly others could follow a situation through to its logical conclusion. Mex was gone - as good as dead – but, as she was forced to retrace the implications for Yakini's benefit, she found a categorical refusal to accept inevitability.

"What can we do for him?" Yakini persisted.

"There is no him. Mex is gone. This is just meat." Yet she still could not take her eyes from his lips and skin. There was a wound on his cheek which looked a few days old. She resented the fact things had happened to him she knew nothing about; her memories of him were all that was left, and they were so incomplete, even during the short time they had known each other.

There was a gap where Yakini might have suggested they should save Mex from any more suffering.

"There's two more over here." Sera said from somewhere else in the room.

"Bergur!" Yakini moved away to be replaced on Julienne's shoulder by her conscience. An idea was taking root in the recesses of her mind. It grew like a tumour, flooding her with false hope. Her mental immune system fought back with currents of revulsion.

"I can't. He'll never forgive me." She muttered out loud.

A monster can only beget a monster, she thought. She could not have sworn her desperation was not selfish but she knew she was going to do it anyway.

Then she moved closer again and placed her forehead to his. Gritting her teeth against the inevitable pain, she triggered a drastic reconfiguration of the implants which peppered her brain like spiderwebs in an attic.

Pools of cold mercury accumulated under her skull and started to push through the natural pores of the bone. Implants she had not used since her escape from MynCorp were sacrificed easily, others, which regulated her every moment, left gaping holes in her psyche as they decomposed. She left enough infrastructure in place to keep her sane, the rest she gave to Mex.

Memories of people and places melted into generic logic gates, and then decayed again, into their component elements. Acquaintances, who might consider themselves to be Julienne's friends, locations where she had found sanctuary, and events which were building blocks in her personality, were reduced to bytes discharging into the grey of her scarred brain.

She howled in pain as the tendrils of fluid technology pushed through her scalp and slithered into his brain. The pain subsided from her end but it had just been transferred to him. Mex had no way to process such stimulus, so she absorbed it back though the inter-implant interface and experienced the agony on his behalf.

Slowly, the threads of intelligent metal found their foothold in his brain and a complete mind was reconstructed. When every last piece was in place she lifted her head and broke the connection between her brain and his.

*

His turned-up tortoiseshell was a bumbling cat-of-meringue on the good sea Mex.

He named her Synonym with froth-flecked anonymity, and set course for fine adventure.

The breeze took its own name from the tongue-like tip of his concentration and buffeted the skinny sails.

Those loved in life frolicked in the bowwave and chattered memories in squeaking whistles.

Mex tried to dip his stamen in the nectar-laced memories which swelled the shell in mocking repetition.

The tension pushed away from his surface scratching, and he emerged flecked in salty spray, like a childhood memory of realised change.

A brook of babbling fuchsia buds popped pink pods in concerned inquisition.

The improbably straight lily sat in the valley between past and future waves and quivered in concentration.

Creepy roots of tantric embrace slithered along the cracks in Synonym's shell and prized an entry beyond measure.

Bristles of connectivity brushed his senselessness in clinging echoes of blazing worlds as wide as his breath.

The lily tore its white pelt from his dislocated burden but left tendrils of mercurial sentiment.

The flapping of thunderous beatniks ordered the other and inverted the current of oceanic Mex.

Incensed, he rose from the introspective waters, like aromatic smokers leaving the shadows of canvas shade.

The sky was a cacophony of misplaced sensibility. The ocean leaked colour
as it lost definition, and the blue bled from water to air,
until he was.

The ocean retreated leaving the taste of crashing surf and smell of rising
thermals.
Mex condensed from a cloud of doubt and certainty into a conflicted mass
of senses and memories.
Superhuman in his mediocrity, he dissected plethoric contradictions from
his sensors and constructed a reality unique in its commonality.

A pale angel bent over him.

Her slender face was creased in worry by muscles too fatigued to separate
the inner and outer worlds. Clumps of blonde hair lay plastered to her
head by dry sweat. Smears of grime and blood masked her face, except in
meandering paths from each eye to her chin. She was more beautiful than
he could conceive, as if the cynicism of accumulated sensory input had
been reset to cloistered purity.

"Julienne," he whispered like the first line of a poem.

"Mex, is that you?"

Her doubt was brutally infectious. What was he that could cause such
uncertainty? He felt the memories of Mex Tyrian rumbling below the
surface of his consciousness, ready to trigger emotions from the barrage of
a sensory world. What more could define a man or woman?

He ignored her question in case it held power of realisation. "The last time I
woke up to find you watching over me, I was missing a limb."

"I remember."

"That's not as reassuring as it could be."

A bulk of flower-coloured muscles cast a shadow over Julienne's uncertain expression. "Sardon left you in a pretty bad state," Bergur said.

"How about you and Kaamil?" Memories trickled backwards from Mex's ravaged mind.

"He didn't get around to us. We just had the Drop drugs to deal with."

"Good," Mex managed.

Bergur grunted an acknowledgement, and moved away to join two impossibly tall figures out of reach of Mex's unresponsive eyes.

"Did we win?" he asked.

"The Nodes are free. José and Nomia have taken them back to Mars to recuperate."

"And MynCorp?"

"Pissed off, I expect."

"I'd anticipate a bit more than that."

"Explain."

Even her brusque refusal to soften demands with social pleasantries was endearing to his newly refreshed world view. He tried to smile but coordinating so many muscles seemed impossibly complex. He removed the expression in case it looked deranged in its partiality. "The Nodes have been running the same corporate strategy program for two decades."

"So?" she asked, but realisation dawned before he could answer. "You're not serious?"

"Totally, I've seen the boardroom of MynCorp. There's nobody there. The Nodes have been running their own jail for years."

"And without them?"

"No jail, no corporation."

"It's too big to fail like that. Somebody will step in and take over."

"Maybe if the Nexus was still intact. I'd be surprised if any of the corporations survive in a form we would recognise. Sardon understood." Mex remembered laughing at the dawning realisation on the man's face. Even as Mex crumbled into mental dust, he had sucked the conciliatory vapour of victory from the moment. After that his mind was a chaotic mess of whimsical and meaningless images. "What did he do to me?"

"He ran a mind-scrape program on you. He probably thought you had enough information for him to save MynCorp."

"Shouldn't I be dead?"

"It didn't complete before the Nexus went off-line."

"Still, a mind-scrape rearranges the brain as a memory retrieval system. My sensory processing should be totally scrambled." For a moment Mex could smell flowers and sea-salt memories.

Julienne touched his cheek so softly he felt the air slip between her fingers. "I had to save you," she croaked.

Mex felt too weak to move but the symbiotic cluster of synthetic neurons in his false arm reached up and took her hand firmly. "What did you do?" he asked softly but with a hard edge of fear.

"I operated to repair the damage."

"That's good, isn't it? Why the worried look?" Mex glanced at the death-grey texture of his last surgical encounter and his voice dropped though

288

concern to accusation. "How much metal did you put in me?"

She pulled back her hand and the corners of her mouth. "I did what was necessary," she said coldly. "If I hadn't dehumanised you by adding some technology into your head we wouldn't be able to argue about it now."

"I didn't mean to imply implants were dehumanising. I don't think of you that way," Mex started but she looked away. He growled in frustration, "Argh, you're so hard to understand."

She turned back to him. "Well, that's not going to be a problem from now on," she shouted and slammed her head forward as if to crunch her skull into his. At the last moment she halted so the skin of their foreheads just brushed.

There was a blinding supernova of mental energy and Mex was inside Julienne's head. The last hour was vivid in her memories; sights and thoughts still percolating through her mind as she looked for meaning.

Julienne lifted her head again, severing the connection for a second time. Mex understood what she had sacrificed to save him, and that she had done it gladly. He knew her detachment was born from fear he would reject the gift as inhuman and repulsive, and implicitly cast her in the same light.

"Come closer," he said weakly.

She bent her head to bring her ear towards his face. This time he raised his human arm and touched the back of her neck with his fingertips. The breath rushed into her lungs and she turned her face toward his. This kiss was shared and reciprocated. As their lips lingered, her forehead fell towards his and their minds connected. Floods of emotion cycled through them both, feeding and growing as it bounced backwards and forwards until they pulled apart with a ragged gasp.

They stared at each other with shared confusion and comprehension.

*

For a long moment Kaamil was back in the isolation of the pilot's bunker, somewhere between stars, but then the incongruity of voices brought him back. He opened his eyes to see the blurry features of Yakini looking down at him with business-like intent.

"He's awake," she said, but the voice was more deeply accented than he remembered and the face, now that he could see it clearly, was longer with a broader nose. She was Martian but not Yakini.

A second Martian face appeared and this time he smiled in recognition. "Yakini, I thought I saw two of you."

"Kaamil, welcome back. This is Sera. She's … an old friend."

"Now that I'm stuck on Earth and all the panicking is over, we need to talk about that, old friend." Sera said.

"Can it wait until we've woken Bergur?" Yakini said.

Kaamil became aware he was lying on a retractable bench in front of a Drop chamber. There were similar capsules for as far as he could focus in all directions. The neighbouring bench was also retracted and a mass of purple muscles was lying on its surface, slowly twitching back to life.

"That's Bergur?" Sera asked, turning to look at the groaning Eridanian. "The Bergur? The one you've been fretting over?"

"Yes," Yakini said shortly.

"But he's …"

"Yes?"

"Very purple."

"And a he, I know."

"You left me for a big purple, male alien?"

"He's no more alien than you or me. Well only a little bit. Anyway, you know it's not as simple as that."

Bergur rose to a sitting position causing muscles to ripple across his abdomen. "What did I miss?" he asked.

Sera backed away one step, as if apprehensive of his sheer size and presence. Yakini put an arm on each of his shoulders and pushed her face against his. "I missed you", she purred.

"Of course you did. You're only Martian," he said. "Who's your sister?"

"This is Sera. Sera say hello to Bergur."

Sera crossed her arms and grumbled a hello.

Bergur looked confused. "What did I do?" he asked.

"We need to have a little three-way talk." Yakini grinned.

Kaamil blinked and found himself in his bunker again. This time the sensation was too real to ignore. He opened his eyes and was back in the Drop ward. He felt the data tethers at the back of his neck twitch and information started to flow.

He cried out in joyful pain.

"Kaamil, what's up?" Yakini said rushing to his side but hesitating before reaching out to him.

"The Suparna. She's back, and all healed."

"Where?"

"In Earth orbit. She's so beautiful. I can see all of her as if I was back onboard."

He felt the rush of telemetry bursting through the quantum coupled transceiver in the base of his neck. It cascaded in overlapping avalanches as if the ship was a proud child rushing to show off her achievements.

"Her engines are back on-line. She's ready for flight and the hull sensors are fixed. I can see the whole Universe through her eyes and ears. I'd forgotten how beautiful it is to see so many stars all around."

He felt the others watching him, but he did not mind. Sharing this moment with friends was marred only by the absence of the one who had made it possible.

"I wish Nomia was here," he whispered. "I'm getting feeds from all round the Earth. There are big holes in the data; whole cities have dropped off the grid. The loss of the Nexus is causing chaos." Then he saw the biggest hole. "Oh no, it can't be." He shuddered as he realised what was happening. A quick look at the Suparna's sensors confirmed the nightmare.

"What's happened?" Mex and Julienne asked in eerie unison.

Kaamil could not answer. He had to see for himself. He tried to run for the door but his legs only provided a drunken stagger. Bergur appeared under one shoulder and Mex under the other.

"Where are we going?" Mex asked.

"Outside. Just get me outside."

They emerged into a clear night and stood blinking at the white glare of a full moon on a cloudless night. Six faces stared open-mouthed at the pristine silver disk of grey maria and crinkled craters.

"They've all gone!" Kaamil said through lungs tight from shock. "It's as if the lunar cities were never built. I was born up there but now it looks as if we never set foot on the Moon."

"Then it's started," Mex said. "They're here."

*

"Kill me!"

The cry prowled the cave, creating shivering crystals in the blood of every soul it touched. Some instinctively turned to look for the quivering pile of skin and bones responsible for the anguished sound. Others focused intently on what they were doing, thrusting up mental shields as strong as their shattered minds would allow.

Nomia rose from the cot she was sat on, exhaustion painted on her face in red and back shadows. She kept her hand on the cheek of the boy she was tending for as long as she could, only withdrawing when her arm was fully outstretched. Then she was totally focused on the girl shivering against the mirror-smooth wall of the cave. Nomia soothed with her hands, calmed with her voice and quietened with waves of projected emotions.

"Hush, it's okay," Nomia whispered rhythmically with the sweep of her hand. "We're all here for you. It's going to be fine."

The girl was swaddled in an orange Martian jumpsuit. She was probably a woman, but the hallow of her cheeks and stringy tendons of her neck, stripped away any maturity and made her azure eyes bulge with innocence.

"Please kill me. Or put me back," the girl sobbed. Her eyes glistened with tears through bone-white knuckles which defended her eyes from the Universe.

Nomia bent closer until their minds overlapped. "You're free now. Just relax and let yourself heal. Everything will be okay. There's magic and beauty waiting for you."

"No!" Anger stiffened her body and voice. "There is too much chaos. It claws at my mind. I feel like my brain is being eaten alive. Send me back. Now."

293

"There is nothing to go back to. You're with us now, and we'll look after each other."

"Why did you do this to me? I didn't ask to be made conscious."

"You were being tortured. You are my sister, how could I leave you?"

"But it was better than this. Dirt and pain, and thoughts everywhere. I can't cope."

"Give it time."

"No. You will take me back." A taut determination disfigured her face as she rose from the ground.

Nomia fell back on her hands, dazed by the ferocity of the mental attack. Daggers of dislocated reality sliced through the cave, cutting holes in the psyche of every mind in their path. The twenty or so Martian carers scattered in random directions, blind to the threat's source. Two fell to the floor clasping their hands around open-throated screams. Dozens of the Nodes wailed and thrashed in their cots. There were forty-three Nodes who had only partially managed to integrate the physical and Verity Space halves of their being. The friction between their conflicted minds had built up a reservoir of potential energy. When the darts of flying pain impacted nearby, reality started to fragment in flashes of bottomless void.

The cave felt like it was folding in on itself, crushing the minds of the thousand frightened Nodes. Waves of fear pushed outwards, temporarily balancing the implosive breakdown in reality. Finally, the fear turned into defeat and every mind began a freefall towards oblivion.

Then there was José.

Order and stability washed through the scene, leaving nothing but the mental echo of the destructive force that existed a thought-beat before.

José helped Nomia back to her feet. She sagged the moment her legs straightened, guilt robbing her of any remaining strength.

"You okay?" he asked.

"What have we done?" She looked down at the unconscious girl lying at her feet.

"Come with me and I'll show you."

José led her away from the hundred cots which had occupied all her time since their return from Earth.

Then they walked through clusters of orange-clad figures, animated conversations energising skeletal bodies. Others sat in pairs silently communing through the touch of linked hands.

"Look over there."

Nomia followed the direction of his gaze towards a couple of dozen cross-legged men and women. They sat in a rough circle, eyes closed and faces calm. Verity Space around them boiled with probed and prodded possibilities.

"Already?"

"They still have a lot to learn about themselves but their ability to manipulate Verity Space is phenomenal. More importantly, can you feel the common underlying emotion around us?"

Nomia let out a breath which had become lodged in her lungs. She unlocked the battered hatches of her mind to reveal the raw wounds within. The emotional currents lapping around her started to seep into her mind, pushing out the pain and fear. There was excitement, wonder and happiness bubbling all around. Underneath was a communal emotional energy acting as buoyancy to all the other feelings.

"Love," Nomia choked as the room blurred through wet eyes. "They're learning to love."

"You did it." José hugged her tight enough to last forever. "You made them whole, and they're beautiful."

"José." The man was probably in his early thirties and was almost tall enough to fill the orange jumpsuit. A look of pride was dampened by the news he had to report.

"Ben, what is it?"

"The lunar cities are definitely gone."

Nomia covered her mouth but a cry of shock spilt around the edges.

"Any sign of survivors?"

"There doesn't seem to have been any warning. There were a few shuttles in flight which survived, but no evidence of a mass exodus. An interstellar cargo ship has arrived in orbit and is taking on board refugees."

"It's probably the safest place to be at the moment." José hugged Nomia but her shoulders just sagged.

"What's going on?" she asked.

"Ben is one of twenty who have shown exceptional awareness skills. They are monitoring Earth for Eidolon activity."

"And they've already reached the Moon. We're nothing like ready."

Ben looked even more uncomfortable. "I'm afraid it's worse than that."

"Meaning?" José prompted.

"We think they've arrived on Earth."

"Then it's all over. We lost."

"It's not that simple. We are picking up tiny flashes in Verity Space as individual points of reality are undone."

"That doesn't make any sense," Nomia said.

"Unless they've changed tactics." José looked as if he had just seen a chink in the armour of an undefeatable adversary.

Nomia started to ask why but then she caught José's mental drift. "During the attack on Mars they suddenly became concerned about harming the sentient algae."

"Exactly, they only want to wipe out human existence without damaging any other life form capable of becoming sentient. On the Moon there is no other life. Everything is man-made but on Earth there is still some bio-diversity to protect."

"So what are they doing?" Nomai asked.

"What do you think Ben?" José prompted.

"If what you say is true, then it feels to me like they have manifested themselves individually on Earth and they are wiping out humans one at a time."

Nomia clenched her fists. "We have to help," she said.

"I agree," José said. "I'll take whoever's ready. Nomia, you can follow when you've had some rest."

"Don't even think about it. We go together."

Ben clearly had more to say. José welcomed the distraction from a pointless argument. "What is it Ben?"

"I know you were very clear but we tried to open a hole. Something blocked us. There's a barrier of ridged reality around the Earth."

"Then we will have to physically travel to Earth," José pondered.

Ben frowned. "Do you think we have time?"

"We don't have to start from here," Nomia smiled. "What was the name of the ship you felt in orbit?"

"The A.I. called itself the Suparna."

"Of course it did." José was smiling too. "We'll be as safe on the Suparna as we are here."

A mental image swept through the cave, centred on José and Nomia. Most faces contorted with fear or confusion but over two hundred pairs of eyes glowed with a common sense of purpose. The dark-haired teacher and the porcelain pale angel borrowed energy from the collective, and wrapped the space in their mental embrace. To those who would remain on Mars they left a map to self-discovery and hope. For the rest there was a change in perspective like an opening door and then they were gone.

Concluded in
Certitude
part three of
The Verity Trilogy.

Follow me at
@MarkOnAJolly
Or send me your thoughts:
TheVerityTrilogy@gmail.com
Anything from a one line comment to a full review.
Receive previews and offers on future instalments of
The Verity Trilogy